In Australia's Northern Territory, NORFORCE Sergeant Jamie McKinnon escorts a group of Americans into Arnhem Land, one of the world's last great wildernesses. Yet what begins as a field assignment becomes a journey into Jamie's own identity.

Danny Carter was a schoolboy during the Korean War, growing up with the mystery of his airman brother's disappearance. As Danny comes of age in a rapidly changing United States, he is determined to locate his brother's lost plane in the face of murder, intimidation and loss.

Danny and Jamie, coming together from opposite sides of the world, learn that revenge extracts a terrible price, and reveal a shocking truth that will shake the world.

Also by Greg Barron

*HarperCollins* Publishers Australia
Rotten Gods
Savage Tide
Lethal Sky
Voodoo Dawn (short fiction)

*Stories of Oz* Publishing

The Hammer of Ramenskoye (short fiction)
Camp Leichhardt
Galloping Jones and Other True Stories from Australia's History
Whistler's Bones
Red Jack and the Ragged Thirteen
Outlaw: The Story of Joe Flick

# The Time of Thunder

Conscience. Brotherhood. Sacrifice.

Greg Barron

*Stories of Oz* Publishing

First edition published 2020 by Stories of Oz Publishing
PO Box K57
Haymarket NSW 1240
ABN: 0920230558
facebook.com/storiesofoz ozbookstore.com

© 2020 Greg Barron
ISBN: 9780648733829
Proof reading: Robert Barron
Cover design: James Barron
Cover photograph: Cameron Blake Photography
Typeset in Bembo and Gilroy by Stories of Oz

To Dad,

*Robert Frederick Barron,*

this one is for you.

There are times when you have to obey a call which is the highest of all; the voice of conscience, even though such obedience may cost many a bitter tear, and even more a separation from friends, from family, from the state to which you may belong, from all which you have held as dear as life itself.

Mahatma Gandhi

# EAST CHINA SEA

## 1950

YOU FLY THE PLANE ONE HANDED, ON A DESPERATE BEARING SOUTH, STARING THROUGH THE PLEXIGLAS BUBBLE AND INTO THE CRYSTAL NIGHT. THE AIR INSIDE THE COCKPIT STINKS OF FEAR MINGLED WITH CHEMICAL TOILET AND GASOLINE FUMES.

A SQUADRON OF SABRE JET FIGHTERS RAKE LINES OF SILVER AND WHITE ACROSS THE SKY IN THE MOONLIGHT. YOU SEE THE SWEPT-BACK WINGS AS THEY PEEL OFF INTO A HUNTING PATTERN, LIT AFTERBURNERS GLOWING LIKE FAST-MOVING COMETS.

YOUR RIGHT HAND HOLDS THE BUTT OF A COLT .45. THE BARREL POINTS ACROSS THE CRAMPED COCKPIT AT YOUR CO-PILOT'S CHEST. HIS HEAD IS BURIED BETWEEN HIS KNEES LIKE YOU ORDERED. HIS NAME IS EVAN GRAY. HE WAS YOUR BEST FRIEND BUT YOU TOLD HIM AND THE OTHERS THAT YOU WILL KILL THEM IF THEY TRY TO STOP YOU.

THE SABRES STREAK TOWARDS YOU IN 'FINGERTIP' FORMATION. EVASION IS YOUR ONLY CHANCE. YOU STAB AT THE LEFT RUDDER PEDAL WITH YOUR FOOT,

LAY THE COLT ON YOUR LAP AND PUSH DOWN ON THE YOKE. G-FORCES FROM THE DIVE STRETCH YOUR FACE AND PULL AT YOUR BODY. THE B50A SUPERFORTRESS YOU FLY IS A GARGANTUAN CRAFT, ABLE TO CROSS CONTINENTS WITH A PAYLOAD OF DEATH, YET SHE MOVES LIKE A DANCER IN YOUR HANDS.

YOU SEE MUZZLE FLASHES AS THE SABRES ATTACK. BULLETS STRIKE THE FUSELAGE OF YOUR AIRCRAFT, LIKE STEEL PUNCHES DRIVEN BY GIANT HAMMERS. SOMEONE SCREAMS. YOU HEAR A HISS OF AIR AS THE CABIN DEPRESSURISES, THEN SEE PAPERS FLYING – LOGBOOKS AND HERSHEY WRAPPERS ALL SUCKED AFT IN A RUSH OF AIR.

AHEAD YOU SEE THE TOWERING WALL OF BLACK CUMU-LONIMBUS CLOUD, TWENTY THOUSAND FEET HIGH, A PHALANX OF DARK GHOST-SHAPES RIDING THE SKY, JOSTLING LIKE HORSEMEN. GUSTS ROCK THE FU-SELAGE AND THE SEA IS A GROWING FURY, WIND-TOSSED WAVE CRESTS BURSTING INTO WHITE TIPS.

YOU KNOW THAT THE STORM MIGHT SAVE YOU, THAT REACHING THE CURTAINS OF DARK CLOUD WILL MEAN A REPRIEVE. YET THE SABRES SWARM LIKE BATS. AGAIN COMES THE CRASH AND WHINE OF FIFTY CALI-BRE MACHINE GUN ROUNDS BREACHING THE FUSELAGE, AND LOUD, UNBEARABLE WEEPING.

SOMEONE CRIES OUT, 'GOD HELP US. THOSE MEN WEAR OUR UNIFORM, THEY'RE OUR BROTHERS IN ARMS – PLEASE MAKE THEM STOP.'

'I TOLD YOU, HEADS DOWN,' YOU SHOUT, WAVING THE COLT BEFORE TURNING BACK TO THE DASH.

ALL LIGHTS FLICKER OFF, YET THE FIRST TENDRILS OF DRIFTING CLOUD ARE JUST HALF A MILE AHEAD. YOU SEE SMOKE STREAM FROM THE STARBOARD OUTER

ENGINE.

YOU REACH FOR THE FIRE-FIGHTING SWITCHES AS
THE FIRST SILKY THREADS OF CLOUD PASS BY THE
SCREEN, AND A SHROUD ENVELOPES THE AIRCRAFT.
YOU LOOK DOWN AT THE GAUGES. THEY SHOW FUEL
FOR FOUR THOUSAND MILES, BUT YOU KNOW THAT
YOUR CHANCES OF MAKING IT A FRACTION OF THAT
DISTANCE ARE REMOTE. YOU THINK OF YOUR BROTH-
ER, AND HOW CAN HE POSSIBLY LIVE WITHOUT YOU.

OUTSIDE, IN THE DARKNESS OF THE STORM, SAINT
ELMO'S FIRE DANCES ON THE WINGTIPS AND NOSE
CONE, LUMINOUS BLUE FORKS OF STATIC ELECTRIC-
ITY, LEAPING AND CONTORTING LIKE GYMNASTS.
SOMEONE IS PRAYING. YOU ARE NOT THE ONLY ONE
STILL ALIVE. YOU LAY THE HANDGUN ON THE DASH
AND CUT THE THROTTLES BACK TO CRUISING SPEED.

IN ALL THE WORLD YOU CAN THINK OF ONLY ONE SAFE
PLACE. YOU STEER THE PLANE SOUTH, KNOWING THAT
IF YOU ARE WRONG YOU WILL ALL DIE TONIGHT.

# ONE

Around dawn a fisherman tending his nets wide offshore from the Filipino village of Cariaga looked up and saw a plane such as he hadn't seen since the war between the Japanese and Americans. Flying unusually low, it appeared to have been damaged, and only three of the propellers were turning.

In Ambon, off the coast of West Papua, two teenage sisters tending the family taro plot saw an American plane. The youngest claimed that she had seen the handsome pilot through the round window at the nose.

In Maningrida, in Australia's Northern Territory, three children from the Kunibidji people stopped their game of keep-away on the beach to watch the plane pass over. Despite its size, they thought it looked old and tired, like the elderly men who stayed in the shade all day with their dogs. Surely, they decided, it would die soon and go to heaven like the missionaries promised happened to all good people.

Further south, a lanky nineteen-year-old camp cook for a gang of buffalo hunters woke up in the mid-morning. They had all drunk too much rum the night before, and the camp was littered with sleeping men. The youth crawled out of his swag and was taking a leak on a nearby tree when he heard a roar in the sky. Looking up he saw a huge bomber, blocking out the sun with the width of its massive wings.

The ear-splitting sound of the aircraft's three working engines woke the camp. The men were still talking about what they had seen when they loaded their Lee-Enfield carbines and rode off on their horses for the day.

In Tucson, Arizona, ten-year-old Danny Carter came home to find three cars parked outside his house. The yard was busy with men, some wearing Air Force uniforms, others in black suits and hats.

Danny looked imploringly at Miss Sullivan, the woman who boarded him while Matt was away, leaning on the handrail at the foot of the front steps. Tears fell down her face. Danny had never seen her cry before. Never imagined her capable of it.

Beside her stood Pastor Siefring, Davis-Monthan Base's chaplain, his arm around her shoulders. Miss Sullivan took Danny's hand. Her skin was cold, and her lipstick pale.

'Come inside,' she said. 'I'm afraid that there's some very bad news.'

They sat Danny at the kitchen table. The chaplain's voice was a dull monotone. 'I'm sorry to tell you that your older brother is missing in action ... believed killed.'

People came and went. The chaplain led a prayer then drove away, but more cars arrived. Men with frightening faces sat down at the table, firing questions. 'Was your brother acting strangely before he went overseas? Did he go to meetings late at night? Was he a communist?'

Danny scarcely heard. Two words repeating over and over. *Matt's dead. Matt's dead. Matt's dead ...*

'Did your brother bring foreigners home with him at any time? Men with strange accents? Have you had any mail from him? Did he leave any papers?'

After a while they left the house, carrying cartons of papers, books, the contents of a filing cabinet, maps, magazines and dreams. Their boots thumped on the wooden stairs as they tramped out to their cars.

Forty years passed. The war in Korea faded into memory. Vietnam divided a generation and left wounds deeper than shrapnel. Saddam Hussein's Republican Guards marched into Kuwait. Kingston Rule ran a record time in the Melbourne Cup and Allan Border's cricket team beat Graham Gooch's England by ten wickets at the Gabba.

Finally, the time came.

# TWO

## 1990

That country. Australia's north. It gets in the blood. Hills the colour of a beating heart. Exposed layers of stone like muscle, sinew, and bone. Wheeling kites; big water; smoke and distance. When you leave, the longing will tear you inside out.

Here, rivers snake past dun-brown country as weathered as time itself, spirits haunt the shadows and myth becomes real. A land fractured as if cracked by sledgehammer strokes, and where modern civilisation is yet to make more than a child's imprint.

Two vehicles barrelled east on the Central Arnhem Road, a couple of hours past Bulman Community, leaving cones of bull-dust hanging in the air behind them. A cassette tape in the player blasted out songs by the Angels, Midnight Oil, and a Yolngu outfit from Nhulunbuy called Yothu Yindi.

The northern quadrant of sky was dark with one of those dry storms that patrol the Top End before the real rains start, with the sun slanting through in brilliant orange, throwing shadows from the moving vehicles on that narrow ribbon of road.

Both vehicles were cut down 70 Series LandCruisers, painted in camouflage daubs of brown and green. These were known in the Australian Army as RFSVs or Regional Force Surveillance Vehicles. The rear trays were stacked with supplies and equipment. On the leading vehicle an upturned aluminium punt was tied down on the racks with brown hemp rope and truckie's hitches.

Sergeant Jamie McKinnon held the wheel in his right hand, finger tapping along with the music. He was not quite six feet tall, sun-hardened and brown, with a raw-boned strength that was obvious in the forearms exposed by his rolled-up sleeves.

Ray, beside him, was locally born and bred, with curly dark hair and the handsome features of the Jawoyn people. His shoulder patch bore the red, orange and green triangles of Australia's North West Mobile Force – NORFORCE.

Like most Indigenous members of the unit, Ray was a bushman without peer, and he had learned the skills of a soldier patiently. A natural hunter and superb scout, Ray never stopped scanning the bush on either side of the road.

In the back seat, her face occasionally coming into view in the rear-view mirror, was a young woman they had been told to call Ms Jones, on attachment from ASIO, the Australian Security and Intelligence Organisation. The order to bring her along had come from the top. So far Jamie hadn't seen her take a backwards step to anyone, most certainly not the corporal back at Larrakeyah Barracks in Darwin who had made the mistake of whistling at her.

Her lips were set in a hard, disapproving line, her eyes hidden by her Ray-bans. The legs that extended from her bush shorts were tanned and nicely shaped, but Jamie had no intention of admiring the view.

They had just come down from a steep jump-up when Ray saw something. Jamie knew the signs before his mate pointed one long forefinger out into the scrub to the north of the road. Jamie had backed Ray up on too many patrols to miss how his head froze in position, eyes narrowing, thick eyebrows coming together. Jamie was already lifting his foot off the accelerator when Ray burst out.

'Hey Sarge, slow up, will you?'

'What's happening?'

Ray pointed down towards a rocky gully on the northern

side of the road. 'See the dust cloud.'

Jamie eased down on the brake, swinging over to the side while he stared in the direction of Ray's finger. He picked it out straight away – a raised figment of dust – spreading too wide for a willy-willy, and too localised for running livestock. He was conscious that Ms Jones was leaning forward on the seat. Her presence irritated him.

Ray rummaged in the glove box and retrieved a pair of binoculars. He lifted them to his eyes, and focussed the lens with subtle movements of his forefinger. 'Definitely something moving in the scrub there Sarge. Not sure … must be a vehicle.'

'We'd better check it out.' Jamie turned to their passenger, 'Ms Jones, would you mind staying in the vehicle while we take a look?'

'Is that really necessary?' Ms Jones asked. Her honey-coloured hair was in a pigtail, threaded through the rear of her black cap. Her bush shirt had dark arcs of sweat under her arms and down her back. It was hot, and even the open windows failed to make a difference.

Jamie jabbed a thumb at the vehicle behind them. 'My job is to get Mister Danny Carter out bush and back safely. That means checking out potential threats along the way.'

Escort duty was usually regarded as a 'soft' assignment, but Jamie had his reasons for volunteering. He had the heart of an explorer, and their route into the escarpment country of southern Arnhem Land was new to him. How could a man with an adventurous soul say no? Besides, the American's interest in an inaccessible portion of Arnhem Land intrigued him.

Jamie engaged the handbrake and stepped out onto the gravel strip alongside the road. The sun hit him hard, but he gave no sign. Ray moved around to the gun rack, passing through two SLR rifles, closing the door carefully so his dog didn't squeeze out.

Jamie turned and looked down into the gully. The dust cloud was growing. *Jesus fucking Christ, what is it?* He hefted his weapon. The SLRs, more properly designated as the L1A1 Self-Loading Rifle, were decades old now, the wooden stocks scratched and scarred. Most of the regular army had long since updated to the newer F88 Austeyr. Jamie slid the bolt, checking the load of dull brass 7.62mm rounds, fingers nimble with long familiarity.

'You ready Sarge?' Ray called.

'Yeah. Two secs.'

Jamie stepped back from the vehicle and ran his eye over Ray's gear. They both wore disruption pattern camouflage uniform, along with black GP boots, green webbing belts and a giggle hat. The only differences in their gear was that Jamie wore sunglasses, and Ray a red, yellow, green and white striped band on his left wrist.

Ms Jones, ignoring Jamie's instructions, was out of the Toyota, leaning on the bonnet. She had binoculars in her left hand and was peering intently down into the gully. Her lips betrayed no emotion, but Jamie noted that she was no longer telling them that they were wasting their time.

Ray called him, 'You right Sarge? Come on, let's go.'

Jamie glanced back at the driver of the second RFSV and signalled for him to wait, before turning to follow his mate. There were no fences to cross, and few obstacles, only wattles with their charcoal-coloured trunks and patches of blood-red stones scattered like marbles on ground that held no moisture, only dust as soft and light as face powder. Even Ray's controlled feet raised a puff with each impact.

Three hundred metres down the slope Ray swung his left hand from rear to front around his waist to signal that Jamie should follow as he changed direction, taking advantage of the terrain to skirt the area of interest unseen. NORFORCE patrols had signals for everything, even for eating and sleeping. They could march and camp for days without a word if they had to.

Another signal from Ray, fingers spread towards the dust cloud, indicated that they should move in fast. They sped up, still using cover but heading directly for the increasing whirl of dust in the gully.

Jamie became aware of the noise, and it was like a needle of adrenaline deep into the brain. A rhythmic clatter. Undoubtedly an engine. Ray pointed ahead to the line of gums that marked the gully, then turned his forefinger in a circle, indicating that they should try to converge at a thirty-degree angle of separation for maximum fire control if it became necessary.

Ray moved on, sliding over the ground as smoothly as oil flowing from a can. No one Jamie had ever met moved like him. They reached the first of the trees. Ray stopped, lifting the rifle to his shoulder as Jamie came up on his flank in support.

Then came a rush of howling turbines. The dark outline of a chopper rose out of a twisting cloud of dust. Jamie recognised the US Navy Seahawk as it levitated slowly. He had seen them on joint exercises dozens of times. Yet the roundels and identification numbers on this one had been painted over with grey.

'Cover!' Jamie shouted, swivelling his neck to watch the huge craft loom over them, swoop across past the LandCruisers, then come back at a height of a couple of hundred feet. For one shattering moment it seemed to Jamie that it positioned itself for a strafing run.

Yet Jamie had already seen that the craft was unarmed. This act looked to him like a demonstration of what they could do if they wanted, of how vulnerable the expedition was. An ominous warning of the stakes at play here.

Jamie didn't need to say a word, or signal to Ray. Both had their weapons up, moving towards the area where the chopper had been. The hanging dust was dispersing now, and they could see where they were going.

They moved cautiously forward to the place where the Seahawk's wheels had touched earth, making furrows in the dust. A strong smell of avgas pervaded the area. The chopper had landed to refuel, probably from a bladder carried on the flight deck. There was no other sign that they had been here apart from a single discarded coke can.

The Seahawk rose vertically to what must have been two or three thousand feet, then made a beeline for the broad waters of the Gulf of Carpentaria, far beyond the unsettled grey of the horizon.

Slinging his rifle Jamie stormed back the way they had come, heading for the second of the two vehicles, making for the driver's side. The window came down. The driver was a NOR-FORCE private, a middle-aged bloke called Wally, only new to the regiment and still with a Darwin beer-drinker's softness about him.

'Was it one of ours, Sarge?'

'No, it damn well wasn't.'

Danny Carter, sitting beside Wally, eyed the rifles nervously. 'What's going on?'

Jamie leaned down so he could look through the open window to Danny. The American was a hard-looking man. The sinews of his neck were thick like gnarled fig-tree roots. Even his voice had a steely quality to it, despite the Virginian twang.

'Just a fucking Navy Seahawk in the middle of nowhere. I think you might know more about that than I do.'

There were two more Americans in the back seat. Tasha, Danny's daughter, and Glenn, her husband. Both were fiercely protective of Danny, but it was the latter who spoke now, 'Sergeant McKinnon, can we be civil about this?'

Jamie aimed his eyes like weapons at Danny Carter. 'It would help if you'd tell me what the fuck is going on.'

Ms Jones the spook had come up behind Jamie. 'Leave him alone, please.'

Jamie turned. 'I want some answers. That was a US Navy chopper with IDs blanked out, on sovereign Australian territory. If I'm taking my men into danger I want to know why. I really don't think that's too much to ask.' He turned his attention to Danny again. 'You're going to get us killed or start a fucking war or something. That chopper was interested in you, not me, and it's from your own country, brus. What the hell are we doing here?'

'I'm sorry,' said Danny, 'but like I just told you, I can't tell you just yet.'

Ms Jones took a fold of Jamie's shirtsleeve between thumb and forefinger and tugged on it hard. 'Can we please just all get back in the vehicles and drive?'

# THREE

The NORFORCE men were part of a unit officially designated as Green Patrol Three, Darwin Squadron, North West Mobile Force. The regiment was a mix of Indigenous and white Territorians, trained to sustain themselves, and if necessary, fight for their lives in the Top End scrub.

The hands on Jamie's scratched old Seiko were showing four-thirty in the afternoon when he swung the RFSV off the road and down a sandy track to the first night's camp. The route was almost impossible to see if you didn't know it, used maybe only once or twice a year.

Jamie had a good scan in all directions as they parked above the river. He left the vehicle, then turned to watch as the second LandCruiser came to a halt. The three Americans, then Wally spilled out, stretching on the track in their Nike runners.

When Wally closed his door and walked down to look at the river appreciatively, Jamie saw that sometime during the day he had ditched his GP boots in favour of a pair of thongs. Hardly a hanging offence but even so …

Barely forty, Wally, looked ten years older. His khaki shirt was straining with his beer belly. He turned towards Jamie.

'Got them here safely, Sarge.'

'That's something, at least.'

Wally responded by walking to the back of his RFSV where he picked the lid off the Engel fridge, reaching inside for one of the icy green cans packed inside.

'Put it back,' Jamie snapped. 'I want this camp set up before you even think about opening a beer, brus. Understood?'

The official daily ration was two, and on a baby-sitting job like this Jamie would normally turn a blind eye to stretching that a little, but not until the work was done, and there was that damned chopper.

Ray and Jamie had set up hundreds of bush camps, and each had a task that had become a speciality. Ray stretched ropes between trees for their hootchies – green tarp-like sheets that peg down on each side, while Jamie gathered and cut firewood, opened camp tables and lugged tubs of food and kitchen utensils into what would become a central cooking and eating area.

Wally helped the Americans pitch their blue Coleman tent, then wandered away to dig a hole for the army-issue thunder box and screen it off with brown hessian.

Within twenty minutes the fire was going, the billy rumbling away, suspended from a soot-blackened tripod, and hootchies stretched tight over their ropes. While Ray lay down on his sleeping bag and closed his eyes – all soldiers learn to sleep when they can – Jamie walked down to the river.

Ray's dog Yella followed, his pointed nose twitching as he sniffed at old mussel shells and dried up bones, hunting the ground head down, nose all but scooping a trail in the river gravel. Part dingo, part camp-dog, he had a hungry belly like a whippet, and a coat of white pig-like bristles.

Ray was besotted with him, slept with him, fed him part of his rations, and caught fish for him. The rest of the unit had learned to tolerate the independently minded canine, but since his two main interests in life were thieving food and perfuming himself with roadkill, that took some effort.

The sound of feet on pebbles disturbed Jamie, and he turned to see Ms Jones picking her way across the black-tipped rocks on the riverbank. She moved well on the broken ground, with plenty of flex in the knee and arch. The power of her thighs was evident in the length of the stride and ease with which she lowered herself from stone to stone.

Arriving beside him at the water's edge, at first she didn't acknowledge him, just looked around in all directions before finally crouching, selecting a stone and skipping it expertly across the surface.

That old boyhood habit of counting came back to Jamie. Nine, ten, eleven … splash.

'Hi,' he said.

'Afternoon, Sergeant.'

'Call me Jamie,' he said. 'Do you really expect us to use official titles for days on end?'

She held his gaze. 'First names encourage familiarity. I'm about to set off on an expedition with five men and just one other woman. Don't you think that keeping some distance might be a good idea?'

Jamie hesitated for a moment, then, 'Okay. I get that.'

Ms Jones moved closer to the water, took a double handful and splashed her face. When she stood again there were droplets on her cheeks.

'It doesn't help,' he said. 'Not when it's this hot. Nothing will cool us down until the rains break.'

Ms Jones shrugged, 'That Private Blake seems to be an interesting character?'

Jamie sighed, 'Wally? Yeah okay, but I'm not going to talk about any of my men behind their backs.'

'Fair enough, but Danny thinks he might have seen him somewhere before.'

'That seems unlikely. Lots of people think that kind of thing.'

'That's true, they do. But leaving Private Blake aside, you had no right to confront Danny Carter like you did back there. Your job is simple: don't ask questions, just take him where he needs to go.'

'Fuck him. I like coming out here – but when there's Yank choppers in the scrub and I don't know what the hell's going on I start getting cranky.'

Ms Jones looked towards the dying glow in the west. 'You're acting like an arsehole.'

The insult took Jamie off-balance. He had been looking at her teeth. They were the whitest he'd ever seen. 'Don't call me that. You fly up here from Canberra, wet behind the ears, and start throwing your weight around.'

'There's a lot more to Danny Carter than meets the eye. Don't underestimate him, or me.' She turned and walked away from the river.

Vaguely annoyed with himself, Jamie watched her go, skipped a few rocks then followed her back to camp, the dog nosing along in his footsteps. The sound of Ray's voice met him half-way up the grassy bank.

'Hey Sarge.'

'What is it, brus?'

'The Colonel wants to talk to you on the HF. He says that there's a fucking American carrier out in the Gulf. Not in our territorial waters or anything, but close enough—'

'That explains the chopper,' Jamie grunted.

'Yeah,' Ray agreed. 'Sure does, brus.'

'I'm on my way,' Jamie said, relieved but worried that his assessment of the strange aircraft had been no overreaction. He looked across and saw Wally looking at him quizzically, pointing at the Engel fridge. It had been a long hot day at the wheel, and besides, he was doing pretty well with the Americans.

'Alright Wally, you can crack one open if everything's done.' He turned to Ray. 'Get me a beer too, will you mate? Sounds like I'm going to need it.'

He was halfway to the radio when the big American, Danny's son-in-law Glenn, walked across. He had been some kind of baseballer, never in the big money, but an elite player nonetheless.

'I think you owe Danny an apology,' he said.

Jamie's change of mood evaporated. 'I don't happen to agree, and I'm busy right now, so can you please get out of my way?' They glared at each other like a pair of bears, then 'Now listen. I'm not here to be nice to you. Just to get you out into the bush without losing anyone. I'm not being told where we're going, why we're going there, and what the hell we'll find there. Then we happen upon a US Navy chopper refuelling in the middle of nowhere, and it looked for all the world like they were going to start strafing us. Do you understand just how fucking unusual that is?'

'I suppose so.'

Glenn's wife, Tasha came across from the tent and drew her arm around her husband's waist. 'Let's not argue,' she said. 'I can understand why you feel the need to know more, but we just can't tell you any more just yet.'

Ms Jones appeared. 'Let's all calm down and get on with each other, we've got a long way to go.'

Glenn slowly lowered his head. 'Fine. I'm good with that.'

Jamie brushed past the ASIO agent. 'I don't need your help,' he said. 'I can fight my own battles.'

'This is not supposed to be a battle,' she replied.

Ignoring her, he stalked to the leading LandCruiser and opened the door. He sat down in the front seat with the door open, feet flat on the ground. 'Shit,' he said to himself, surprised and annoyed at how riled he was getting on this trip. Taking a deep breath, he picked up the radio handset.

'Green Patrol Three Leader, come in base, over.'

'Base Leader. Over.'

The CO, Lieutenant Colonel Lineham's voice had been a comfort throughout Jamie's career. From Victoria River Downs to Coburg, that gravelly rasp had brought good sense and assistance, when necessary, without fuss or judgement.

'A couple of things,' came the voice through the speaker. 'Ray told me about the chopper. I'm going to send another vehicle and two more men. When you turn off the Arnhem Road leave coloured tags on the turns so they can catch up.'

'I'd feel more secure with more of the blokes,' said Jamie. 'That chopper rattled me.' He paused. 'Ray just told me that there's a Yank carrier out there.'

'Sure is.'

'Which one?'

'The *Carl Vinson*, apparently.'

'Shit,' Jamie grunted. One of the new supercarriers.

'We can only assume the chopper was one of theirs. There'll be a protest from us through the usual channels – it won't make the press of course – and the RAAF are going to fly deterrence missions over the area so the Yanks will think twice about going up again. ASIO is handling it – keeping everything hush hush.'

'Good. But can you please tell me why?' Jamie was watching the camp. Wally had caught himself an olive python, a couple of metres long, and was showing off to the Americans, letting it squeeze his arms, all the while keeping a firm grip on its head. Tasha was taking photos, in between squeals. This was a welcome distraction, Jamie supposed.

'No, because I don't know much more than you. I'm out of the loop, sorry. I'm pissed off but what can I do?'

'Yeah, it sucks.'

'One more thing. I've seen the weather forecast. There's rain coming, a trough heading south. Be ready for it.'

Jamie wasn't surprised. The rains were overdue, with the country near breaking with tension, crackling with static, waiting for moisture. Ray's people called this the Time of Thunder, when clouds crackle and growl, warning of the coming storms.

The conversation over, Jamie hung the mike back on the hook and stood up.

'Hey Wally, let that snake go.'

The big man grinned. 'Okay Sarge, you worried that Ray'll cook it up?'

'No, I'm worried that the fucking thing will bite you, and we'll have to get you medivacked. They're not poisonous, but those bites get infected. So, let it go, and while you're at it lay off the racist crap.'

'Sure thing Sarge.'

Wally grinned and carried his catch to the thick bush alongside the camp.

'Not there,' Jamie shouted. Take it down the track a bit for fuck's sake.'

Wally shrugged, retightened his grip on the reptile, and

walked away.

That night, the fire dying down and the last of the patrol heading into bed, Jamie climbed into his hootchie. He unbuttoned his shirt and trousers and pulled on a pair of King-Gee shorts. His last act was to lift a medallion on a steel chain over his head. He pressed it to his lips, then placed it under his pillow.

In minutes he was fast asleep.

# FOUR

An hour after dawn, the RFSVs rolled out of camp, bull bars wrapped with rags and dew beaded on the sprung aerials.

Back on the main road the first barrier was the Wilton River causeway, where pandanus fronds hung over silken water, and locals sat under shady trees, shuffled cards or drank, while kids played chasies in the dust. Yella got his front legs up on Ms Jones's lap and barked at a couple of bored camp dogs.

When they were halfway across Ray said, 'You'd better stop here, Sarge.'

'Why?'

Ray pointed back to where the other vehicle had stopped on the causeway. Tasha was out of the car in ankle deep water, using her Nikon, taking photos against the shining beauty of the river pouring smoothly downstream, a grey heron standing sentry beside it, beak poised like a spear.

Tasha walked past them, still taking photos, then back again, all flashing white teeth and smiles. Pausing at the window as she went past, she said; 'I can't wait to get these rolls developed – I've never seen colours like these. Not anywhere.'

Half an hour later, while they streamed eastwards two hundred metres apart, four Fa-18 jet fighters from RAAF base Tindal streaked overhead at low altitude, engines shrieking over the rumble of the diesels.

'Looks like the Colonel's stirred things up,' Jamie commented, and Ray nodded agreement, craning his eyes up to the windscreen as they powered on. They sky was slowly changing colour – not quite blue, not quite grey either, and tiny droplets fell from that undecided sky, spotting the screen lightly, and when Ray ran the wipers, mud pooled at the base of the screen.

They spread out so there was a kilometre between the vehicles, not enough to let the dust fully settle before the next came through, but about as far apart as Jamie wanted them.

The vehicle behind flashed its lights and Jamie pulled over, getting out and walking back.

'We need to turn here somewhere,' Danny said through the open window.

'There is no "turn here somewhere",' Jamie said.

Danny pointed to the north, then held up the instrument on his lap. It was the first civilian GPS Jamie had seen – a Magellan 1000, and he was not convinced of its usefulness. 'The GPS says that we need to go that way.'

'Hey Ray,' Jamie called. 'Give us a minute will you, mate?'

The door opened, and Ray appeared, Jamie went to meet him, leading him out of earshot. 'Mate, Danny Carter says we have to go north from here, is there a way?'

Ray stared into the bush for a minute or two, scratched his beard. 'Yeah, there's a way Sarge. An old track, not used too much these days.'

'So, you reckon it's worth a try?'

Ray shrugged, 'Yeah Sarge.'

The two greenskins walked back across to the others, where Danny Carter was waiting expectantly.

'Now Ray says he knows a way north from here, but it's not much of a track.'

'Great, thank you.'

Jamie turned and called. 'Mount up, you lot, we're going in.'

Jamie left Ray with the motor running and tied a blue marker ribbon to a woollybutt trunk on the side of the road to mark their route. Then, back in the RFSV he followed a wisp of hard ground between paperbark swampland on either side, interspersed with dark green livistona palms, with fronds so wide they all but blocked out the sun.

Ray drove with a gentle momentum, dodging and weaving around mature trees. Every now and then the way was blocked by immature saplings. In this case he slowed, edged up until the bullbar was just touching the trunk, then poured on the power, pushing it down, trampling over with leaves and branches scraping the undercarriage.

'It's a shame you have to kill trees like that,' Ms Jones said, leaning over from the back seat.

'What do you want us to do?' Jamie grinned. 'Dig them up and transplant them.' He winked at Ray who smiled back.

Over a set of low hills, they were back into grasslands the colour of moselle. Old trees along the gully lines had been flattened. Legacy of some old cyclone. Jamie knew just how bad those storms could be, having lived through Cyclone Tracy when it swept away Darwin on Christmas Day 1974. He would never forget how his family learned to live without a solid roof, running water and power, using tarps to channel rainwater into buckets. One of his vivid memories was of lining up at distribution centres for rations of rice, tinned foods and flour.

Up until then, Jamie had a happy childhood. He was a brown kid living on the flats near Rapid Creek, with a house full of half-brothers, cousins, running through that colourful, steaming hot and cosmopolitan city like they owned the place.

The young Jamie knew little of the wider world. Even the notion of Canberra and a Prime Minister was vague to him. He was caught up with school, Aussie Rules football, food, fishing, and fun. Late every Saturday morning his mother would make him walk with her to the shops down on Cavenagh Street and they'd return home with two paper bags of last-minute specials – Friday's bread, meat offcuts, wilting vegetables and some canned food.

That night, in a cooking pot, Jamie's mother would make a

stew, stirred with a red ironwood spoon one of the uncles had carved for her. That stew would be reheated over and over to last them through the week. Laundry day was Sunday, and every week their mother washed the bottom sheet of their beds and the top sheet was rotated down. Monday to Friday they walked barefoot to Saint Mary's school down on Lindsay Street, right in town, where the nuns gave them hell for six hours.

When Jamie got nits Mum would shave his head and rub tea tree oil on their almost bare scalps. Jamie could still remember the smell and the sting of it on the bites.

Thinking of his mother always affected Jamie's mood, and when they stopped to boil the billy an hour up the track the melancholy was yet to leave him. Tasha did most of the preparation, bustling around in a bright orange singlet, laying out mugs and sliced date loaf still fresh from the bakery in Darwin. Jamie lazily noticed the straps of her bra as her singlet moved around.

It was their first real chance to talk. Jamie learned that Tasha was a trained biologist, working at the National Museum in Washington, DC. Her specialty was ferns, and she spent up to six weeks each year in a particular mountain range in Colorado, collecting and observing.

Some people you can see the child in more easily than others. Tasha was like that. Jamie could see the class helper in her, the lack of confidence with people that might have stemmed from being an only child. Danny treated her differently than most parents of adults Jamie had known – more indulgently – but also with an emotional need.

Tasha's black hair was always perfect, held back with a coloured band that changed each day, as if she had brought an endless supply. She dressed in shorts and button-up shirts and had good walking boots and gaiters.

After a while Glenn came and sat beside her. They were a good couple, with obvious feelings for each other, and Jamie wished that they had gotten off to a better start.

Using his hat on the wire handle Jamie lifted the billy from the crackling dry-stick fire and threw in a handful of Lan-choo tea from the box. He stood up and looked around. Ms Jones was tapping away on a portable NEC computer – the first Jamie had seen – in the back seat of the RFSV. The contrivance was, she told him, referred to as a laptop, and it had a power plug that fitted the vehicle's cigarette lighter.

'Experts and their gadgets,' smiled Jamie, and the others laughed.

# FIVE

Since the expedition was operating under the auspices of the Australian Army, each camp was constructed accordingly. That night Ray ordered a stop beside a lily-studded billabong, sunken into a plain of grass and scattered trees that stretched into the distance.

'What's this place called?' Jamie asked. He didn't try to remember the name Ray recounted, just enjoyed the music of the words, spoken in an ancient tongue. Standing on the LandCruiser's running boards he looked down along the waterhole. From that height he could see a kilometre or more along its length, an ancient oxbow that must have once been a river channel, carved out of the plain by the relentless flow of water.

'Looks like a nice long hole. Plenty of fish, I bet.'

Ray smiled back and held his arms out to indicate a big fish. 'Yeah, barra, catfish in there. Plenty cherabin, bony bream for them to eat all the time, so they get fat.'

'Might have time to launch the punt in the morning before we head off,' Jamie said. 'Let's get things organised and think about it.'

Ray waggled a finger at him. 'Now don't you upset Miss Jones again, Sarge.'

Jamie grinned, 'I'll try not to. She sure doesn't like being upset. And it's Mezz Jones, not Miss Jones.'

Camp hygiene was a priority, and Jamie selected an area for the pit latrine, well away from the waterway and screened by a brace of jagged boulders. The thunderbox itself was standard army issue, folding galvanised steel plate, streaked with rust but perfectly strong.

Glenn grabbed a shovel and headed down with Jamie. The American started to dig while the NORFORCE sergeant pounded in star pickets for the burlap screen. The ground was soft, and the hole took shape quickly. They manhandled the thunderbox into place and levelled it up, wriggling it into the dirt until it sat flat.

Glenn leaned on his shovel, breathing just a touch heavily after the exertion, sweat gluing a clump of his blonde-brown hair so it sat at right angles to the rest. 'You probably think catering to a bunch of Yanks is a pain in the ass.'

Jamie picked up the sledgehammer and rested it over his shoulder. 'No, it's interesting. My father was American.'

'No shit?'

'Yeah.'

'Is he still around?'

'He died before I was born.'

'I'm sorry.'

'Don't be, it's ancient history, and I'm proud to have a Larrakeyah mum and American dad.'

A heavy volley of thunder startled Jamie, and he turned in time to catch the breeze on his face. Looking up past the tree-tops he could see dark clouds moving fast, blocking out a good third of the sky. 'Looks like we might get a storm ahead of those rains,' he said. 'That'd be a relief.'

With Glenn trailing behind, he hurried back towards the camp, where Ray was adding the finishing touches to their hootchies.

'Hey brus. Are we going to cop this storm or not?'

Ray grinned back. 'Yeah. I think it's finally going to rain this time, Sarge, but it won't last long.'

'Hey everyone,' Jamie called, 'better get your gear under cover.' The good storms almost always moved in quickly. The ones that rumbled on the horizon for hours came to nothing.

Wally hadn't moved, still sitting on a stump, staring vacantly.

'Did you hear me for Christ's sake?'

'Yeah, yeah, alright,' Wally muttered, and started packing things up. Jamie walked back to his own vehicle, just as all hell broke loose.

For six months, since April, no rain had fallen. The soil was desiccated, sucked of moisture by air creeping northwards from the country's red heart. The first gust of that storm came with a smell of moisture so strong it was like a physical release, a momentary disconnection. At the same time dry leaves dropped from their stalks and descended in their thousands.

'Hey, you lot, better get under cover,' Jamie shouted, but he had no intention of getting out of the rain. Standing in it was a physical need. Back when he was a kid that first rainstorm was a matter of great excitement, and they'd gather out on the street, faces turned upwards, bodies trembling with anticipation.

The sky was now painted deep black from one side to the other, with different layers of clouds, closer and further away moving at different speeds. A fissure of lightning speared overhead, and the crack that followed was like a thump from a subwoofer in Jamie's chest.

The rain started with a pulse of heavy, huge drops, followed by a momentary relapse into calm, and then it started. Rain filled the air from ground to sky, and there was Jamie standing, drinking in the taste and sound.

Rain-blurred figures stood around him, even Ms Jones. Not even she could resist the saturating sensuousness of it.

'You can get in one of the cars if you like,' Jamie shouted, but for the first time since they'd met, he saw that she was laughing, lightning flickering on her face.

'Why would I do that?' she shouted back.

They laughed together, and Jamie tried not to notice how her sodden shirt clung to her body.

Ray stripped off his shirt and danced, face filled with joy. He danced in the way his people had done for fifty thousand years, when the first rain of the season washed away the dust.

His bare feet slammed into the earth. He sang a song that was older than the pyramids of Egypt, older even than the celebrated Neanderthal paintings in the caves of France.

It was part of his story, this rain.

After thirty minutes of deluge, the storm moved on, leaving the air cleansed, with new smells brewing. The rain had brought the bush to life, the insect sounds now a roar, birds rushing and darting. As night fell, flying foxes left the trees along the waterhole, flying overhead in endless waves, their ammonia smell hanging thickly in the air.

Stranger creatures too – land crabs crawled out of the earth with the rain – nippers held like weapons against Tasha and her camera lens, torches and exclamations. The air cooled only briefly, and the heat, as it returned full force, had a steamy new level of humidity.

Later, however, with dinner cleared up, and everything done, Jamie wandered up to the RFSV and dragged a battered black case out of the rear cargo bay. His old Maton guitar had covered almost as many miles as the LandCruiser. It had a bruise beneath the sound hole from a fall when Jamie had leaned it against a vehicle once, and a few minor scratches, but it was otherwise a beautiful instrument, oiled by years of sweaty hands.

Danny was passing a bottle of Scotch around the fire, and the NORFORCE boys had their ration of iced cans. Jamie strummed a G major chord, metallic bright and just a little out of tune so he leaned his ear down close to the sound hole and twiddled the tuning heads until he was happy.

Tasha asked Jamie if he knew any Joni Mitchell, and he sang Big Yellow Taxi, repeating the second verse because the words to the third had slipped his memory. Ray had been watching him for a while, firelight reflected in the dark of his eyes while he waited for Jamie to play a song he liked.

Jamie teased him with a country version of Marianne Faithful's Lucy Jordan before moving on to the hard stuff.

'You want me to play Johnny Cash brus?' Jamie asked him.

Ray's teeth flashed as he nodded. 'Yeah.'

'What song?'

'Maybe the one about the boy called Sue?'

As Jamie sang the song he could see Danny mouth the lyrics, thinking that of course he must have grown up with this stuff.

They all shouted: My name is Sue; how do you do?

Jamie segued straight into Ring of Fire, bunging on the deep voice, all the effects, even the accent. Yet, it had been a long day, and he was ready to hit the hay a little after ten.

Ray's eyes twinkled. 'That rain we had, Sarge. Pretty sure that'll get the fish biting in that waterhole.'

Their eyes met. If you have that hunter-gatherer gene in you, no matter who you are and where you're from, you can't resist the call, and Ray was right. The rain had energised the bush. The air itself had a new and tantalising perfume. Rain had brought life, and all the creatures – even fish – would know it.

Jamie looked at Danny. 'I don't think anyone's going to be ready to hit the road until about nine anyway, so Ray and I might throw the boat into the waterhole at dawn, just for an hour or so.'

It wasn't exactly a question, but Danny acknowledged that Jamie was in some way seeking his permission. 'Fishing's not my thing, but that's okay, I guess, as long as we're not delayed in any way.'

'Good stuff,' Jamie said, then to the others. 'Any of you people want to come.'

Wally grinned back. 'Someone's got to cook breakfast while you blokes have fun. I'll stay here.'

Glenn was first to throw his hand in. 'Sure thing. I'm up for it, what time?'

'Say five thirty if we're going to be back before breakfast.'

Glenn's face lost some of its initial glow of enthusiasm, and Danny said. 'He won't turn up – he won't leave my daughter. They've been trying to have a baby for years ...'

'Dad,' said Tasha sharply.

Jamie caught the twinkle in Glenn's eye and turned to Tasha.

'Maybe you could both come – there's room?'

Tasha shook her head. 'Not me, that's sleeping time. Besides, it'll give me a chance to take some specimens.'

Jamie turned to the final member of the party, ready for a lecture about not wasting time. 'Ms Jones?'

He already had a reply to her emphatic 'no,' prepared, but she surprised him. 'You know, I love boats. Back home I do a bit of water skiing.'

Jamie wasn't surprised – she had a water-skier's body. But there was a wistful look in her eye, as if that were in another life. 'Where's home? Canberra?'

'Yeah, Canberra.'

'Well why don't you come out on the waterhole with us?'

For the first time since Jamie had met her, she looked un-decided, showing him something beyond the glassy persona she breezed around with.

'I guess I'll come along if that's okay with you.'

'See you at five-thirty if you want. No harm if you change your mind.'

'I'll be there,' Ms Jones said.

'Good. Night all.'

Jamie strummed a final chord, hefted the guitar, and walked off towards his hootchie, unable to pin down why he felt so pleased with himself.

# SIX

A flock of magpie geese moved through the pre-dawn sky in dark, elegant waves. To Jamie, the surf-like rise and fall of their wingbeat was a familiar comfort as he walked towards the LandCruiser. He had suspected Ms Jones wouldn't show, so early in the morning, but surprisingly, she was there, ready and waiting, clutching a water bottle.

'Glenn's not coming,' she said. 'He decided to stay in bed – stuck his head out the side of the tent as I walked past.'

'No worries,' Jamie replied. 'More room in the punt for us. He's a fair lump of a bloke.' He climbed in and drove the Land-Cruiser down into the edge of the waterhole. Ray was on hand to help him lift the tinny down. The pair of them taking a side each, lifting it down, sliding the hull into the water with a mut-ed splash. Jamie added their gear: rods, petrol tank, knives and buckets, while Ray clamped the old Johnson outboard ono the transom and connected the fuel hose.

The three of them, with Yella at his place in the bow, were soon aboard and motoring out from the bank while the sun still glowed from below the horizon. Jamie gripped the tiller handle in his left hand, steering them across water so still and black it might have been Hades. Mist in tiny wisps spiralled upwards. Jamie could taste it, cold on his lips and tongue, as he idled the punt downstream, buttocks vibrating on the hard aluminium seat.

Ms Jones sat quietly, dressed in khaki shorts and a work shirt. Ray was silent beside her, head turning in all directions as things caught his attention.

Then, when Jamie cut the throttle and nosed up to a school of bony bream, Ray plied his cast net from the boat, standing rock-steady amidships, throwing the knotted circle of mesh so precisely that he had to release most of his catch, and keep just a dozen small fish alive in his blue flour tin, half filled with water.

They motored on downstream, past islands studded with freshwater mangroves, and surrounded by thousands of green lilies, flat on the water, with blue flowers extending like eye stalks at intervals.

Ms Jones clapped her hands excitedly. 'This place is amazing. Just beautiful.'

Jamie slowed at a snag-filled reach that looked promising. Cutting the motor to drift with the tide, he produced a spare casting outfit for Ms Jones, equipped with a small 'eggbeater' reel.

'Do you know how to use these reels?'

Ms Jones didn't answer, but merely took it from his hands, spun the handle a few times, then looked at him as if to say, just watch!

Together, with live bait and lures, they worked over the structure. Ms Jones's first few casts were a little ragged, but she was soon in the rhythm. Jamie sneaked a glance at her. The dawn light and reflections off the water suited her. He wanted to look at her all the time, but there was so much else to see – a good-sized freshwater croc scrambling from the bank into the water with a splash just nearby – a small bow wave betraying his position until he disappeared into the deeper water.

Ms Jones fished in silence, and Jamie gave thanks for that, not being enamoured of chattering anglers. Silence is part of the attraction, part of this world, and the noisy often miss clues and nuances that reward the listener.

After a few minutes Ray's hand line started disappearing over the side and he hauled in a bull-headed catfish that would have weighed a couple of kilos. Handling it carefully he hacked off its head with the blunt knife he always used and dropped the rest in the boat where it rolled around in the bilge water. Ray never seemed to worry that this kind of handling might affect the taste.

They moved several times without any barra strikes, but still they kept at it, hammering every kind of structure, or around any sign of bait fish. The lure tossing became engrossing, the world receding to only that act. Jamie warmed up, and he took off his shirt, his medallion nestled in the hairs at the centre of his chest. It seemed like they had scarcely started fishing when his watch showed almost seven thirty. Time to head back.

'We'd better get going,' he said, 'but we can troll along the bank as we go.'

Ray shot him a dirty look but cut the hook from his hand line and tied one of the two or three lures he owned – an old red Nilsmaster – on to the end. Then, the rods twitching with the action of the lures, and Ray holding his line with grim concentration, they trolled slowly back the way they had come, cutting in close to the sunken trees on that deep left-hand bank.

Half-way back Jamie's rod buckled over and the reel hummed with a good run. Even as he knocked the motor back into neutral a barramundi of around seventy centimetres in length burst from the water.

Jamie was conscious of the time and worked the fish hard. After a couple of strong runs, it lay beside the boat, Ray netted it neatly and dumped it, flapping on the floor of the boat, bright silver; red-eyed and beautiful.

'Dinner?' asked Ms Jones.

Jamie grinned back. 'Yep. Dinner. Now if you don't mind, we'd better power back or we'll be late. Hopefully there'll be another chance for you to get your own fish before the trip's over.'

'I don't care,' she said. 'I'm happy just to be out here.'

Twisting the throttle until the outboard roared, Jamie watched the hair fly from Ms Jones's head in the slipstream, and her attempts to hold it back. She was engrossed, and it gave him an opportunity to observe her. There was nothing classical about her face, but his mother used to say that beauty needs a little strangeness, and her glow of sheer good health was undeniable. He dug in his fishing bag and passed her a rubber band.

She took it, regarding him quizzically. 'You carry everything in that bag?'

'Not everything, but plenty of rubber bands. We use them for down-rigging baits. Other things.'

'Cool, thanks.'

Jamie couldn't take his eyes off her as she flung her head back and tied those flowing tresses out of her eyes. It was the moment that he saw her properly for the first time; hair tied back; face tilted into the slipstream to drink in the scented air.

She turned towards him. 'Do you still want to know what my first name is?'

'Yes, of course.'

'My name's Holly, are you happy now?'

Jamie nodded and settled back into driving the boat. He mouthed the word inside his head.

*Holly.*

*He liked it.*

*He liked it a lot.*

# SEVEN

That moment when you leave the roads you have travelled before, and turn off into the unknown, trails that are scarcely trails, where only the Traditional Owners, bushmen and hunters in the old days have passed. You become an explorer, and every tree, every termite mound is new.

Flies swarm in through the open window, and you turn off the music, because the grind of the diesel engine, squeal and crunch of tyres on gravel and the cawing of crows are the only sounds necessary.

Cloud builds across the sky into a uniform deep grey, and heavy rain showers come and go, leaving red-brown puddles on the track, and streaky runnels down the hillsides, scraping at those ancient genes we all carry. Stone and water. Raw elements. Life.

Every hill has shadows, each layer of stone tells a story, and every stream bed a history that binds millions of years into a story. Your connection to this land is a high tensile web, and euphoria begins at the base of your neck and spreads into your heart.

That was how Jamie felt that day. When he turned and caught Ray's eyes, they each knew how deeply the adventure was affecting them, in different ways. This was a journey into the heart of Arnhem Land, on a road that existed only in Ray's memory, to uncover a mystery Danny Carter would not divulge and did not yet know himself, in its entirety.

Jamie was enjoying the drive far too much to waste time thinking. The landscape grew more and more spectacular. Much of the time, in the background, they saw flat topped mesa-type ridges, but sometimes nothing stood out for long stretches, just savannah grasslands with scattered trees. Once they entered an area of rounded, globe-like hills, with stones poking in all directions like echidna quills.

The track had never been graded. It just followed the lay of the land. Small trees sometimes had to be nudged over with the bull bar so they could proceed. Red kangaroos crossed their path in proud, muscular mobs, and once, a wild donkey stallion, as solid and heavy as the landscape galloped across the track, confused by the noise and dust of the vehicles, his hide sharp-furred like Velcro, shedding in places, leaving bald callused leather beneath. His mane stood up sharply and muscles in both fore and hindquarters bunched as he ran.

'This country used to be a station, way back in the pioneer days,' said Ray. 'All round here to the sea and back again.'

'I didn't know that.' Jamie loved hearing Ray's stories.

'Arafura Station, owned by a bloke called Captain Joe Bradshaw. Us mob drove his people out, by and by. Speared his cows and burned his house. They speared Chinese gardeners, but they never hurt the station missus. Her name was Kate Rodgers, and she was a proper fighter too.'

They came to a creek steeply cut from the matrix of the plain, descending sharply down, and into a deep brown bed, already running strongly from the rain.

'You sure this is where people cross?'

Ray peered down into the ravine-like depths. 'Yeah, but there must have been some heavy rain around here. Hope we haven't left this trip too late.'

'I hope not too, brus.'

Ray raised a bushy eyebrow quizzically. 'You gonna get us stuck down there are you Sarge?'

'Not if I can help it.'

The sides were of eroded clay, and Jamie pointed out a possible route that wound precariously down one side, through the creek, then finally up the far slope. The muddy watercourse itself was almost waist deep – still easily negotiable with care.

Wally lit a smoke. 'I'll go first,' he said, 'show you mob how it's done.'

'Alright,' Jamie said, 'but we'll let the women walk just in case something happens.'

Jamie hadn't heard Holly come up behind him, and the look in her eyes warned him that he'd said the wrong thing.

'Excuse me, Sergeant McKinnon. That's rather condescending isn't it? Make the women walk?'

'Holly, I don't have time for this. I just meant for Wally to cross the creek without passengers.'

'Maybe so, but please choose your words more carefully. In my job I fight sexist pigs every day of my life – I thought you might be different. What about Danny, who happens to be a male? Isn't he walking as well?'

'Of course, it was just a slip of the tongue – I meant all the passengers. Jesus, do you have to be so touchy?'

'If you weren't so insensitive, I wouldn't have to be.'

Furious at himself, Jamie watched Wally take the RFSV over the lip and power down the steep slope.

Too fast you bloody idiot.

He tried to brake, but instead the locked wheels skidded the last few metres, the lower edge of the bull bar hitting with a thump at the bottom.

With no hesitation Wally slammed into the creek, white-brown water churning from the wheels, cleaning the mud-caked tyre grips in the process, rendering them ready for the climb.

Halfway up the slope the RFSV started losing traction, wheels spinning madly. Blue smoke erupted from the pipe, and the engine roared. Yet Wally did not let up, pouring on the power until he hit the redline.

Slowly, inch by inch, the vehicle made the slope, spraying barrow-loads of grit and dirt back down the slope. At the top, the engine note changed, and the vehicle barrelled over and out of sight.

Still smarting from Holly's anger, Jamie climbed into the other LandCruiser. Even in that state of mind, he didn't try to emulate Wally's display of raw power. He shifted into low-range, and stayed in second gear on the way down, plunging through the water at walking pace, back to first gear for the climb, avoiding the channels made by the other vehicle's wheels. Jamie needed to apply power for the last of the slope, but the 4.2 litre diesel had barely raised a sweat when he pulled in past the other vehicle and walked back to watch the others make their way across.

After safely negotiating the creek, later that day Wally managed to get his RFSV stuck. It was a nothing situation, he just lost concentration, and dropped one of the leading wheels into a hole. The limited slip diff wasn't enough to provide traction for the other wheel to pull it out.

Jamie used a chain rather than a snatch strap to drag it out, preferring the direct control, but fifteen minutes was wasted. Tempers flared unnecessarily, and when Ray was checking over the wheel for damage he called out to Jamie. 'Hey Sarge,' he said. 'You'd better come and have a look at this.'

When Jamie walked across, Ray was holding up a matchbox sized black box with a tiny wire aerial attached.

'What the hell is that?'

'I dunno.'

'Where was it?'

'Right up under the wheel arch. Magnetic – must be.'

Jamie turned it over in his hands, then spotted Holly and called her over.

'Do you know what this is, Ms Jones?' he asked as she neared.

She came closer, took it from his hand and held it up to the light.

'It's a radio transponder, used for tracking vehicles.'

'Just what I reckon, so how did it get on this car?' His eyes turned on her. She stepped back a pace.

'I had nothing to do with it. Why would I want to track this vehicle when I'm here travelling with it.'

'Who else would be carrying this kind of hardware around?'

'I didn't attach that transponder. To be honest I've never seen one like it.'

'Well someone put it there. I guess they could have slapped it on back at the barracks, or when we stopped in Pine Creek. We know the Yanks are interested in what we're doing, maybe it was them.'

Holly shrugged, 'Well you can bet there'll be one on the other RFSV. Let's find it.'

She was right, they found another one in the corresponding wheel well; right front, but there were no others, despite careful searching.

Jamie sat the little tracking devices on a fallen log and smashed them to pieces with the butt of a trenching tool. They were solid little things, but he kept pounding until they were just a mess of splintered circuit boards and hanging wires. He threw the components into the rubbish bag in the back of his LandCruiser and moved towards the driver's seat.

After notching up another dozen slow kilometres on rough ground, Ray suggested that they stop for the night in a clearing where the ground was sandy and somewhat dry, and the remnants of last year's grass was giving way to the first green shoots of the new season. A small creek looped past. Jamie suspected that it would be just a dry gully in the dry season, but right now it was a metre deep and thick with suspended clay.

'We'll boil water from that stream before we drink or cook with it,' Jamie told the group as they set up. 'Just to be on the safe side. Wally, do you mind taking your rig down another ten metres over that way, then we can use that old log to sit around the fire?'

'Cheers Sarge, I'll do it now.'

'Where do you want the hootchies, Sarge?' Ray asked.

'String them between those two she-oaks, and steer clear of that old gum – looks like a couple of those branches are ready to drop.'

Half an hour from dusk, when the work was done Ray

pointed through the dry woodland to a rocky mesa at least five hundred metres away. It was taller than the others, and crowned with red–gold cliffs.

'See that there?' Ray asked, grinning.

'Yep.'

'I know that place. It's special. Come on.'

'Why not? Just give us a sec.'

Holly walked up just as they were leaving the camp. 'Where are you two going?'

Jamie studied her face, trying to figure out if she had forgiven him for his earlier blunder. 'Climbing that hill. Ray wants to show me something.'

'I'm coming too, wait on.'

By the time Holly had her boots on, the party had swelled to five, with only Danny and Wally remaining behind.

# EIGHT

They strode out across the plain of crackling dry spear-grass, with Tasha's Nikon capturing everything from termite mounds to agile wallabies looking quizzically up from amongst the grass stalks, then taking flight as Yella made mock dashes at them, stopping short to sniff the ground where they had laid up through the day.

Most of the time, however, Yella just ran in aimless arcs through and around them, leaning into the curves like a motorcyclist, running to iron out the creases of all those hours on the back seat, and for the sheer joy of being alive.

One half of the sky was dark with cloud and the other, mostly clear, with the sun rounding up stragglers and chasing them, bright with orange pennants, into the grey mass. The rain was holding off for the moment, making Jamie more hopeful than before that they might make it to their destination before the heavens opened fully.

Jamie fell in with Holly, and he looked at her sideways, wondering if the angry words at the river crossing were going to affect what had seemed to be a developing friendship.

'Sorry I cracked up at you today,' she said. 'I guess you were only trying to be safe.'

'No … I'm sorry. I've been thinking about it all afternoon.

Maybe I have to change the way I think sometimes. There are women in NORFORCE, but I guess it's a man's world, and they just fit in.' Jamie had never met a woman like Holly, who was prepared to fight and argue for her place.

'Do you know anything at all about feminism?' she asked.

'Nah, not really.'

'Well there are some things you need to know. One is that there are two main types – radical and socialist feminism. The first group believe that sexism has always been present in society, the second feel that it's a manifestation of capitalism. I'm being simplistic, but that's the general idea. Basically, both attempt to challenge ingrained patriarchy in our society and achieve true gender equality.'

'So which kind of feminist are you?'

Holly smiled, 'A bit of both. Back in Canberra, most women I know are feminists. Some of the men too.'

Jamie gave a crooked grin. 'How can a bloke be a feminist?'

'By believing in the fight for equality. It's only fair, don't you think? Why would anyone want to live in a society where people are discriminated against because of their gender?'

'I guess that's true,' Jamie said. 'I've just never really thought about it before.'

Holly made a face. 'Well it's time you started.'

The mesa came fully into focus, chiselled of stone, with broken scattered chunks at the base, then cliffs at the halfway point. Ray led the way up the slope, waiting once to let a brown snake slide away from their path. The going was rugged – loose boulders embedded with pebbles of quartz – interspersed with tussocks of spiky grass.

Using a forearm to wipe the mingled sweat and rain that built up on his face and eyes, Jamie stopped and looked ahead. He could see the overhang of stone and the ledge deep inside. Even from a distance ochre designs on the stone wall inside were visible.

Drawing closer Jamie saw that most of the painted figures on the ledge were faded animal shapes rendered in natural colours. He sat down on a rock and let the beauty of the sight raise the hair on his arms and legs, feeling the power of dead generations lying heavily on this place.

Before him was a kangaroo-man, with his clutch of boomerangs, skirt and tassels. Another figure was chucking a stone axe towards a gang of small human and animal shapes. The majority were painted in soft clay pigment, applied to the surface with brushes of pandanus leaf or chewed sticks.

More animals; emu, pig-nose turtle and barramundi, high arched back sweeping down to a narrow head. These were not the intricate, more recent, x-ray patterns Jamie had seen on platforms to the north and west, but Mimi art, a form that even Ray's people regarded as ancient, apparently painted by mythical beings that had long ago lived in this country. The human and animal forms did not show internal organs, but were highly stylised, instantly recognisable.

Many had suffered from water damage or mineral coatings, and had faded irregularly, some to the colour of the parent sandstone, others to hybrid greys, whites, and red or yellow ochres.

Tasha checked with Ray if taking photos was okay, and that was fine. As fast as she could get the Nikon out of the case her lens was clicking, and Glenn stood like a colossus, obviously moved. Jamie liked him a little more.

Ray squatted alone, smiling, satisfied with the act of giving them pleasure. The respectful way the outsiders treated the site must have helped. No one tried to touch the painted stone or made excessive noise.

Holly perched on the rock next to Jamie, almost touching him at the hip. 'This is amazing, but I can't help feeling guilty. We could still be driving.'

'Travelling in the half-darkness in this kind of country is a bad idea. You can't see washouts and terrain. Of course, we do it when we have to, but not with um—' Jamie looked at her warily, 'civilians along with us. Besides, you like it here. I can see it in your face.'

'Of course I do. I've seen photos of this kind of thing,' she said. 'But no representation on paper could do it justice.'

'This blood runs in my veins, on my mother's side,' Jamie said.

'I can't put into words what I feel when I visit these dreaming places. I'm like a tree, some of my roots are deep underground. Some of them I don't even know.' It sounded clumsy, to him, but Holly seemed happy, swaying against him for a moment.

Ray stood at the end of the ledge and crooked his finger. 'Come on. There's another place, up high.'

Jamie stood, with Holly close behind him. Ray held out the palm of his hand and shook his head. 'Sorry. No women for this one.'

Holly looked thunderstruck, and Tasha reddened, camera on the sling around her neck. 'What do you mean, no women?'

'Men's place only. Glenn, you come too.'

Holly's face was already red from the climb, now it turned bright purple. She opened her mouth, as if to say something, then closed it again.

The irony was burning in Jamie's gut. 'I guess that's one for the radical feminists,' he said. Then, 'Sorry, I shouldn't joke about it.'

'It's okay,' Holly said at last. 'See you soon.'

With the females waiting on the ledge, Ray led the men around the face of the cliff. Jamie followed his example. The world below opened up into a diorama of brown and green studded trees, watercourses and hills.

'Did I happen to mention,' Glenn said as they moved along a narrow ledge, 'that heights make me feel woozy?'

Ray seemed to think that statement was funny, chuckling under his breath. Consequently, it seemed to Jamie that his mate picked out the steepest and most vertigo-inducing route, just to piss Glenn off. Sometimes, though, it was hard to work out when Ray was having fun with someone, or if he had other reasons.

Near the top, Ray stopped at the edge of a long platform, like a terrace cut in the edge of the cliff. There he squatted, motioning the two men to the ground. Staring intently down along the platform Ray started to sing. It was a haunting sound, too soft to generate an echo, as natural as rustling leaves.

At one point he picked up a stone and threw it. Then another.

'What's he doing?' Glenn whispered.

Jamie half turned, hairs prickling up on the skin of his arms. 'He's waking up the spirits of his ancestors, so we don't surprise them. Asking them for permission to go on.'

The song stopped, and Ray stood, motioning them to follow, moving along the terrace, and stooping into the yawning mouth of an overhang. His eyes adjusted quickly, and Jamie shivered with the sacred air of the place.

Nothing mattered then. All the thoughts that plagued him. The insecurities, the feeling that nothing, in civilian life at least, ever worked for him, that everyone seemed to have their shit together except for him. Jamie was back, rooted in the soil.

The walls were covered with art, still in the Mimi style, but fewer animals now. More ceremonial figures in head-dress. One was a slender woman, breasts hanging out on either side, with barbed spearheads sunk deep into hips, knees and head. Jamie was aware that this was a powerful symbol of sorcery.

Cracks in the walls were filled with rows of bones and skulls, some still in their paperbark coverings. And through it all was woven a representation of the serpent himself, Bolung – so often misappropriated by European culture. Such a powerful mythic being that the lore of his passage runs across the boundaries of Indigenous nations across the continent.

His python head, tongue extended, pointed back towards the figures on this wall, like a warning. His tail curled and weaved through his lands and creatures, encircling them possessively.

Ray squatted down beneath that gallery, and Jamie watched as he closed his eyes tightly, and twin lines of tears flowed like blood from his eyes.

Sometimes, the depth of Ray's connection to the land made Jamie envious. The product of years of learning at the knees of old men and women, absorbing the wisdom accumulated over a thousand generations.

Ray's first tear fell to the dust, turning into a dark ball, and it was as if Jamie used him as a conduit, the smell of his sweat, the salt of his tears. At that moment he felt it as powerfully as a dream. He felt their hands in his. He saw their faces.

The voices of the past combined with the present. Jamie knew then what Ray meant when he spoke of 'listening to the earth', and his belief that music is already inside a person – that instruments and voices serve only as a reminder.

After a while Ray seemed to exit his near trance-like state. With hardly a word he led the way out of the overhang and up the final stages to the summit of the hill. The top was not as level as it appeared from below, but was made up of fractured sheets of stone, crushed together in places to form jagged ravines.

Ray chose the highest peak, shaped like the ruined, lopsided battlements of a castle. Now, with the sun nearing the horizon, searing rays beaming through the smoky distance, the light was ethereal, beautiful. The landscape, laid out below, was like nothing else on earth. Orange, fiery ground, needled with dull grey trees, and scarred with the beds of ancient watercourses.

Glenn cleared his throat, 'My father was Irish. He used to talk about the 'thin' places, where heaven and earth are closest together. This has to be one of those. I've never seen or felt anything like it.'

Goosebumps bristled first on Jamie's arms, then roved over his body like squalls. For just one moment he was not parentless and alone, but part of the continuum. All his connections, living and dead, seemed to be here, in some fourth dimension that he could sense but not see.

They did not speak again, just sat, filled with their own brimming cup of wonder. It wasn't until they heard Tasha calling from far below that they turned their backs on the thinnest place Jamie had been and started to descend.

# NINE

After filleting and skinning the barramundi, Jamie dusted the fillets with salt, pepper and a squeeze of lemon. He fried them in a dab of butter, bringing them out still moist, the flesh breaking into natural sections and turning translucent, pearly white.

After a meal that even the Potomac-dwelling Americans admitted was one of the best they'd had, Jamie washed up and Danny dried. The NORFORCE boys had rigged a canvas tarpaulin as a general cover, eight feet up in the air. Light raindrops pattered on the surface.

'So how close are we?' Jamie asked the American.

'Very close. Before lunch time tomorrow so long as we can keep moving.'

'Good to hear. I just wish you'd tell me what the hell this is all about.'

'I can't, not yet. Hey, but by the way, Glenn was telling me on the road today that your father was from the USA.'

'That's right, but he died before I was born.'

'What was his name?'

'Joel McKinnon. He was in the Territory on business.' Jamie lifted a glass he had been washing, held it up against the light of the gas lantern, then washed it again. 'He worked for a company that made agricultural equipment – tractors and such. He and my mother … fell in love.'

'A shame you never had the chance to know him. How did he die?'

'One of those pointless tragedies. A fire.' Jamie kept his eyes on the soap suds and dishes, never on the older man's face. 'I guess I put my hand up for this mission because of the American connection. It's not generally my thing, I'm not really a people person but as soon as I heard about it, I couldn't get it out of my head. So, I … volunteered.'

The older man cocked his head strangely for a moment, 'McKinnon, you said?'

'That's right.'

'Well, if ever you want to find out more about him, just let me know. I can help. I know what it's like to have a hole in your life like that.'

'Thanks, I'll keep it in mind.'


The third RFSV arrived the next morning, just as they were ready to move out for the day. The newcomers were Mick and Nico, part of Jamie's usual patrol. The men shook hands and slapped backs like brothers.

Mick took off his giggle hat and wiped his almost-bald head with a red handkerchief from his pocket. As well as patrol corporal, he was a top bush mechanic, and was known through the regiment for once, on a field trip into the Coburg Peninsula, having used WD40 to cure jock-rot, that annoying, intensely itching fungus that infects the inner thighs, under and around the testicles. Mick swore blind that the aerosol, usually used to start cars or free seized bolts, had cured the problem.

Like most Darwin Greeks, Nico's descendants come from the island of Kalymnos. The islanders migrated to replace Japanese pearl divers after World War Two, but soon dominated the city's building trade. Nico's family lived in a white mansion with columns and even a garden fountain in Parap. He'd rejected a guaranteed role in the family business for the military, and Jamie respected him for that.

Nico was into running, soccer and cricket, as well as being ranked seventh in the Territory in Mixed Martial Arts. He had his sights set on the upcoming SAS selection trials over at Robertson Barracks in Perth and had lately upped the intensity of his fitness regime.

Jamie was relieved to have them here. Not just two extra rifles, but good solid mates. He dragged the billy out for a celebratory cup of tea.

From that point on the going was tough. They wound through the only drivable pass in a maze of stone pillars standing end on end in the wilderness like cigars.

With no longer even a remnant of a vehicle track to follow, they were guided only by Danny's GPS and a compass. They detoured around stark hills and deep gullies, crossed creeks churned with brown, and sweated bullets in the heat and humidity, vehicles hardly moving fast enough to kick up a breeze.

Finally, as the rain that had spotted their screens all morning stopped, and a glaring bright sun emerged from the clouds, they clattered over loose rocks to the lip of a deep sandstone gorge. They left the vehicles parked under whatever scraps of shade they could find while they walked to the edge and looked down to where a ribbon of water wound along the gorge floor below, occasionally backing up to form sluggish pools or narrowing into white rapids. Jamie could see along a kilometre or more before it kinked to the north.

Jamie knew a little about the geology of these sandstone escarpments. That the strata had been laid down eighty million years ago, when Cretaceous seas filled the lowlands, and ancient creatures swam in those warm waters.

The seas withdrew over a thousand millennia, leaving the strata high and dry. Terrestrial plants and animals filled the void, as the ages advanced – torrential monsoon rains created runnels, creeks, and rivers, scouring their winding paths through weak points in the matrix.

'It's beautiful, isn't it?' Holly said, arriving beside him with hardly a sound.

'Beyond words,' Jamie agreed. 'And this is just the start of the Arnhem Land escarpment country. There are hundreds of miles of it, all the way to Kakadu Park. No one has seen all of it.'

'Look at my arms, I've got goose bumps,' Holly said.

Jamie turned to look. The sun had tanned her skin golden brown and it suited her. 'You have the gift then,' he said.

'What gift?'

'To feel the land as well as see it. Not everyone is like that.'

Danny walked across with Tasha's hand in his. Father and daughter were a touching sight. 'According to the GPS, the site I'm interested in is very close – walking distance from here.' The American was visibly agitated, near breathless.

'Thank God for that,' Jamie breathed, but he had to admit to his own twinge of excitement – that they might finally find out what the hell the trip was all about. 'Let's plot your coordinates on a map so we don't get ourselves lost.'

'No problem,' said Danny. 'We can do that.'

'Are you ready for this, Dad?' Tasha asked.

'I've been ready for forty years.' Danny said.

Jamie was only just starting to understand how big this moment was for Danny. His face showed some measure of that – beads of sweat on his forehead, a strange clarity in his eyes, as if he were no longer fighting a battle, but letting himself get carried along by the stream.

Up until then this had been a mission and no more. Now it was really sinking in to Jamie that they were going to see something special, something that had been hidden for a long time.

After a few minutes with the map, they left Mick and Nico with the vehicles and set off along the top of the gorge. The vegetation grew thicker, and after a while they were forced to walk in file along a game trail littered with the round droppings of kangaroos and much larger clumps from wild buffalo.

'We must be close now,' Jamie mused aloud, stopping to check with the map.

Five minutes had come and gone when they descended into a deep and jagged gully, sharp grass stinging against Jamie's legs, through the khaki. The funny thing was that Jamie was watching where he walked, not scanning the scrub, and it was a sudden shout from Danny that gave it away.

'My God, there it is.'

Jamie looked up and could not believe his eyes. Half leaning against the rocky sides of the gully, was a black mess of ruined metal towering three storeys above their heads, joined to a tapering cylinder of dull aluminium, smashed by what must have been impact with the ground. A rear hatch yawned open. The port-side tail wing had settled somewhat into the ground, having bent like foil from the impact with the earth. Vines roped and curled and knotted around the wreckage. The barrel and breech block of a heavy machine gun lay half embedded in the earth nearby.

'Holy shit,' Jamie breathed. 'So, this is the reason we came all the way out here?'

This, Jamie realised, was not just some minor transport plane, but the rear section of an intercontinental bomber. This was important. People had almost certainly died here.

The gun turret gave the battered wreckage a warlike visage as Danny, and Tasha behind him, moved to the open, shattered end of the tube. A goanna, over four feet in length, with black curved lion's claws on the extremity of each speckled leg sprang out from the darkness inside.

'The plane must have struck with incredible force to have separated like this,' Danny said. 'Surely the main fuselage won't be far away. I can't imagine it would get far without the tail.' He looked at Wally, who was staring up at the fin with his jaw open.

'Holy fuck, hey brus, this is so cool.'

# TEN

The RFSVs were showing the wear and tear of driving in harsh conditions. Dust and mud of various earthy shades coated every surface and was clotted beneath the windscreen wipers. The rags that were wrapped around the black steel of the bull bars had collected a thick layer.

When the main party got back to camp Mick had the bonnets up, shaking dust out of air filters and checking oil levels. Jamie went straight to the Engel and pulled out a beer, tilted his head back to drain half of it in one pull. The others slowly gathered round, fetching drinks. Ray filled the billy from a jerry can and placed it on the campfire Mick and Nico had built in their absence.

'So that tail fin comes from a USAF bomber, an old one?' Jamie asked Danny.

'Correct.'

'Where's the rest of it?'

'That's the million-dollar question,' Danny said. 'We thought it was still together – the aerial photography wasn't clear about that – so it's a little disappointing. It must have broken up on impact, and the rest of it will be nearby somewhere.'

'Why is it so important that we find it?'

'I can't tell you that quite yet.'

'I'm getting sick to death of hearing that.' Jamie turned to Holly. 'Can you tell me any more?'

She shook her head. 'Not at this stage.'

'Bugger off all of you. I'm going down the gorge for a bogey and the rest of you can sit here with your secrets for all I care.'

Jamie walked to his pack and removed a pair of board shorts and a towel. Then, without looking back at them he headed down along the cliff a hundred metres to where there was a narrow game trail winding down. A startled wallaby bounded out of the grass nearby and continued down the slope with supernatural skill. Those agile wallabies were one of Jamie's favourite creatures, with fawn like faces with tiny stripes down from the ears, their brown coats shaded with russet gold and orange.

The gorge itself, he saw as he made his way down, was formed of solid rock in ridges and waves, cut through by a channel of water studded with protruding ochre-coloured boulders from bowling-ball-size to some with the girth of small cars. Surface reflections chased bubbles down each stage of rapids, and pandanus palms drooped low over the fringes.

The stream ran clear between timeless pools shelved with rock. Jamie picked a spot out of view of the people at the top and stripped off, shivering pleasurably as he waded into the water. He wallowed quietly, mind racing, while tiny shrimp and fish tickled the skin of his back and thighs. Before long the others came down too, but he ignored them, closing his eyes and letting the earthy smell of the water and the peace of the gorge infuse his system.

Later in the afternoon, back at camp, an old man appeared. One second there was just the scrub, and the next he was there, standing stock-still waiting for someone to invite him into the camp. He wore grimy denim jeans held up by a knotted length of blue and yellow Telecom rope, and a Western shirt, too big for his bony chest. A bolt action .22 rifle was slung over his right shoulder.

Wally who had been half snoozing in a camp chair, opened his eyes to see the visitor. He gave a sharp little sound of alarm and stood up.

'It's okay brus, I know him,' Ray said, standing up from his place at the fire and walking across to clasp hands with the visitor, who smiled broadly, reached into his top pocket, produced a tin of tobacco and rolled a cigarette.

'Hello Grandfather,' said Ray. 'It's been a long time.'

'Yeah, long time. You lookin' alright, Ray.'

Jamie approached, and inclined his head in greeting. 'You're Ray's grandfather?'

'That's right, all about here my country.' The old man lit his smoke, and it hung out of his mouth as he shook Jamie's hand, studied his eyes and smiled. 'You Ray's greenskin mate?'

'Yes, we're mates from way back.'

Jamie loved old men like this one, his missing teeth, and scraggy old clothes. His eyes were glassy from sandy blight – trachoma, and the grey stubble on his face almost white. His chest and arms were raked with jagged raised scars where he had gone through initiation half a century or more earlier. The wisdom in his head, Jamie suspected, would fill a shelf of books.

The old fellow's eyes alighted on Danny, who was sitting beside the fire with his hands wrapped around a coffee. Still holding the rifle, the old man walked across that campsite, then squatted near the fire, laid the gun down on the dirt.

Jamie said, 'Hey Ray, do you mind if I ask your grandfather if he's seen a plane fuselage around here? If anyone knows where it is it'll be him.'

'Sure boss, ask him.'

Jamie squatted. 'We're looking for an old aeroplane.'

He picked up a twig, cleared an area of dust as a slate and drew a fuselage, body and wings.

'Do you know where it is?'

The old man pointed at the tail. 'That the only part left.'

'Where's the rest of it?'

The old man lifted both hands wide, then slapped them together. Finally, he moved them heavenwards, wiggling his fingers. It was a masterful gesture, clearly meaning that the plane had disappeared. 'Gone.'

Danny's brows knitted together. 'Something that big can't just disappear.'

Tasha had been out collecting specimens and walked back into the camp. Her eyes widened at the sight of the old man in the camp.

'It's okay,' Jamie told her. 'This is Ray's grandfather.'

She put her sample bags down on a table and turned. 'Oh hello, pleased to meet you.'

The old man's reaction to Tasha was remarkable. He left the others and stood in front of her, taking her hand and smiling. Then he dropped to his knees and pressed his ear to her belly.

The old man laughed loudly, and turned to Ray, chattering away in his first language, and pointing at Tasha while she smiled nervously.

'What's he saying?' she asked Ray.

Ray's grin was as wide as the gorge itself. 'Grandfather says that you're growing a fine baby in there, and that you are going to be a beautiful mother.'

Tasha burst into tears and called for Glenn, who came running as if there had been an accident. An hour later, the old man had gone, leaving only the smell of burning tobacco behind him.


It was almost dark when Holly climbed into the front seat of the LandCruiser, closing the door behind her. Jamie saw that she had the portable computer running, using the cigarette lighter as a power source. He half watched her as he started preparing for the evening meal, carrying trays of food and cooking gear from the rear of the vehicle. For an hour or more she remained inside, hunched over the screen. He wondered what the hell she did on the machine.

Then, with roast potatoes cooking away in the hot ashes, and a camp oven bedded down with coals around the sides and the lid, filled with one of Ray's basic but tasty stews, Jamie saw Holly close the lid of the laptop, sit it on the dash, then walk off to the latrine.

He sidled up to the vehicle, opened the door and pretended

to look in the glove box. Then, checking that no one was looking, he lifted the lid. The screen came on.

```
FM SECSTATE WASHDC

TO AUSTGOVERNMENT

DIA WASHDC

INFO AMEMBASSY CANBERRA


S E C R E T


E.O. 12356:  DECL:OADR

TAGS:

SUBJECT:  WRECK OF USAF BOMBER SERIAL NUMBER
46-006/047


SECRET THE PRESIDENT AND CONGRESS OF THE UNIT-
ED STATES OF AMERICA VIEW WITH GRAVE CONCERN
THAT US CITIZEN DANIEL PORTER IS BEING ESCORT-
ED TOWARDS A POSSIBLE CRASH SITE OF A KOREAN
WAR VINTAGE BOMBER.

THE EVENTS OF THAT MISSING AIRCRAFT, EVEN FOR-
TY YEARS LATER, REMAIN OF CRITICAL CONCERN TO
OUR GOVERNMENT, AND NUMEROUS UNRESOLVED QUES-
TIONS REMAIN.

WE REQUEST THAT THE OPERATION BE TERMINATED
AND THAT OUR FORCES BE PERMITTED TO UNDERTAKE
THEIR OWN SEARCH.


JAMES A BAKER

SECRETARY OF STATE
```

Jamie looked up to see if Holly was on her way back yet. She wasn't. He studied the keyboard, there were arrow buttons like they had on the IBM PC machines back at headquarters. He reached out and held the down button, allowing him to read on.

SEC- CLASSIFIED CABLE

FROM FOREIGN MINISTER AUSTRALIA

TO JAMES A BAKER SECRETARY OF STATE

TAGS:

SUBJECT: CRASH SITE INVESTIGATION, NORTHERN TERRITORY OF THE COMMONWEALTH OF AUSTRALIA


SECRET THE GOVERNMENT OF THE COMMONWEALTH OF AUSTRALIA ACKNOWLEDGES YOUR POSITION, BUT MUST RESPECTFULLY DECLINE PERMISSION FOR A UNITED STATES LED FORCE TO OPERATE INSIDE OUR SOVEREIGN TERRITORY. NEVERTHELESS, WE DO UNDERTAKE THAT ONCE THE CRASH SITE IS LOCATED WE WILL ALLOW TECHNICIANS SUPERVISED ACCESS TO THE SITE.

AT THE MOMENT, HOWEVER, WE MUST INSIST ON MAINTAINING THE INTEGRITY OF OUR BORDERS. OUR GOVERNMENT IS CONFIDENT THAT YOU WILL UNDERSTAND OUR REASONS.


T.E. PIERCE

DEPARTMENT OF DEFENCE

CANBERRA

```
FM   SECSTATE WASHDC

TO  AUSTGOVERNMENT

DIA WASHDC

INFO AMEMBASSY CANBERRA


S E C R E T


E.O. 12356:   DECL:OADR

TAGS:

SUBJECT:   WRECK OF USAF BOMBER SERIAL NUMBER
46-006/047


SECRET THE PRESIDENT AND CONGRESS OF THE UNIT-
ED STATES OF AMERICA REMAIN UNSATISFIED WITH
YOUR RESPONSE AND ARE CONSIDERING A RANGE OF
OPTIONS.


JAMES A BAKER

SECRETARY OF STATE
```

The document ended with blank space, and Jamie used the arrow key to return the document to the position it was in when he found it. He closed the lid and placed it carefully back on the dash and was out of the vehicle moments before Holly sauntered back up the path from the thunderbox. He turned away, thinking furiously.

# ELEVEN

Up at first light, Jamie joined Nico on his morning run. They headed back along the track for a few kilometres, building the pace to a murderous level, punishing each other on the slopes. He enjoyed driving his body to the limit, his mate beside him, matching him pace for pace.

Nico was shorter and bulkier than Jamie, and stronger on the climbs. He was a pretty good dancer, and Jamie had seen him in action, out on the town, in Darwin's Smith Street night clubs, dressed in white jeans and open shirt. Occasionally, in the bush, when he thought he was alone, you'd come across the young Greek-Australian spinning on his heel, eyes closed as if he were lost in an imaginary rhythm, hips shaking.

Ray gave Nico heaps about it, but Jamie knew that Ray too was partial to a turn or two on the dance floor. After midnight at Kirby's back bar in Katherine, Barunga band Blekbala Mujik or local act Ged's Wedding live on stage, Ray owned the dance floor, with a can in one hand, shaking to the beat, eyes closed, oblivious to the glare of the stage lights, everything but the music itself.

Now, there was no question of yielding to Nico, and Jamie pushed himself to the limit on the return. He had a leaner, rangier build than the young Greek, but with a cast-iron constitution. Old-fashioned kind of strong.

They jogged back into the camp, neck and neck, to find the smell of cooking eggs and Ray's half amused smile over the pan.

Jamie stood, hands behind his head, struggling for breath, ignoring him. Ray regarded exercise for the sake of it strange, joining in only when ordered to. Yet he never gained an ounce of fat, and could out-walk any of them, even Nico, at a pace that never varied.

'You look like you're gonna spew up, Sarge,' Ray said.

'Shut up Ray,' Jamie said, but Ray's grin was so open and wide he couldn't resist a smile in return.

While tea brewed, and a new batch of eggs sizzled, Jamie set the long-range radio to ABC National on 657 AM and listened to the news. At first it was filled with Saddam Hussein tightening his grip on Kuwait, and his fencing with the UN Security Council over Resolution 678.

'You reckon the Yanks will go in there, Sarge?' Nico asked.

'Probably.'

'What about our boys?'

'Maybe a few more ships, but not ground troops. Too far away. Not our business, not really.'

Apart from a ferry disaster in Africa, and farm subsidy talks in Europe the rest was politics – Hawke and Keating's intrigue over the national leadership and WA Inc shenanigans in the West.

When breakfast was over, Jamie called them together. He had thought long and hard about how to approach this. The cables had scared him. This was important, and he wanted the truth before they continued.

'We need all the information on hand, and we need it on the table.' Jamie said. 'How can the boys and I help you find the plane if we don't even know which direction it was travelling; where it came from?'

'It came from the north,' Danny said.

'Asia?'

'Yes.'

'Japan?'

'I ...' Danny looked helplessly at Holly.

'Tell him.'

'Korea.'

'Thank you. What kind of plane was it?'

'A B50a Superfortress.'

'Now I've seen the tail fin, so I have some idea, but how big was it overall?'

'Huge. A hundred and fifty feet wide and a hundred long. It had four engines. Each one developed more horsepower than five Kenworth trucks. It could fly at four hundred miles per hour with a range of five thousand miles.'

Jamie went to the LandCruiser and returned with a battered leather map case. After a quick sort through he unfolded a 1:250 000 survey map of the area on a folding camp table.

'Okay Danny. Show us how and from where the plane came in.'

Danny used a stick to draw an imaginary line from north to south along the map. 'The plane came this way, still on a south-erly heading, the same bearing all the way from Korea. As it started to run out of fuel it descended,' the stick slowed, 'and hit the ground.' Now Danny lifted the stick away from the map and pointed in the direction in which the tail fin had been found.

'I'm guessing that the rear section of the plane hit first. The impact made part of it break off and would also most likely have made the nose strike upwards momentarily. Then, unable to fly, the main frame might have skipped on for a short distance, say a kilometre maximum.'

Having been involved in searches before, Jamie weighed in before they started second-guessing this assessment too much. 'So, our best bet is somewhere within a one-kilometre radius of the tail. That's where we'll start. Fair enough?' Jamie looked from face to face. Slow nods. 'I don't know about you lot,' he went on, 'but I'm dying to find out what the hell is inside that plane – something bloody interesting judging by all the fuss.' He caught Holly's eye and she was just a little too slow to turn away.

Using map grids as a reference, Jamie divided the arbitrary search area up and split the party into two groups, one with him and one with Ray. Mick would remain at the vehicles to monitor the radios and maintain a base.

While the others slipped their boots on, Ray leaned close to Jamie. 'Ha Sarge, funny you put Ms Jones in with your mob.'

Jamie bristled, 'There are only two groups, Ray, Holly had to go into one of them.'

Ray raised his eyebrows. 'I reckon she's hot for you. Maybe you all the same for her.'

'Shut up Ray.'

Jamie walked away, shaking his head. Holly could have gone with either group but maybe, Jamie admitted to himself, he liked having her around.

'Keep the walkie-talkies on your belts switched on at all times,' he told them. 'Five minutes into the scrub and it all looks the same – we don't want to lose anyone.'

Jamie allowed the other group to set off first – Nico, Glenn, Wally and Ray, then turned to his own party, running his eyes over their clothes. Danny had jeans, hiking boots and a Thomas Cook shirt, and Tasha pretty much the same. Holly had top notch gear: Alt-Berg boots with jeans, and stout canvas gaiters. Jamie himself wore his DPCU trousers and shirt, giggle hat, ankle high GP boots and an SLR rifle slung over his shoulder.

'All set then?'

'Yes. Lead on.'

They started off, and Jamie found it hard to get used to people who instinctively wanted to bunch up and talk, rather than fan out in rehearsed patrol positions. Danny walked on his left side, and Tasha the other as they moved along the lip of the gorge. Only Holly maintained her position out on the flank.

Tasha, apart from her obvious interest in plants, asked questions constantly. Jamie identified animals as they passed – a herd of five or so water buffalo grazing some two hundred metres away – lifting their great horned heads, chewing as the humans passed. Their hides were coated with thick dried mud from their last wallow.

'If we need meat, we can shoot one,' Jamie said.

'You're joking, surely,' Tasha said.

Jamie shrugged. 'We're trained to live off the land. That includes red meat.' He dropped the subject; some people don't like to get too close to the source of their nutrition. NORFORCE personnel, however, were well known for their liking for meat. A good part of their yearly budget went on compensating cattle station owners for stock they shot and ate in the course of their work.

They saw a couple of bush turkeys, and once, a brown snake weaving, unhurried, through the grass. Tasha, however, in line with her field, was most enthusiastic about the vegetation, everything from turkey bush to kapok.

Somehow, she managed to have a small botanical field guide open much of the time, identifying plants and occasionally taking samples and photographs. Stinkwood, woollybutt, cypress – she trimmed leaves and fruit off them all, slipping her samples into tiny plastic bags that she secreted in her pockets.

The group had bunched up even further. Tasha's botanical enquiries were interesting but distracting. 'That's enough for a bit,' Jamie declared. 'We're not going to find anything at this rate.' Then, voice raised: 'Let's spread out, twenty paces between us. Check constantly for the people on either side of you. If you get separated just sit tight and use the walkie talkie to call in.'

They moved into a parallel file, knocking down trails through tall spear grass, winding past scrubby eucalypts and chest high termite mounds. They followed the cliff face itself for a thousand paces, then turned away for another fifty before walking parallel to the edge once more.

It was dispiriting stuff, hour after hour, but Jamie didn't push them too hard, stopping for lunch in the shade for a good while. It was pleasant, he and Holly next to each other, with Tasha photographing tiny ferns that colonised the wet rocks where water soaked through from some artesian reserve inside.

When they had finished eating Holly dried her hair, wet from rain showers and sweat, with a towel from her bag, and set about brushing it.

Jamie tried not to look at her, but he couldn't help it. In the end he gave up and asked her a question. 'So how did you end up in ASIO?'

'Well, not to boast or anything, but I was headhunted. I'd just graduated from ANU with an honours degree in political science. I'd applied for a few jobs but hadn't heard anything when I was approached about a career in ASIO.'

Jamie grinned, 'So a black car pulled up out the front of your house and they took you down to headquarters?'

Holly put the brush aside. 'Funnily enough, it was pretty much like that. The money was good, and it seemed like an interesting challenge. It turned out that I was good at it, particularly field work. I've been in the game for four years now, still green, but I'm going okay.'

'Are you married or anything? Boyfriend?'

Holly rolled her eyes, 'You've got to be kidding me. I can hardly manage to see my girlfriends occasionally, let alone try to keep a man happy. In any case, I seem to scare them off. Too serious. Guys seem to go for the girls who are out-there, crazy and carrying on like pork-chops. I'm not like that.'

'I like serious,' said Jamie.

Holly smiled. 'Well that makes one bloke out of ten million. What about you? Girlfriend?'

'Not for a while.' Jamie looked down at his feet.

Holly put her hat back on her head and tucked a few stray strands back under the brim. 'You just haven't met the right girl or no time?'

'I dunno. It just hasn't happened.'

'I'm sure it will, sooner or later.'


The afternoon was no more productive than the morning, and both search teams were back at camp by five. It was a welcome morale booster when Nico produced a cricket bat and tennis ball. Only Danny couldn't raise the energy for the game.

They used a wattle trunk for a wicket beside the neat and tidy campsite, with the orange Coleman tent and jungle green hootchies spread out in the clearing. The scent of meat and stewing vegetables filled the air, while Ray turned up the sound system in their RFSV. Joe Geia and his band, No Fixed Address, rang out from the speakers, bright reggae upstrokes echoing down in the gorge.

'Do you always have to play that black armband, shit?' complained Wally. 'I've got a Barnsey cassette in the other car.'

The others ignored him, and when it came to the chorus they sang along.

We have survived, the white man's world.

And you know you can't change that!

Cricket was a favourite of Yella's, and the outfield had to work hard to retrieve the ball ahead of his needle-sharp teeth. If the dog got there first, he had to be caught, then the ball prised from his narrow jaws and wiped of a coating of saliva.

Glenn caught on quickly, clean bowling Nico on the third delivery. Scowling, the young private declared the American's bowling action illegal. Called on to officiate, Jamie sustained the dismissal, and Nico sulked in the outfield.

To avoid any further discussion on the matter, Jamie took up the ball, sending down his trademark off-spinners that bounced jaggedly out of the dirt.

He removed Holly's middle stump on the first ball, and she dropped the bat in disgust, standing with hands on her hips. 'Hey, you shouldn't bowl so hard, it's not fair.'

Jamie stared back at her, crestfallen. 'That wasn't even fast. You really want me to go easy on you because you're a woman?'

'No, stupid. I want you to go easy on me because I can't bloody play cricket.'

'I give up,' Jamie said, and tossed the ball to Nico, who paced out a run-up that would have exhausted most men.

Wally hammered Nico's delivery into the air, and Yella grabbed it on the bounce, running off with the ball.

'Hey, you fuckin' mongrel dog.'

Wally chased him comically, then hit him on the rump with the cricket bat. The dog yelped, dropped the ball, and ran off under the nearest vehicle with his tail between his legs. Wally picked up the ball between thumb and forefinger.

'Fuck. Now it's all wet.'

He hadn't seen Ray walking towards him. 'Hey brus. You've got no right to hit my dog with a bat.'

Wally threw the ball to Nico and stood with his hands on his hips. 'Well maybe try controlling the mongrel thing for once. If there's one thing I can't stand it's a man who can't control his dog.'

'Don't touch him again, hey?' Ray growled, and Jamie saw the warning signs on his face.

Wally dropped the bat, just as Ray shoved him hard in the chest with both hands.

Wally made a fist and was in the process of drawing it back when Jamie hurried in, grabbed the arm and twisted, holding the big man immobile and helpless.

'You shouldn't have hit the dog like that, Wally, but Ray, you're over-reacting. Now both of you, get on with the game.'

'I'm tired of his racist shit too,' Ray said.

Wally turned his head, baring his teeth at Jamie. 'Let go of me, or you'll bloody well regret it.'

Jamie let go, but pushed Wally lightly between the shoulder blades. 'This is going on report, right?'

'Whatever, do what you like. I don't give a shit.'

With that, the game was over, and they all wandered off. Ray went over to the fireside ready to start dishing out. Wally stayed standing until they were all gone, glowering over at Jamie.

The song went on:
*You can't break my bones by putting me down,*
*Or by taking the things that belong to me.*

# TWELVE

Using the HF radio, Jamie called base, requesting a flyover from a Nomad patrol aircraft out of Tindal. He gave them the coordinates, and they patched him through to the pilot. The two men chatted about the possibilities, and the conversation ended with Jamie being promised a thorough grid search over eighty square kilometres using infra-red, standard optics and real time observation.

The third day from their arrival, while they waited for the Nomad, Jamie widened the ground search. They tramped backwards and forwards in near silence, sweat on their bodies and dreaming of a spider-webbed cockpit, cracked gun turrets, and a gargantuan aircraft.

Jamie heard the Nomad arrive around late morning, then spotted it in the north western quadrant, a dot growing into an ungainly winged machine. It remained overhead for two and a half hours, crisscrossing the area at around five thousand feet, deploying its capable electronics suite. While the NORFORCE crew ate lunch, the Nomad ran a final pattern down low with, Jamie imagined, the crew craning their necks out the windows with field glasses.

Two hours later the plane droned away, and the two teams set off for another grid search on foot, driving the LandCruisers to their starting points, covering ground so cold that they could not help a defeated slouch to their shoulders.

The only real excitement that afternoon came when Tasha decided to try to approach a buffalo calf. This was a dangerous mistake that resulted in her being charged by a huge cow she had not seen, as black as Hades with horns as wide as a man's spread arms. Jamie was forced to fire a couple of rounds into the air to discourage the charge and enable a tactical withdrawal.

'I only wanted to pat it,' Tasha defended herself, but no one bothered to laugh.

That evening, while Danny and Glenn drank a quiet bottle of Hunter Valley Cab Sav the younger man had brought in his luggage, Jamie again spoke to the Nomad pilot. They had seen nothing visually and the boffins had failed to come up with anything resembling an aircraft in the imagery.

The tail section, Jamie heard, was so well shielded with vegetation that they had apparently only found it on the IR prints because they knew it was there. The standard exposures showed nothing.

Jamie followed up with a call to base and didn't try to hide his despondency. 'It's just not here,' he said, 'and though the rain's only a nuisance right now, I can tell that it's building.'

'If you think that you're wasting time, then pull out,' said Colonel Lineham. 'Canberra can send in its own people if necessary. You're the man on the ground, so I'll leave it up to you.'

Holly was waiting for Jamie when he put down the mike and left the vehicle. Jamie could see she was agitated at being excluded from comms with the RAAF boys.

'What's happening?'

'Well they didn't find anything at all, I'm starting to think that this is a waste of time. The Colonel said it's up to me if we want to pull out or not.'

'Of course, it's not a waste of time, you've seen the tail fin with your own eyes. The rest can't just have disappeared.'

Jamie shook his head slowly, 'I understand that, but where the hell can it be? And we can't run the risk of being stranded by the rains.'

Leaving Holly to stew, Jamie led Ray, Nico and Mick away from the camp and they squatted on the track facing each other. Jamie filled them in on the results from the search. They had themselves trampled down the grass for a circle of some kilometres away from the site and found nothing.

'What do you blokes reckon?' Jamie asked. 'Do we keep up the search, or head for home before the rivers start rising?' They all knew that once major watercourses like the Winton River spread their wings the patrol could be stuck for weeks, if not months.

The three faces looked back at him, none wanting to be the first to speak. Jamie knew Nico had been stewing, because his heavy black brows got close together when he was like that.

'Come on Nico, what're your thoughts?'

'I personally reckon we should piss off home first thing to-morrow, Sarge. We've brought the Yanks up here, it's not our fault the rest of the plane hasn't survived.'

'It can't just disappear,' Jamie said.

'No,' Mick put in, 'but think about it – a thing that size. If it was here the Nomad would have found it.'

Nico pouted. 'Maybe it was an explosion, see? Maybe one of the tanks exploded and blew it into fifty thousand little pieces.'

'Surely, we'd find some of those little pieces, and I imagine that the petrol tanks would have been fairly low. Maybe that's why they crashed.'

'Maybe, but shit, we've done our job. The plane's gone. I say we do what you said last night – pack up and fuck off out of here in the morning.'

'What about you Ray?'

Jamie valued Ray's opinion and Ray knew it. He didn't want to meet the sergeant's eyes; he always did that when he went against what he perceived to be Jamie's wishes. 'Sorry Sarge, but my grandfather was here when that plane crashed. If he says that the rest of it has gone, then that's what happened. Let's go back, maybe have a day on the Winton fishing.'

'Mick?'

'I agree with Ray and Nico. Don't forget that aluminium will burn away if it gets hot enough. Must have been some kind of explosion. Maybe even a missile strike way up high.'

'A missile strike, here? From what? Let's not go overboard.'

Mick just shrugged and offered nothing further.

Jamie hugged his knees and looked at the sky, 'Fair enough if that's the way you blokes feel, but I'm the one who's got to tell Danny. I don't think he'll be happy. And do you really want the Federal Police or whoever they send out here on our turf?'

'Maybe. It's their job, not ours,' Nico said. 'Walking around in the long grass all day is giving me the shits. And as for Danny Carter, he was lucky to get this far. Seems like a wild goose chase to me.'

'What about the carrier out in the Gulf?' Jamie asked.

'We haven't seen any more choppers,' Nico said. 'Chances are the Yanks have worked the same thing out as us. There's nothing here but that tail section – and you can bet they've had those freaky spy planes of theirs looking.'

'What are our exact orders?' Mick asked.

'The Colonel left it up to me to negotiate with Danny. If I think we're wasting our time and pull out he'll back us up. He's seen the results from the Nomad now too.' He paused. 'What are your thoughts, Wally?'

'I reckon we give it another day or two, shit, it's not like it's hard work.'

'No,' Jamie said, 'but sorry, but I agree with the others. We've brought Carter here – done our job. It's time to go – the creeks are rising, and we don't want to get stuck.'

The patrol must have looked a touch daunting as they all walked back to the camp, because the rest of the party all stood to meet them. Jamie guessed that they'd known what the NORFORCE men were talking about. Danny stood from his camp chair, a wine glass in his hand. He looked tired, disappointed; haggard even.

'The blokes and I have had a chat. If the rest of the plane was still in existence, we'd have found it by now. The Nomad saw nothing either. I'm afraid we'll have to pull out in the morning.'

Danny said nothing, just stared back at him. Holly was not so reserved.

'What are you talking about Jamie? We've got a mission and we haven't accomplished it.'

'That plane wreck would have taken up most of a football field. The Nomad would have seen it. We would have seen it.'

She opened her lips again.

Jamie raised a finger. 'No Holly. This is not your decision, it's mine.'

Even when not sleeping well Jamie could usually make it through to about 0100 on the first dig. Sheer physical exhaustion is the best sleeping drug on the market, and Jamie had overdosed on this good stuff in the last couple of days of fruitless leg work.

Not only that, but the frustration of feeling so close, of genuinely knowing that the wreck they sought so desperately must be here, had eaten into his well-being.

That night, total exhaustion took him into the early hours, when he began to dream.

He dreamed of his youth, always with a footy not far away. Then the beer, and the drugs, and the hard nights on the streets before he found the army. He dreamed of his mother, and the huge yawning space in his heart.

Up until that point, his eyes stayed closed. It was a noise out in the night that caused them to flick open. Someone who spends so much time sleeping in the bush soon gets a sense of what's out there. Insects of course, crickets and beetles. Frogs with their throaty African drums. Nocturnal mammals like quolls and large antechinus have their own sounds, scratching through the dirt and nosing around. Human footsteps make a noise that a quadruped can't replicate. Two legs have a unique rhythm, even when the owner is moving stealthily.

Jamie lay still for a few seconds, still not reacting to any great extent. The chances of an intruder just seemed too ridiculous to contemplate. Then, a moment later he heard a sharp pop, a tearing sound, and the hiss of air.

Jamie was already moving before he had fully articulated the thought. Someone had just punctured a tyre on one of the LandCruisers.

Sleeping in shorts, he swung up, reached for his SLR parked at the end of the hootchie, and slipped out into the night, barefooted. They had swept the leaves from the camping area as a fire safety precaution and his bare feet were near silent as he crept, keeping his silhouette low, towards the vehicles.

He saw a figure crouched beside one of the wheels. Another light pop, a hiss, and the LandCruiser sagged down on one corner. Jamie didn't shout, nor warn the vandal in any way, just started running, and he was already changing his grip on the rifle, so it was more of a club than a firearm.

The person was up and darting off well before Jamie was in striking range. If he'd hoped for a glimpse of a face, he was disappointed.

The fugitive was also fast, taking off down the track at a speed Jamie had to stretch hard to match. Only minutes earlier he had been sleeping, and there was a sense of unreality to now chasing a dark-cloaked figure down the track. It was almost supernatural, after all, who were they? Where had they come from? After a hundred metres in the relative clear, just as Jamie was starting to gain on them, they diverted left into the trees.

It was a good manoeuvre – low light always suited the hunted more than the hunter, and they were dressed to take advantage of it. There was nothing in Jamie's training to suggest that ploughing into the scrub at night, dressed only in a pair of boxer shorts, was a good idea. If the person had an accomplice, he might well be placing himself in harm's way; an ambush perhaps.

Yet, trusting his gut, Jamie followed, holding the SLR in front like a bar, catching whipping branches before they struck. He was still running when a dark figure came around a tree trunk, knocked the barrel of his rifle away and gave him a chop to the neck that left him stunned.

It was an expert blow, aimed for the carotid artery, and Jamie reeled back. The striking hand fully immobilized him. He felt himself falling, cushioned only by a spindly branch from some benevolent tree that broke the force of the blow before it landed. Jamie had never felt anything like it, dropping into a semi-shocked state. He released the rifle involuntarily, and sank to his knees, watching the dark figure disappear into the bush, unable to stand and chase after him.

# THIRTEEN

Returning at 0400, Jamie woke the camp. They had been awake ever since, sitting around the fire in an alarmed huddle. Ray had spent almost an hour casting around the spot where Jamie had been attacked by torchlight. He found no trail to follow, just one or two marks in close, and beyond it nothing at all.

'Whoever this is,' he said gravely. 'He knows how to move, Sarge.'

It seemed incredible that the mystery assailant could out-fox Ray's considerable skills. They were dangerous. The NOR-FORCE men were the trackers, the ghosts that hid in the bush and melted away. Whoever this was had beaten them at their own game.

'Probably that wild blackfeller who was in the camp yesterday,' said Wally.

Ray's eyes burned, but he said nothing. The warning signs were not lost on Jamie and he stepped in. 'Don't be an idiot Wally.'

'Well …'

'Just shut up for fuck's sake. Change of plan,' Jamie said. 'Someone either in this party or outside of it has got it in for us. We stay and see this through. There is someone out there, and God knows what their motivations are. I'll check with the Colonel when we do the sked, but I'm sure he won't want us to leave until we know who was in our camp last night.'

Nico pointed at Holly. 'How do you know it wasn't her? She probably knows all kinds of tricks – and she didn't want us to leave.'

Holly crossed her arms in front of her chest. 'Of course it wasn't me. That's ridiculous.'

Danny, who had said nothing to this point chimed in. 'I think the only way to solve this is to keep looking. We haven't even started inside the gorge itself.'

'We can see down into it from up here,' Nico spat.

Glenn stiffened in his seat. 'What if floodwaters carried the wreck downstream? It's had forty years to do it.'

Jamie considered the idea. They had all been down to swim, a couple of times, as well as to fill water containers, but no one had yet rounded the first bend. It was within his nature to want to do that, aircraft aside, very much, even with the rains growing steadier every day.

Jamie met Nico's eyes. The young Greek-Australian was ready to go home. He had made it known that he thought this was a wild goose chase.

'I guess,' Jamie said, 'it could fit in with what Ray's grandfather said about the rest of the wreck having disappeared. It's definitely worth a shot. Especially if there are any deep pools there.'

'It's a bad idea, Sarge,' Ray said.

'Why's that, brus?'

'I've never been right up this part of country before, but I was talking to Grandfather when he came here yesterday. He was telling me that down in the gorge, there's some bad country. Sickness country. Further downstream.'

Jamie clasped his shoulder. 'Hopefully we won't have to go that far down. Will you know when we get there?'

Ray did not answer his smile. 'Yeah, I'll know.'

Nico flared, 'You said we were going home, and now just because—' he glared at Holly. '—someone lets down our tyres and

Glenn comes up with another bullshit idea isn't enough reason to change.'

'Holly didn't do it, Nico.'

'You can't be sure of that.'

'She was here when I came back – in her tent.'

'You said you were unconscious for a bit. Wouldn't have taken much to get back here and climb into her sleeping bag ahead of you. What the hell is she doing here, anyway?'

Holly's eyes were huge when she was angry, Jamie decided. 'I work for ASIO, okay? I work for freaking ASIO, so I'm on the same side as you. Can we all just move on, please?'

Danny stood up. 'I agree. All I can hear is arguing. All of you, just shut up for a moment. Don't say one more word.'

They watched in silence as he stalked to the orange tent, then came back a moment later with an old cigarette tin so faded and scratched it seemed incredible that the metal hadn't worn through. He sat back down and opened the tin on his lap. There was no sound apart from the trickle of water down in the gorge and a butcher bird's high-pitched whistle nearby.

'Now I know you people have got other lives and that some of you think this is a waste of time, but I want you to know what this is like for me.' Danny delved into the tin and removed a black and white photograph, holding it up so the others could see. It was of two men in uniform, standing against a window with a city behind them. Both had their arms extended and thumbs raised. 'That's Matt, my brother, on the left.' Danny looked around so the moment was not lost on them. 'He was the pilot of the plane we're looking for.'

'Holy shit,' Jamie breathed. 'Now this is all starting to make some sense.'

'That tail you saw yesterday,' Danny went on, 'belonged to my brother's plane.' He paused, and then his voice cracked a little. 'Matt raised me from when I was little. I loved him like … he was my world.' He delved back into the tin. Another image. Then another. 'This is real to me. My life has been … a lot of pain because of what happened here. I implore you to help me. Another couple of days.'

Jamie also choked up, deep in the back of his throat. 'Tell us what happened, for God's sake. Start from the beginning.'

'You really want to hear it?'

Jamie stared at Nico, saw him slowly settle down into a seat, then said, 'I think we need to.'

Danny Carter took a deep breath. 'My father,' he said, 'died of a heart attack while parking his car outside the North Cleveland Baptist church when I was a baby. He was sixty, and my mother was thirty-five – she was a dime actress working at local fairs – haunted shows and all that.

'My old man left all his money to her, but his brothers contested his will on the basis that she was a gold-digger and a woman of low morality. They won, leaving us broke, like dogs – living in one room at the Adam Baldwin Memorial Home for Bankrupts and the Socially Disadvantaged, in Lakewood, one of Cleveland's poorest suburbs. This crumbling mansion, a poorhouse by another name, was a shithole – unpainted boards, thin chicken soup and stale corn bread. Every failure had a story. We heard them all.

'Mom lasted just twelve months before she died of tuberculosis. I was four years old. It was Matt who filled my world. Matt became a man at the age of fourteen, getting out of bed at dawn to vacuum bars and clean toilets before school, then delivering groceries for two hours afterwards. By the time I started fourth grade, we were out of the poorhouse and into assisted housing.

'Matt was my mother and father. Helping with long division was no trouble. He encouraged me to work hard at everything. On the weekends he found time to throw a football or baseball around. "One day," he whispered across our bedroom when the lights first went out. "I'll be a pilot. Fly in the sky like a bird."

'We lived that dream together, talking long into the night when Matt was accepted for basic training. At first, he was flying Douglas A-1 Skyraiders. After that he got his rating for the twin-engine Dakota Transport, months ahead of the rest of the guys in his class.

Danny lifted his mug from the ground beside his chair, wiped the rim on his shirt, then sank to one knee to fill it with tea from the billy. He drank it black and grimaced at the first taste before he went on.

'Davis–Monthan Air Force Base outside Tucson, Arizona, was Matt's fifth domestic posting. I had just turned twelve, and Matt was flying the US Air Force's largest bomber, the B50a Superfortress. Eighteen months later, the Korean War raging, Matt was posted far across the Pacific Ocean to Guam. Our first long separation. He told me not to be scared. After all, we lived off-base with a lady called Miss Sullivan. We both knew she'd look after me, and Matt wrote almost every day.

'Yet the weeks dragged by like years, and one afternoon I came home to find cars and people outside the house. That's the day they told me that Matt had died. There were lots of them, asking questions. Even now it seems like a dream.'

# FOURTEEN

WHILE DANNY TOLD US THE STORY, WE PASSED PHO-
TOGRAPHS AND LETTERS FROM HAND TO HAND, THE
RUSTED OLD TIN AND ITS HISTORY A SYMBOL OF THE
TIME THAT HAD SLIPPED AWAY AND THE SWEAT OF
HIS HANDS AS MAN AND BOY.

MOST OF ALL WE LISTENED, WITH ONLY THE BREEZE
IN THE TREES AND THE CASCADING WATER DOWN IN
THE GORGE. WE CAME TO UNDERSTAND THE DEEP LOVE
HE HAD FOR YOU, A LOVE THAT HAS NEVER FADED.

# FIFTEEN

Danny loved the Arizona desert. Unusual things happened there. Roman legions, bright with scarlet cloaks and iron weapons fought Gallic hordes in the dry streambeds. Dinosaurs grazed the valleys. The lonely boy created a mythical world more stimulating than reality.

One wintry afternoon Danny ceased his play and looked towards the silver Rincon mountains and dying sun. Miss Sullivan put supper on the table at six o'clock and he dared not arrive late. Standing, he shouldered his satchel, aiming through the mesquite and creosote for home, avoiding the occasional empty cigarette packet and coke bottle on the path. The sky was clear and blue, bisected by twin vapour trails from a pair of jets.

Pausing on Beacon Hill to catch his breath, he spat in the dust, and peered at the aircraft as they thundered overhead, shaking the ground. 'F4 Meteors,' he said to himself. He had a book with smudged colour plates of every military aircraft in existence. Sabres, Sea Furies, Stratojets, Mustangs. He knew them all.

He saw the row of houses at the city's fringe. Distance swallowed the detail, but he knew his own place by the white facade and red roof. It had been home for almost five months – since Matt's posting to Davis-Monthan, or Don't-Matter as the flyers called it.

Soon the houses were so close that smoke from a burning rubbish pile stung his nostrils. Danny crossed the road at a run but stopped on the sidewalk when he saw the cars. Visitors, so common when Matt was home, were unusual in his absence.

Tony Cassetari, Matt's best friend, leaned on his blue Chevy with whiskey on his breath and red rims to his eyes. He wore the uniform of a first lieutenant, Air Force, with the red and black patch of the 43rd Bombardment Wing. Pastor Siefring from the base waited beside him.

Danny looked at Miss Sullivan. She had ironing draped on one arm and tears fell down her face. He had never seen her cry before – never imagined her capable of it. The pastor had hold of her hand.

Tony led Danny inside, letting him gulp down a glass of milk. Pastor Siefring broke the news of how the USS *Colby* had picked up enough debris in the East China Sea to confirm the deaths of all eleven men on board Matt's aircraft. Danny watched Tony unscrew the half pint of whiskey he took from his dress shirt pocket and take a jerky mouthful. He felt sick. His spine seemed too weak to support his head.

The sound of engines and car doors came next. Men came to the door, bursting into the house and asking questions. Looking through Matt's precious bookshelves until they found copies of novels by Maxim Gorky and Ray Bradbury … placing them in sealed bags and carrying them away. They emptied drawers and carried his things away in boxes.

'Did your brother love America?'

'Of course he did.'

'Did he ever talk of visiting Russia?'

'Why would he?'

'Did your brother go to meetings?'

'Never. When he was home he stayed home.'

Of the following hours, Danny remembered little, only Miss Sullivan leaning over the kitchen table, staring. Her hair flopped down over one eye as she spoke, so she had to wipe it away. A table leg creaked.

'You can cry if you want to,' Miss Sullivan said, 'no one's going to blame you for crying.'

Danny stared at the whiteness of his hands against the mahogany table. The kitchen clock ticked away in the stillness.

'I can't keep you, you know that, don't you?'

'I know.'

'Matt paid the rent until Christmas, you've got until then, at least.'

Silence.

'Do you understand what I'm telling you?'

'Yes Ma'am.'

She reached out and touched his forehead. 'Sleep now, and if you wake up hungry, just call for me.'

The hallway lights flicked out. The door closed. Once he was sure that she had gone Danny switched on the bedside lamp and stood on unsteady legs. He walked to the dressing table, his reflection in the wide, curved mirror, gripping the iron handle of the second drawer. From inside he withdrew a hinged tin that had once contained one hundred Rothman's Pall Mall cigarettes. The tin was pale cream, illustrated with fine buildings, columns, a carriage and cherubic clouds.

Back on the bed he lifted out the neat pile of letters and placed them to one side. The photographs he fanned out in both hands, thick black and white prints with a wide border.

The earlier prints showed Matt and Danny together – in Cleveland at first, then here in Arizona. The most recent were of Matt alone or with his flyer comrades at Andersen Field, Guam; Quonset huts fringed by patches of jungle, and aircraft parked in their hundreds out on the apron. Danny's hands shook when he came to the last print. He had received it only the previous day. It showed Matt, flight helmet off, standing in front of the giant Boeing aircraft. Dark shadows filled his eyes and he looked quizzically at the camera.

Danny had started a countdown to his brother's return on his wall. Now, there would be no homecoming. Never again.

Three days after the memorial service at Davis-Monthan Field Danny answered the door just after supper. It was Tony, all oiled dark hair and whisky fumes. He swayed on his feet at the doorway and spoke with exaggerated care as if frightened of making a mistake.

'I want to take the kid out for a bit,' he said.

Miss Sullivan demurred, 'I don't think you should drive at all.'

'I'll be careful,' he said.

Danny stepped closer to the door and looked back at the older woman. For almost a week he had stayed inside, moving from his bedroom to the kitchen for meals when she asked, dutifully sitting with her while she knitted her endless scarves and sweaters. Now he needed some respite.

'I want to go with Tony,' he said.

The airman took a firm grip on the doorjamb and the swaying ceased. 'Just for an hour?'

Miss Sullivan nodded, 'Okay, just for an hour, and please drive carefully. God knows it might be good for Danny to spend time with you.'

Danny knew that he was causing trouble for Miss Sullivan – making her come to him in the night when strange shadows crossed the walls and garden noises made him afraid. Maybe she would be relieved to have a break from him.

Tony squatted down, and to Danny it seemed he tried to judge the intensity of his grief – as if anguish left scratches and claw marks on a person's face. Standing, the young pilot put an arm on Danny's shoulder.

'Let's go,' he said.

Danny didn't know where they went. Tony just drove – one hand on the wheel and the other resting on the neck of a whisky bottle between his legs. For almost fifteen minutes Danny was content to sit in silence, watching the night lights fly past, the heater warming the car.

Along Congress Street Tony finally pulled off the road opposite a Mexican food joint. Men and women in jeans and jackets stood outside, talking and eating in groups.

'I wanted to tell you something,' Tony said. He paused for another swig of whisky. 'If I could I'd wait a year or two, until you're older, but I might be the next to go, then you'd never find out.'

'Tell me,' Danny said.

Tony's breath, thick with alcohol, stank worse now that he faced Danny, but the boy didn't care.

'No one's getting told nothing about the crash. Matt and his crew got orders sending them out to Guam, and just a few days later they're all dead or missing. We don't know if they were on a mission or training. Even the Colonel doesn't know what the hell is going on but get this—' Tony lifted the bottle again. Danny heard the bubbles tick through as he drank, '—their orders came direct from General Macarthur.'

Danny had heard of the famous general but couldn't see the significance. 'I don't understand.'

Tony leaned closer, 'Kid, neither do I. There are things I can't tell you about the unit – things Matt couldn't tell you either, but we ain't equipped to deliver flowers. There's a hell of a lot more to this than meets the eye – and I'm gonna find out what. A B50a has four engines – she can fly okay on just three, or even two for a bit – it ain't easy to bring an airplane like that down.'

Danny shifted slightly in his seat.

Tony shook his head. 'God only knows how Matt would have reacted on a real mission. He used to say that he loved life too much to take it away – reckoned he was in the wrong job – always talked about flying airliners instead. Your brother had a heart of gold, and I loved him for it.'

A Chevy truck pulled up opposite. Half a dozen men piled out of the tray and onto the sidewalk. Danny took out a handkerchief and blew his nose. 'Why did Matt have to die?'

'I don't know, but I'm gonna find out,' he said, 'you and me – between us we'll find out.'

'Like a pact?'

'Sure, yeah, like a pact.' Tony's eyes looked queer in the light. 'I guess you miss him a lot, huh Danny?'

Danny sniffed. 'I want to be just like him.' He knew those words did not truly express the way he felt. He not so much wanted to be like Matt, but to be him.

Tony lowered his eyes, 'We all do kid, we all want to be like him.' He leaned forward. 'Matt loved you Danny, you know that, don't you?' The boy nodded, wishing Tony would stop. 'He talked about you all the time – when you got a good grade – when you hit a home run down the park. He had your photograph in the cockpit. He was so proud of you.'

Danny didn't want to cry, but he couldn't help it.

As Tony drove Danny home, he sang the unit song:

*Men of the 43rd*
*half-man, half-bird.*
*Foes of freedom,*
*we'll smash asunder.*
*Down below they'll,*
*Hear our thunder.*

Danny tried to join in, through the tears, and Tony stopped the car at last. 'I won't walk you inside – that old broomstick will just nag on me, but I'll come to see you again, promise.'

Danny didn't want Tony to hear him blubbering. He opened the passenger door and went out into the cold, stopping to watch the Chevy squeal through a U-turn and disappear into the night.

'I'm not sure whether I should tell you this quite yet,' Miss Sullivan said when he walked inside, 'in case it doesn't work out, but I had an idea tonight.'

'What?'

I've got a cousin. Her name is Suzanne. She doesn't have any children of her own. I telephoned her tonight and guess what? She's driving over to see you with her husband – all the way from Kansas.' Danny saw how Miss Sullivan's bottom lip caught on her teeth while she waited for his reaction.

'Why?'

'Oh silly, if they like you, they'll take you with them – you'll have a real home. They've got a farm, more than a thousand acres, and a big house.'

'Why would they take me with them?'

Miss Sullivan took him in her arms and pressed him against her chest. 'Oh silly, because some people – most people – need somebody to love.' She rubbed his hair. She smelled of Sunlight soap. Danny closed his eyes and breathed it in, trembling in her arms.

Miss Sullivan's cousin and her husband pulled up in a beige Mercury coupe at eight in the morning three weeks after the chaplain came to call. Danny sat on the sofa in his best suit. Miss Sullivan went out and returned, leading a slim young woman in a yellow dress. A tiara in her hair made her look, to Danny, like a princess, yet her arms, he noticed, were finely muscled.

She took his hand. 'I'm Suzanne, Frank will be here in a minute – he's checking the oil in the car, though goodness knows why he had to choose this exact minute to do it.'

Frank walked in a few minutes later, seemingly as wide across the shoulders as the door. His skin was brown, and his eyes creased so you wouldn't doubt that he worked all day under the sun. He wore a John Deere cap high on his forehead.

'You're Danny?' Frank asked.

The boy nodded, watching the way Frank summed him up.

'This is awkward for all of us – Suzanne and I thought it might be best if we go out for the day together. By supper we'll all know if we want to take this business further.'

'I'd like that,' Danny said.

Out at the car Miss Sullivan kissed him on the cheek. 'Good luck,' she said. 'You deserve a break.'

'Why don't you come with us?' Danny asked, suddenly afraid.

Miss Sullivan shook her head. 'Suzanne needs time with you, not with me. She and I can get together some other time.'

Suzanne slid her seat forward so the boy could climb in, folding his knees and ankles so he had room to sit. Frank started the engine and the big V8 roared.

'I like your car,' Danny said, leaning forward in the seat. Matt owned an old Buick, but it had been off the road for so long grass had grown up around the wheels.

'Thanks.' Frank reached the end of the street and turned west.

Suzanne pointed through the window at a brand-new church on a big block beside the park. 'Is that your church Danny? Paula tells me you're a Methodist.'

Danny nodded vaguely. He had become used to life without the constraints of Faith. It seemed that if he went to Kansas things would be different.

'We're Presbyterian,' Suzanne went on, 'would changing over bother you?'

Danny sat with his hands on his knees, 'It's the same God, I guess.'

Frank laughed, 'That's right, I often think that He doesn't much care if you're a Methodist, a Quaker or even a Catholic so long as you honour and obey Him.'

As if she could read Danny's thoughts Suzanne turned back to look into his eyes. 'Don't get the wrong impression, we're not holy rollers – just simple people who go to church on Sundays, aren't we Frank?'

'Sure, that's right.'


Together they strolled the broad sidewalks of downtown Tucson. Suzanne bought Danny new clothes, while Frank wandered, hands in pockets, from cigar shop to hardware store, gruffly pretending not to watch boy and woman bonding together.

They ate lunch in Reid Park – hot dogs and soda on the green-painted tables. Danny saved the last portion of his bun and rolled small lumps of the soft bread into balls between his thumb and forefinger. These he aimed at the squabbling pigeons.

'Tell me, Danny,' Frank said. 'What do you want out of life?'

'I don't want to go to an orphanage.'

'I'm sorry.' Frank shifted on the bench. 'I know things are hard for you. Losing a brother in any circumstances is difficult enough, for you it must have been an enormous blow. I hate asking awkward questions but you and me and Suzanne need to get to know each other pretty quick and that's hard to do without asking a few curly ones.' He paused. 'Miss Sullivan told us that you don't have any real family. Is that true?'

Danny had vague memories of his mother from those precious years before she passed away, and somewhere back in his memory there were aunts. He could not picture any one of them. Matt had said once that they were ashamed of his mother and her poorhouse boys. He shook his head.

Suzanne licked a smudge of ketchup from her lip. Sometimes, it seemed, she wasn't like an adult at all. 'What about you Danny?' she asked. 'Have you got any questions for us?'

'How come you haven't had children of your own?'

Frank's eyes slitted up in the sunlight. 'You speak your mind, no doubt about that. Suzanne and I would have liked to be blessed with children but the Lord hasn't seen fit to let that happen.' He waved a hand at his wife. 'If ever you've seen a hen without a chick it's Suzanne here, she's so desperate to mother something she ... well you should see her with the darn cat.' He dropped his head. To Danny's surprise the big man's voice cracked. 'I hate seeing her like that.'

The young woman said nothing. A tear ran down each cheek and her green eyes offered him a glance deep inside, into the wells of sadness there.

Danny stood up from his seat, brushed the crumbs from his trousers and walked twenty paces until he stood facing a stand of oaks near the swings. Lives turn on a series of major decisions. This was one of them, and he was wise enough, even at the age of twelve, to know it.

One day, years earlier, when Danny had been in trouble at school, Matt hadn't scolded him, just sat next to him near the front steps, on the grass, and talked, thumping a baseball into a mitt while he did so.

*I know you don't remember our mother all that well, she died a long time ago, but she always used to say that if you're not sure what to do, if you don't know what's right, just close your eyes and feel it from inside, all the way from your toes and into your heart. Listen to what that inner voice tells you. It knows, every time. Sometimes the right way is hard, sometimes it might even mean hurting someone close to you ...*

Now, with a pair of pigeons stalking him for more of the soft bread, Danny closed his eyes and pictured Suzanne. The young woman with the pain in her eyes. He began to listen, to the wisdom in the earth and in the lives of past generations and those yet to come. It was nothing to do with religion, or ideology. It was just there.

Danny knew what to say. There was no other choice. Turning around, hands hanging at his sides, he walked back to where Frank and Suzanne waited. 'I want to come with you,' he said.

Frank stopped talking and stared. Suzanne smiled. 'Why, Danny, that's …'

'I mean, if you want me to.'

Frank looked at his wife, then Danny, and beamed. 'I think we'd both be pleased if you did.'

Danny had no time to reconsider his decision. By then he was in Suzanne's arms.

# SIXTEEN

The school bell ringing in his ears, Danny hurried through the classroom door. He rolled the bike, a brand-new Western Flyer, gently off the rack and wheeled it, as school regulations required, past the rose garden, through the gate and finally to the road. The bike had been Danny's fifteenth birthday present from Frank and Suzanne, and he loved it dearly.

The years in Kansas had helped assuage the pain of losing Matt. Danny had almost forgotten about the hard men in suits, distracted by summer days on hay carts, golden ears of corn in the day's last rays of sunshine, fresh apples from the orchard, small town dances in halls, girls and baseball games.

Moncrieff, Kansas was not a large town, but the main street ran wide and straight with two blocks of faded shop fronts and offices with brass plaques. Poplar trees burst from garden beds at intervals along the sidewalk and the hotel retained a hitching post out front for those farmers who still preferred to ride in to slake their thirst.

Frank and Suzanne's farm was a shade less than three miles west – up to half an hour by bicycle depending upon distractions along the way. Danny lifted himself onto the seat and pushed the pedals. The solid rubber wheels carried him halfway across the road before a shout caught his attention. It was Eddie Feeney.

'Hey Danny, walk with me a bit.'

Danny was anxious to feel the wind on his face. Even so he applied the brakes and swung off the seat – Eddie was the only true friend he'd made in Kansas.

'Hi Eddie,' he said.

'Got any dough?'

Eddie's father had broken his back in a car wreck, and the family struggled to supply themselves with basics like shoes. There were no spare coins for frivolities.

Danny dug in his pocket. He had two dimes and a nickel. 'Some,' he said.

A shop window carried a poster advertising World Series baseball. Joe DiMaggio glared out in colour, about to swipe a baseball a mile or two. Eddie cocked his right arm like a pitcher and fired an imaginary ball at the paper representation of everyone's hero.

'Strike two,' he shouted, then turned to smile at Danny. 'They say that the Yankees have drafted Mickey Mantle from Kansas City.'

'I heard that too.'

'You got enough for two sodas?'

'Yeah, but I got chores – I'll give you a dime if you want but I need to get home.'

They reached Merrill's Hobby Shop, and Danny turned, slowing up to examine the delights in the window display. Toy soldiers lined up in their dozens and a model panzer advanced through their ranks. A miniature train chuffed endlessly along a track, through the tunnel and over the bridge.

The sound of a car engine caught Danny's attention. He turned and looked. A glossy burgundy coloured car, with wide-set headlights and a low grille had just come to a halt across the road.

Eddie had an abiding interest in all things mechanical. 'De Soto,' he said, 'looks brand new. Don't even recognise the driver, mustn't be from around here.'

Danny stared also – not at the white wall tyres and shiny chrome hubcaps but at the occupants. Four men. The driver wound down the window. A pedestrian stopped to talk to him. People on the streets stared, and even some of the shop owners left their places to stare at the brilliant car.

With a roar and squeal of tyres on bitumen, the car pulled away. Danny stared after it, suddenly chilled. There was something different about the men. They reminded him of some of the fliers he had met so many years ago – even out of uniform they had a military look.

'What's wrong with you?' Eddie asked.

Danny shook his head. 'Nothing. I'd better get going.' He grabbed the handlebars and started to run.

'Hey, what about the ice cream?' Eddie called. Danny dug into his pocket and pulled the coins out. They clattered on the footpath behind him.

'Hey, have you gone crazy or something?'

Danny wasn't listening. He reached the road and swung up onto the bike, pumping his legs and accelerating. A car horn sounded. The wind roared past his ears. He maintained that speed past the Texaco gas station on the edge of town. Rows of wheat ruffled in the breeze on both sides of the road – uncountable acres of amber wealth stretching from horizon to horizon.

Three miles passed quickly. Danny rode the bike into the tool shed, pushed down the stand, and walked towards the house – a single storey place with smoky heat shimmering from the chimney. He paused on the porch to remove his boots and entered the kitchen.

This was Suzanne's domain: immaculate benchtops, a wooden bread keeper, a shelf of Fowler's Jars filled with bay leaves, flower, curry powder, and sugar both brown and white. A fly swat sat on the window sill ready for any insect suicidal enough to enter.

'You're breathing hard,' Suzanne said. She pressed the flat of her hand to Danny's forehead. 'My, you're hot too. Are you feeling okay?'

'Fine, I rode fast today.'

Suzanne wiped her hands on the apron. 'I made some brownies.'

Danny ate two of the soft chocolate cakes with a glass of milk.

'There's a letter for you too,' she said, handing him an envelope. It was postmarked Tucson, Arizona.

Holding the letter to his chest Danny walked to his room, sat the letter on the bed then changed out of his school clothes. Changing after school was one of Frank's rules. He had a rule for every occasion, and Danny had found that once he learned them life was surprisingly easy.

Sitting on the bed he carefully tore the letter open. It was from Tony Cassetari. His letters arrived every month or two, with cheery news or sometimes just a joke. Danny read and reread them until the paper started to tear along the folds, and kept them in the cigarette tin next to those from Matt.

*Dear Danny,*

*This is a sad letter, because I don't know how soon I'll be able to write you again. My crew and I have been back at Tucson now for over a month, but I'm leaving the base, and maybe the USA for good.*
*I know a little more about Matt's last mission. The story is too long and complicated for this letter, and as yet unconfirmed, but I want to tell you that he is a hero.*

*When I've taken care of some things and found out more, I will come to see you.*

*Your Friend*

*Tony*

Danny read the letter three times, then opened the bedside drawer and slipped it inside, into the tin of treasures. Later, he would read it again. Slowly, thinking about Tony's words, he changed into overalls and ran back along the corridor past the kitchen.

'You want anything else to eat before you go out?' Suzanne called from the kitchen as Danny pulled on his boots.

'No thanks,' he replied, running out the door and across the back yard so fast that Winston, the old Rhode Island rooster, flapped noisily out of his path.

Feeding the pigs, then the chickens, took half an hour, and thereafter Danny was theoretically free to play. Often, however, he found it more interesting to seek out Frank and the hands.

He passed the small fenced-off garden with the six white crosses. Frank had explained how each represented one of Suzanne's miscarriages, a term Danny understood only vaguely. Once, in his early days at the farm he had stumbled on Suzanne weeding and tending the tiny plot. She had stood, leaning on the rail and pointing to the evening sky.

'I see my babies in the sunset,' she said, 'a shape, sometimes just the suggestion of a face. I believe their souls live on. I don't believe that God would snuff them out without setting their souls free just because they weren't yet born.'

A tractor chugged away somewhere to the west and he walked in that direction, past the orchard, soon reaching the first large paddock. The tractor pulled an ancient cart, trailing a baler in long circles around the field. Danny ran to catch up. Frank and one of the hands, Willy French, followed the cart, picking up the bales from their rows and throwing them inside.

There was not much Danny could do to help here. The big rectangular bales were heavy, and the cart stood at chest height. While he could lift one, he could not do so fast and constantly.

Frank made the work look easy. He bent over and lifted the bale high, drawing back his arms to drive it into the cart in almost the same movement.

Danny stopped running and walked alongside. 'Have you got any jobs I can do?' he asked.

Frank lifted another bale and tossed it on the cart. 'You could give Pat a spell from the tractor and send him back here to help me.'

Danny ran ahead and waved at Pat, a good-natured Irishman with a straw hat and perpetual grin. The tractor stopped, idling, and Pat stepped down. 'Frank said I could drive,' Danny said.

'Sure you can,' Pat said, 'and what does he want with me?'

'Loading the cart,' Danny said, aware of sending Pat from this comfortable job to a difficult one. Still he climbed the tractor and eased her into gear, the engine building revolutions as he opened the throttle.

Ahead, the bales dribbled in neat lines from the machine. All Danny had to do was keep close to that line and drive on slowly. It felt great to sit so high above the golden pasture with the first cooling breeze of dusk in his hair. A meadowlark swiped by so close to his head that he felt the wing beat.

Frank called a halt within an hour and climbed up on the wheel rim for a ride back. The other men sat on the hay bales of the cart. Danny heard occasional laughter even over the engine throb.

Fence posts threw long shadows across the track as they drove past fields mauve with flowers. The sun now cleared the horizon by just a hand's breadth. Danny drove slowly, conscious of Frank's silent scrutiny.

'Stop here and let the men off,' Frank said close to Danny's ear as they passed the labourers' quarters. Danny eased in the clutch and shifted into neutral while the workers piled off the cart.

'We're not gonna unload tonight?' Danny asked.

'No, it can wait 'til morning. Those bales won't go anywhere by themselves.'

Danny pulled the tractor over outside the hayshed. 'Did I do okay?' he asked when the clattering engine and the echoes off the buildings had died.

'You did a man's job well,' Frank said. They walked towards the house in silent companionship.

Before supper Danny went back to his room, found Tony's letter and read it again, trying to understand the meaning behind his words. I want to tell you that he is a hero. He reached for the box and took out the last photograph Matt had sent, trying to read his expression. Was it pride, or anger?

Matt had owned the kind of face that rarely strays far from a smile. Danny studied the narrowed eyes, and the hands clasped around his middle. Matt had used that gesture sometimes. When?

His brows were creased just a little. Was he nervous?

The letter that had accompanied that final photograph was on the top of the pile. Danny lifted it and carefully smoothed out the paper. He began to read.

It began like so many other letters before it, with a joke. Dear Danny, Guess what? They've decided to make me a general at last. Danny smiled, but at the third paragraph he stopped, and reread one sentence three times. Three months to go, and I fear I'll never make it.

Danny suddenly felt a chill that brushed through his hair, bringing it erect from neck to crown. Matt was trying to tell him something that the censor would never pick up. He read on through three unassuming paragraphs: I've always lived in hope that when the time came it wouldn't be me. I was wrong. On earlier readings Danny had always assumed that the sentence referred to an anecdote in the previous paragraph.

Then there was a single word. Kaesong. It had no connection to the surrounding sentences but sat on its own at the end of a paragraph.

Matt was trying to tell him something, Danny realised. He picked up the photograph again and looked at the face he had loved. The image was clear. Matt was afraid. He was telling him that he was in fear for his life, and now it was too late to help him.

Danny closed the box and stepped silently from the bed. From the shelf above the desk he took down the glossy Reader's Digest atlas. On the bed he studied first Guam and the Marianas, then Korea.

Danny found the city in the north. Kaesong. He put the atlas and tin away and turned off the torch. Lying back under the covers he said the word once more. Kaesong. Matt had been frightened. Frightened of Kaesong.

The living room was not much bigger than the long mahogany table and grey upholstered lounge chairs but was cosy in winter. Frank's radio set sat on the dresser, broadcasting news, music and serials.

When dessert was over Danny carried plates out to the kitchen and rinsed them under the tap. Suzanne arrived a few minutes later with the cutlery and glasses.

'I'll help wash up,' Danny said.

'You dry,' she said.

Danny selected a towel and waited while Suzanne filled the sink. Her movements were rapid and efficient as always.

'Did you learn anything new at school today?'

'We learned Gypsy Rover for the school concert.'

Suzanne smiled and started to sing.

*The gypsy rover came over the hill,*
*Bound for the valley so sha-dy...*

Danny joined in until they ran out of verses. By then only the pots and pans remained.

A pair of vehicle headlights, visible through the dining room window, stopped near the front gate. Danny ceased drying and looked. Frank stood up from his almost inviolate after dinner routine of reading the newspaper from cover to cover and parted the curtains.

'I wonder what they're doing,' he said, walking through the kitchen, 'darn strange at night. If they're still there in five minutes I'll go out and see what the trouble is.'

Danny continued with the drying up, but no longer felt like singing. He worked steadily and finally put the last item away.

'Well that's five minutes,' Frank said, 'might as well go and see. They've still got their headlights on – soon have a flat battery if they keep that up.' The screen door slammed.

Suzanne touched Danny's shoulder. 'Go out with Frank and see who's there. I'll wipe the benches.'

Danny sat on the porch step and pulled on his boots. He walked to where Frank waited with the long stainless steel torch he kept beside the hat stand, with its bulbous end, bright with reflectors.

Boots crunched on the gravel drive as Danny struggled to keep pace with the big man. 'It's not polite to park outside a man's home like that,' Frank muttered.

As they neared the road Danny stopped walking. 'It's them,' he said, so sharply that Frank stopped walking also.

'Who?'

'I saw them in town this afternoon. A big De Soto with four men inside.'

 The car roared up the drive, followed by another. The first car had police markings. Danny could see the shadows inside, behind headlights that radiated side beams and left white spots on the eyes.

Frank took Danny's arm. 'I don't care who they are. I'll see them off.'

A door opened and Wal Pride, the local sheriff, stepped out. Danny knew him by sight – a tall, chubby man with an easy-going manner and an oversized six-shooter in a holster at his side. The second car, the burgundy De Soto, nudged in behind and men got out. Car doors slammed.

Danny moved closer to Frank. A hand dropped to his shoulder protectively. 'What brings you out here, Wal?'

The sheriff stopped just short of the porch, then turned back to look at the other men who were coming up behind him. 'Sorry Frank, I hate to disturb you folks tonight but—' he pointed at Danny. 'It's to do with the young fellow here.'

'Wally Pride if you've come here to waste my time I'll—'

The sheriff took a folded document from his top pocket. 'This is the search warrant, Frank. It's signed by some fancy judge in Kansas City, but it's legal.'

Frank stepped back so he could read the document using light from the kitchen. Danny could hear Frank breathing loudly through his nose as he always did when concentrating.

'Well I never,' Frank said at last. 'Search my house? What's the world coming to when an honest man and his family can't relax in peace without having their house searched?'

'Sorry Frank, but the best thing is to get it over and done with.'

One of the men stepped up to Frank, standing so close it was like he was aiming to bump him with his chest. He was young, just seven or eight years older than Danny, yet he wore a perfectly fitted suit and had a face as lean as bone. 'Take us to the kid's room.'

Silent men filed through the house and on into the bedroom. Past Suzanne standing silently, arms at her sides, and lips pale as moonlight.

Then, standing against the wall with Frank, Danny watched them go to work in the room, pulling clothes and school books from drawers and shelves. One threw the covers off the bed and used a knife to slit through the mattress, searching inside as if something might be hidden there.

'Hey what do you think you're doing?' Frank asked. 'That's enough.' He stepped across the room, and then something happened that rocked Danny to the core.

The man delving inside the mattress turned away from his task, cocked his fist and drove it into Frank's mouth, provoking an instant and copious flow of blood. As if that wasn't enough, he punched him again in the head and the big, gentle man hit the deck like a falling pole.

The man's lips were thin and set in a cruel, semi-permanent sneer. He barked some instructions then paused in front of Danny, shaking the pain away from his hand.

'You are Danny Carter, correct?'

Danny said nothing, merely stared, hatred and fear filling his heart.

'Talk to me, son, or you are in for a dose of shit you won't want to repeat. Have you had any form of contact from your brother?'

Confusing emotions welled and eddied in Danny's heart. The question seemed almost incomprehensible at first. Finally, he started to shake his head. Long suppressed hopes jumped to life. The world that he had built in this place was flying apart.

'Answer me boy.'

'Is Matt alive?' Danny asked.

'You tell me.' The man snapped back.

Frank sat up, holding his face in both hands, blood trickling from between his fingers. Danny tried to go to him, but the stranger grabbed his shoulder and pulled him back roughly, thrusting his face close. 'You've got three seconds. Have you had contact with your brother?'

'No,' he said at last.

The man's eyes were like blue marbles. His lips writhed like rattlesnakes. 'Your brother was a traitorous son-of-a-bitch. He sold his country down the river and if he's still alive now it's only temporary. If we find him alive, he will hang from the neck until he is dead.'

The words had the force of bullets, pinning Danny against the wall, his heart beating against his ribs like piano hammers on strings. 'You're lying.'

One of the men withdrew Danny's cigarette tin of letters and photographs from a drawer, scrabbled inside then tucked it under his arm. He seemed pleased with the discovery.

Danny ran forward and tried to pry the tin from the man's arms. A firm hand pushed him away.

'I'll be seeing my lawyer first thing tomorrow morning.' Frank choked out, blood running down his chin, onto his shirt, but the strangers were leaving the room, ignoring him. Danny waited, breathing hard, shaking with fear, but he could not let the man take the letters. He started to run, but Frank stopped him with a hand on his shoulder. 'Let them go,' he urged. 'We'll raise hell. We'll get your things back.'

Danny looked into Frank's eyes. To the honest farmer the box of letters and memories meant little, but to the boy they were everything. He broke away and burst through the screen door that led from the kitchen.

Outside, car doors opened and closed. Danny focussed on the man with the tin.

He sprinted, covering the intervening distance in ten short steps. He was fifteen, and farm-boy strong, big enough to crash into the unsuspecting man and set him off balance. The tin fell.

Danny snatched it up and started to run back towards the house, but Frank stood on the porch, a long bloodstain down his shirt.

'No, Danny. Give it back to them. Give it back and let them

go. We have the law on our side.'

Yet Danny was learning that the law is not something rigid. Law can be manipulated; bypassed, ignored by men of power.

'Take the little son-of-a-bitch,' someone shouted. 'Grab him.'

Danny turned and faced the dark paddocks beyond the tank stand. Darkness was his only chance. *They* would steal his memories until there was nothing left. He glanced back. Suzanne emerged from the house. Danny locked eyes with her and she screamed his name.

Knowing that Suzanne and Frank could not protect him, Danny faced the night, and broke into a run, the tin tucked under his arm. Shouts and blundering footsteps sounded behind him, but Danny had come to know every square foot of this farm. He ducked under gates faster than those who followed could climb or open them. Sometimes he stumbled on rough ground. Rabbit holes. Stumps. Still he ran on.

Ten minutes passed before he scaled a solid timber and wire fence, conscious that he was leaving Frank's property behind. He stood on the other side, hesitating for the first time. Wanting to go back.

A vivid image of Suzanne filled Danny's head and he had to lean on a post while a sense of longing overcame him. He wanted to be back in bed, with Suzanne pulling up the warm covers and kissing him goodnight.

No. *They* were there, waiting. Tears filled Danny's eyes. Maybe Matt was alive. The man had asked. Matt was afraid. Of Kaesong. He needed help. But how could he leave Suzanne and Frank?

I'm sorry, but if Matt is alive, he needs my help. I have to make it so they can't hurt him.

With the back of his hand he wiped the tears away, and with strength and resolve building in his heart, he ran on into the night.

# SEVENTEEN

They were relentless, pitiless. Twelve months later, they found Danny in St Louis, bedraggled and half-starved from living on the streets. Framing him for crimes he had not committed they locked him away from the world, first at Algoa Reformatory.

The tin of letters and photographs was well hidden, in the walls of an abandoned fur warehouse by the river, but that was small comfort as he was dragged from lock-up to reformatory.

On his third night in Algoa *they* came to see him. A guard took him to an interview room where two neatly dressed men were waiting. One had an unforgettable face. He and Danny had met before, on that night at the farm, when he had punched gentle Frank. To Danny he was the most frightening person he had ever seen. Tall, with a lean, cruel face, and pitiless eyes. Like the room itself. Cold stone. Hard floor.

'Hello Danny, my name is Lieutenant Temple. My men and I belong to an organisation called AFOSI, the Air Force Office of Special Investigations.'

'I don't care who you are. Leave me alone.'

'Not until you give me what I want. I want the letters your brother was sending?'

'They're hidden where you'll never find them.'

The second man picked Danny up by the shirt and threw him against the back wall. His head smacked backwards against the concrete, and he fell sideways onto his arm.

The American stood over him, staring down, 'You've let yourself get in quite a predicament. You should never have run that night.'

'I told you. LEAVE ME ALONE.'

'I want you to tell me the truth, Danny.'

The wall was damp against his back. 'Go to hell.'

The American lowered his voice. 'Give me your full cooperation and I will help you to the best of my ability. Refuse it and I will use all my influence to make sure you rot in custody.' He took a step forward. 'Where would your brother go? Where would he hide? You must know something.'

'I don't, you sons-of-bitches.'

The second man kicked out with a polished black shoe, knocking Danny down, following up with a second blow to the nose. It bled immediately, a flood of red that cascaded down onto his shirt front. Hot tears flowed out of his eyes and the fear that threatened to consume him swelled and roared, combining with longing and shame until it seemed that a strong wind shrilled through his mind.

'I don't know,' he said again, softly this time. The anguish shook his body and he cried into his hands. 'One day soon Matt is going to find me, and when he does he's going to punish you for what you have done.'

Temple lowered his voice. 'Don't you understand that the best way to find your brother is to work together?'

'No, get away from me. Leave me alone.'

'Have it your way,' Temple's voice fell to a whisper, 'but you'll never have him. Not ever. If we catch him, he'll swing from a rope. Forget him boy. Even if he's still alive he's lost to you. Lost forever.'

When they left Danny stayed crumpled on the floor of the room, weeping as if he might never stop.

★

Algoa stripped Danny of dignity and left him in a wilderness – without hope. All links with Matt had gone. The years seemed interminable at first, but the months somehow stretched into years, and eventually he had trouble remembering what it had been like on the outside.

When he turned eighteen they moved him to the centuries-old Jefferson City Penitentiary. It was there that another piece in the jigsaw fell into place.

With three months to serve at the jail Danny was conscious only of surviving. He shared an E-Hall cell with a real friend, Lloyd Irons. The pair had endured the apprenticeship of Algoa together as a team. Lloyd was redheaded and athletic; strong and fast. Even here at the jail they kept each other safe, for Lloyd had taught Danny one essential skill – how to fight.

The cell had three bunks with straw tick mattresses, and a barred window with a green painted sill. A beam of sunlight shot in, illuminating the airborne dust.

Even with his shirt off sweat covered Danny's chest – it had been a hot, dry summer. The warders – many of whom were farmers earning money on the side – told of crops lying crisp and brown in the fields where they had wilted, and of the end-less hot winds that robbed moisture from the soil.

Danny tried not to think of the cool pond back on the farm in Kansas, nor even of snow and cool breezes. He tried not to think of the wind and the rain and the stars at all – but simply endured.

'Yard time boys, out you go.' It was one of the guards – Ted Little, who, like most of his colleagues was more interested in a quiet life than antagonizing prisoners. The guards at Jeff City wore no uniform, but rather denim and work shirts.

Men filled the yard, talking in groups or sitting. Only a few actually exercised. Danny sat with Lloyd and an older convict called Thomas. Ted Little was never far away, and Danny watched him carefully to make sure he didn't stray out of sight. At least a dozen men wanted to make Danny their punk and avoiding them took all his time and attention.

In Jeff City a punk was a man who allowed others to have sex with him, willingly or otherwise. Most killings and beatings were related to punks – jealousy, unwillingness, outright refusal and retaliation. Homosexuality was the biggest difference between Algoa, where the practice was less common, and the adult pen, where perhaps one out of three men used others for sex, at least on occasion.

Older men competed for new arrivals. Danny owed his continued freedom from these attentions to his association with Lloyd. He still remembered how fear had sunk in over those first few days – men staring at him as if, on the outside, they might have looked at a girl. Danny walked carefully, looking in all directions. In the yard he stayed close to a guard like a shadow. He worked in the kitchen and kept a weapon handy at all times. He stared at no one, offended no one, and so far, he had been lucky.

Old Thomas wiped his mouth with the back of one hand and pointed a crooked finger at a passing man. 'New feller,' he said, 'just got here this morning.'

Danny looked incuriously at the man. He was nondescript, wearing the same green outfit as all the detainees. He had a beaky nose, and a face unshaven blue.

'They reckon he's a war veteran,' Thomas continued, 'flew an airplane in Korea.'

Danny stopped dead in the act of lighting a cigarette. 'A pilot?'

'Sure. That's what Ed Jolley told me.' Ed Jolley was a guard – a St Louis teenager with a mouth too big for his own good.

'How did he end up in here?'

'Came back from Korea and found his wife had installed a new guy in his bed. He shot 'em both with his .45.'

'Jesus.'

'That's what I'd do too,' Lloyd said, 'I wouldn't tolerate it if my woman cheated on me.'

Thomas slapped his own leg and laughed. Danny hated it when the old man laughed because the wide-open mouth placed his rotten teeth on display. 'You ain't never had a woman, so how would you know?'

It was true, Danny knew it; but Lloyd was riled. 'Hell, you don't have to do something to know what it's like.'

Thomas leaned forward, smirking. 'There you are dead wrong – you don't know nothing 'bout women 'til you've had one – you might think you do but you don't. Me? I've had hundreds.'

'Hell Thomas, you ain't ever been out of here long enough to get one, let alone hundreds.'

Danny stood. 'I'm gonna go and have a word with that guy.'

The new arrival walked aimlessly, but Danny saw that he never strayed far from the guard.

'Hi,' Danny said.

'Beat it, kid.'

'A guy said you were in Korea.'

'It's none of his business where I was, and it ain't yours either.' He started to walk away.

'My brother was over there, but he went missing. His plane went down.'

The man stopped without turning. 'What outfit was he with?'

'The 43rd Bombardment Wing.'

'Never heard of them. I flew an F-84E for the 428th.' The hostility left the man's face and all Danny could see was fear. He sidled closer but kept his voice low. 'Kid, do you know a guy called Lester Holmes?'

'Sure do. He ain't in the yard right now, but I know Lester's not someone you want to mess with.' The prison had cliques – Negroes, St Louis toughs and white rural folk. Each had one or more leaders. Lester Holmes was the unchallenged king of the St Louis boys. People got killed when he blinked.

'I know that – but I got trouble, I killed his cousin for screwing my wife. I heard he's gonna do me in the first chance he gets.'

Danny accepted the information without comment. Revenge was the way of the world he now knew. 'Where's your cell?'

'C-Block, with two old guys who look like they'll hold me down for that Holmes son of a bitch for two bits. I gotta get out of there.'

Danny looked across at Ted Little — he was watching them talk. 'What's your name?'

'Wilson, what's yours?'

'Danny. For five bucks I can get you moved into our room — we've got a spare bunk. It's just me and Lloyd and we'll help you keep out of Lester's way.'

'Five bucks in real money or this prison voucher bullshit?'

'Greenbacks. You got any?'

'I'm not saying I have, or I haven't.' The possession of real money was punishable by a week in the hole — besides, a man known to own a wad died quickly.

'Come over and meet Lloyd, he's my buddy in the cell. I need to see a guy who works as clerk for the screw in charge of room shifts. I need the money first.'

Wilson exhaled, making a 'p' sound with his lips. 'Alright, look, I ain't got a cent — maybe I'd better just check in with the warden — they'll put me somewhere nice and safe on the second floor.' Checking-in meant declaring to the guards that you feared for your life and wanted protection.

'Don't do that,' Danny said, 'you'll never get respect, no matter how many years you're here.' He wanted to keep Wilson close — he was a flyer, just like Matt had been. 'I'll loan you the five bucks — I won ten playing stud a few days ago.'

Danny left Wilson with Lloyd and scanned the crowd. The man he wanted leaned against a pillar waiting for business. Every man with half a brain turned their job into profit — trusties delivering cigarettes, cooks preparing special meals — having the ability to change rooms on demand was as good as money in the bank.

Danny pressed a five-dollar bill into the man's hand and spoke softly. 'You know that new guy who came today? Wilson's his first name.'

'Sure, I saw him.'

'I want him in my cell. Danny Johnson, and Lloyd James. Can you do that fast?'

The man nodded. 'Two hours, I promise.'

Danny walked away. Wilson seemed like a good guy — he was

already in earnest conversation with Lloyd. It would be nice to have him in the cell.

Only after supper did the starlings, birds that had the run of the jail, settle peacefully. The prison hummed with low conversation, and was never truly dark, for the corridor lights burned night and day.

Danny lay on his side, listening to Wilson.

'General Goddamn Macarthur,' he said, 'if he had of stopped our Marines on the North Korean border, I reckon the war would've been over in a year. No, he kept them marching north, until China came into the war. Jesus, back in mid-1950 it was all over, and then Macarthur had to invade the North.'

'How long were you there?' Danny asked, eyes glazed with hero-worship and the pleasure of being near someone who had been there.

'Two tours – '50-'51 then most of '52. In between my tours I sorta guessed what Liz had been doin' with that creep John Holmes but didn't really wanna believe it. Then when I was back in Korea a friend wrote me and coughed up what was going on. Can you imagine what it was like to be stuck in a goddamn Quonset hut on the edge of the world, knowin' what another man was doing to my wife? I'll spend every day of my life in this jail, and Lester Holmes might cut my throat, but I tell you – I'm still glad I done it.'

Danny nodded, 'Tell me about the war – flying. Tell me about flying.'

'Jesus, it breaks my heart just to think of how it felt. Have you ever driven a car with the top down?'

'I've never driven a car,' he said. 'Only a tractor.'

Lloyd piped up. 'I have – and it sure does feel good.'

'Well flying an F-84 is like sitting on a bolt of lightning. Sometimes we'd have a mission – like to drop fifty pounders on some Chink positions. Other times we'd just go up and it was up to us to fly around and find a target for ourselves – mebbe a Chink tank, or a resupply column.'

Danny saw how the sweat on Wilson's face shone in the corridor lights. He used his hand like a model jet screaming in close to the ground. 'I loved that the best,' he said, 'strafing just fifty feet up. Down there you could see every round strike – men going down like skittles.'

'Must have been good times,' Lloyd said.

'The flying was good, but there was a lot of time in between – boring some of it, and when God made Korea he said "I'm gonna make this the biggest bitch of a place in the world," and so it is. Korea is just a whole bunch of hills – and the winters are so cold you don't ever get warm. In summer it's hot enough to melt a candle.' He paused. 'It's damn hot enough here – I'm sweatier 'n a courthouse bible.'

'They say this is the worst drought in a hundred years.'

'They always says that,' Wilson said, 'now if you boys don't mind, I'm gonna get some sleep.'

Danny smiled and rolled onto his back, knowing that the images Wilson had conjured would be with him all through the night.


The first contact from Lester Holmes came the following morning. Lloyd led the way to the dining hall and their customary position at the end of one long steel bench. It was a lowly place – the best seats had views of the entire room, so the diners had warning of any impending danger. Thomas sat next to the three cellmates.

While they were eating their mash a short guy with a mop of black hair hanging off his head approached. Danny recognized him as one of Holmes's flunkeys.

The guy mumbled, smiling through broken teeth, 'Which one of you guys is Wilson Dowdy?'

Wilson put down his spoon and looked up. 'I am. So what?'

The messenger giggled, 'Lester said to tell you to say your prayers, 'cause you be dead by nightfall.' He turned and left almost immediately. Warning another prisoner about an attack was a common practice in Jeff City, particularly amongst those who liked to keep the other prisoners in their thrall. It served to make sure both the victim and the general prison population knew who was behind the killing, even if another man's hand held the knife.

Danny kept swallowing his oats. He had learned early in his time at Algoa to clean his plate before someone bigger did it for him. When he had finished, he leaned towards Wilson.

'I'll see Ted Little, maybe he'll let us stay in the cell today.'

Normally Danny went to school for three hours in the morning and worked in the kitchen in the afternoon. It wasn't too difficult for a prisoner to stay in the cell if he preferred to.

'We still got to come here to eat.'

'Okay, but that narrows it down to just one time when Lester can make his move – and we got about ten guards here during supper.'

'I'm done for,' Wilson said. 'Hell, how can I keep away from the guy for one day, let alone for a few weeks, an' he's got years to kill me.'

Thomas grinned. 'You could kill him first – that might do it.'

Wilson's mouth turned down. 'I thought about that idea – but I ain't no knife-fighter, and not a killer either – not really. Sure, I shot Mary and that asshole she was fucking but I was hyped up – I don't know if I got that kind of killing feeling in me.'

Lloyd turned to spit on the floor. 'Sure, if it's him or you I know what I'd do – kill him. I've got a knife hidden that you can use.'

'That's crazy,' Danny said, 'Wilson'd just get sent to the chamber.' He wanted no part of any plan to kill Holmes.

'Jesus Danny, people are always getting killed here, and no one gets charged half the time.'

'That's just because no screw can prove who did the job. What if Wilson got seen? I can't imagine Lester's buddies protecting his murderer, can you?' Danny paused, realizing that his voice had grown just a touch loud. 'Killing won't solve anything, and besides – it's wrong.'

Thomas laughed, 'Here you are, enjoyin' a stay on the bloodiest forty-seven acres in America and you're complainin' about what's wrong?'

Danny half rose, men were already filing back out of the dining room. 'I've got three months to go and I'm free – I'm gonna keep my nose clean. Now get up and keep Wilson in the centre – anyone comes near us we run for the cell. Wilson'll be safe there.'

Lloyd shrugged. Danny sensed he was unhappy at having to protect Wilson – things were dangerous enough without bringing a dead man into their cell – it was difficult not to be selfish in this place.

# EIGHTEEN

All day they played chess and talked in the cell. The rows were quiet, with the rest of E-hall off working or exercising. Occasionally a guard walked past.

'This still ain't gonna work,' Wilson said, 'Lester said that he's gonna get me today and I believe him.'

'He'll have to try at supper time.' Lloyd said.

'It's the only chance he'll have – and we'll take it real easy – come as late as we can so they can't hide a stabbing in a crowd.'

'Maybe you could get sick,' Lloyd suggested, 'if you're sick you don't have to go to the dining hall.'

'Yeah,' Danny said, 'but at the sickbay Lester will be able to get him anytime – all sorts of people walk through that place. All Lester'd have to do is call in sick himself and you're gone.'

Wilson sat on his cot with his face in his hands. 'Just stop talking about it for five minutes, will you? This is like being on death row. I ain't going to supper – I'll say I'm not hungry and you guys can bring me back something – just enough to keep me going. That takes care of today and tomorrow's another thing entirely.'

Without work the day passed slowly, but at supper time Ted Little unlocked the door. 'Out you go,' he said.

Danny turned back and pointed at Wilson. 'He doesn't feel

like going down to supper – can we bring him back some?'

'If y'all can talk Sid into giving you extra go ahead.' He looked at Wilson, who was lying back on the bed. 'Don't come whinin' to me if you're hungry later.'

'I won't.'

Danny looked back once, relieved. All day supper had loomed as an impending catastrophe, now it seemed that any problems would be deferred until the following day.

During the meal Lester Holmes himself came over to the table. His face was black with stubble, and his eyes dull. 'Where's your new friend at?'

Danny was halfway through a mouthful and was too scared to answer. It was Thomas, who was too old to be a threat to anyone who spoke up.

'He ain't well – laid up in the cell.'

Lester had the uncomfortable habit of moving his head as he talked – as if to an invisible groove. 'Well, when you see that cocksucker tell him that I always do what I say I'm gonna do.'

'Too late now, Lester. Day's near over.'

'He shot my cousin – blew a hole right through him – now that ain't the right thing to do. He's got to pay, man, and I mean it.'

Thomas shrugged, 'Your cousin was screwin' Wilson's wife – what didya expect him to do about it? Nothin'?'

Lester shook his head again as if ridding his ear of a fly. 'Just tell that guy what I said – and don't interfere or you're just as dead as he is.'

Danny watched Holmes withdraw carefully before he turned to Thomas. 'You've got a big mouth. I don't know anyone else who'd talk to Lester Holmes like that.'

'I don't mean to – I just open my trap and words fly out like I got no control over them.'

Lloyd scratched a section of scalp and caught a louse. He used a fingernail to squish it on the tabletop. 'I guess he's so worked up about Wilson that he couldn't be bothered with a loudmouth old con like Thomas.'

Danny finished his plate and took a big swig of water to wash away the taste. 'Finish up,' he said, 'I think we'd better get back there.'

In the quiet hour after dinner, the only time of day when bellies felt more than a little full, Danny flicked through a National Geographic magazine. Lloyd sat next to him and made lurid comments about the images of women from around the globe.

'What type of bird did your brother fly?' Wilson asked.

Danny looked up from the magazine. 'A bomber – B50 Superfortress.'

'Shit, now that's a curious thing.'

'Why?'

'Had the weirdest mission one night – had to get this rogue B50. I never did find out what the hell it was all about.'

The magazine fell onto the floor. Lloyd picked it up. Danny stared at Wilson. 'Tell me what happened.'

Wilson tilted his head back and stared at the ceiling for a few moments as if he were remembering, then turned back to Danny.

'Well as I recall it was about midnight. I'd been asleep for about an hour. The siren went, and they briefed us in the air.'

'Anyhow, that B50 crossed the Korean coast near Kwangju, and first we tried to force her down into the sea. That didn't work, and the orders came through to shoot the thing down.' Wilson took a crumpled cigarette from his top pocket along with a flat book of matches. He took his time, and finally blew a broad stream of smoke from his nostrils. 'I'll never forget that plane. Big? By Heavens, she was like a flying submarine with wings. She had a brown bear painted on the fuselage behind the cockpit.'

There came the sound of shouts then running men, but Danny hardly noticed. Already he felt the choking feeling, and the tears ready to travel. He tried to stop it coming. 'What happened?'

'Well that pilot must have been some kind of hotshot the way he weaved and dived to get away from us. We shot that plane so full of holes it must have been blowy as hell inside, but still they kept going.'

'Did she go down?'

'That's the strange thing. I guess she must have, but we never saw it happen – she got into cloud – a big storm front north of Formosa and we lost her. My tanks were near dry by then and we had to turn for home.'

The shouts came closer. Danny heard the clang of opening doors. Wilson looked up, a worried crease in his eyes.

'What else?' Danny urged.

'Flight of Sabres came up from Kadena and were going to wait around and see if they could find her – I never heard anything. I guess that bomber might have survived but where would the crew take her with the whole goddamned US Air Force after them?'

The questions crowded Danny's head so that he couldn't think which to ask first. He caught the first whiff of smoke, and the shouting increased. Lloyd got up and looked through the bars. 'Jesus, they're startin' a riot,' he said.

'The orders to take down that plane came from the top,' Wilson said.

'Who?'

'Macarthur himself. Anyhow – it was the weirdest thing – I always wondered what the hell it was all about.' Wilson was in the process of standing to see what the commotion was outside when a key turned in the door lock. It slid open on electrically driven runners.

Danny looked up to see Lester Holmes and two other men on the threshold. Each carried a short steel bar.

Lester looked at Danny and growled. 'Get out the way, this is between me and your friend there.'

Danny ignored the warning, trying to insert himself ahead of Wilson, but Holmes thrust a hand at his chest and sent him sprawling.

Wilson darted forward – trying to get out of the cell and into the corridors where he could run, but Lester's steel bar caught him on the temple with a sound much like a baseball bat hitting a ripe plum. He went down, and the three men stood over him, raining blows on the inert body.

Danny stood back, unable to move, too sick to cry out or move. It was over in just seconds. The three men dropped the bars and left the cell. Lester turned back at the threshold.

'You guys saw nothing, right? Or you get the same medicine.'

They heard whistles, then a siren. Danny went to Wilson where he lay on the cell floor, barely room for his body, between the cots. His head looked like a misgrown watermelon, with a deep groove on the top where a bar had penetrated. Blood oozed from his hair.

'Back to your cells, back to your cells,' a guard shouted.

Danny tilted his head skywards and sought air with his mouth open so wide the sides of his lips felt like they might split.

# NINETEEN

One day, three months later, Danny was called from his cell and released. His time was up. He had vague thoughts of going to Washington to find General Macarthur, but by the time he had fetched his cigarette tin of letters and photographs from its hiding place in St Louis he had changed his mind.

Then, through the fire of summer Danny travelled east. His first stop was Louisville, where he picked lettuce for keep and five dollars a day. At Charleston, West Virginia he dared not veer south to Beckley in case he lost his way to Washington. Instead he continued east through the mountains. A pair of undergraduates, both serious young men from Ithaca, New York, picked him up, drove him through to Staunton, then north close to Hagerstown. They encouraged him to tell his story and listened in silence through the long miles.

Danny was astounded at the way the two young men criticized all the powerful institutions he had been taught to revere, along with their own Cornell University. The taller and older of the two took the keenest interest in their hitchhiker. 'So what are you going to do now?' he asked.

'I want to find out about my brother.'

'That's not a career – just an understandable obsession.'

Danny felt less worldly than the two close friends in some ways, but far more experienced. He had seen death in its uglier forms, and few places display the human core more dramatically than prison.

'You should study – you're smart enough,' one of the young men observed.

'Study what?'

'Well what sort of things interest you?'

Danny shrugged. He wasn't sure.

When the car pulled over and Danny had to leave he offered some of his dwindling cash from the work at Louisville.

'Forget it – we're in this for the experience – you might end up in a book someday.'

It was easy to envy the pair, and the curious kind of freedom that only a safe, affluent background can provide. When the Chevy sedan flew past, roaring off with a burst of smoke from the exhaust, Danny lifted one hand in farewell.

Danny camped in a pine forest, where the air felt thick and full of menace – so still that smoke from his cooking fire rose up in a single unbroken column, dispersing only as it gained height. He ate bread and ham, purchased during the day in Hagerstown, and lay on his side to sleep.

The wind came in the early hours. The first stinging gust pushed pinecones to the earth and creaked in the deepest bones of the trees. Danny woke and shuddered, sensing that this was not ordinary weather.

His campfire had died hours earlier, leaving the forest black, only the tops of trees whipping to and fro against a coloured sky. More cones thudded to earth and Danny had the notion that the forest was no longer safe. He gathered his belongings by feel and walked with his hands extended to avoid running into sharp branches.

Leaving the shelter of the trees Danny found that the wind force trebled. He realized that he had to find shelter. Frank had talked of the terrible twisters in Kansas – black tubes that reached the sky and destroyed everything in their path. This storm was different — it gave the impression of vast and irrepressible force.

Danny reached the fence he had climbed to gain entry to the forest and slipped through and back onto the road. The wind was on his right as he hurried east, but then the rain started — big drops that stung even through his clothing.

Farmhouse lights flicked on as men and women found their sleep interrupted by the storm. Still Danny hurried on, holding his cap with one hand and protecting his face with the other.

Finally, he reached a crossroads. A semi-enclosed brick bus shelter stood on the right-hand side. The opening faced away from the wind and rain. He hurried in and sat on the bench seat, giving thanks to the Maryland workmen who built so soundly.

His clothes were saturated but there was little he could do about that. At least he was out of the rain, and had a little food. Danny closed his eyes, but an increase in wind speed and intensity forced them open. A barn across the road lost its roof with sharp crack and long tearing sound. The event was scarcely visible in the heavy rain, now driving almost parallel to the ground, so heavy that the road ran ankle deep in water.

Just one car passed, moving skittishly along the road, like a creature desperately looking for refuge. Danny felt the brickwork of the shelter at his back move slightly under the pressure of wind. A sheet of corrugated iron flew past, hit a post on the road verge and curled around it like a slice of cheese.

The preacher in the Moncrief church had spoken of Armageddon — when the world would be destroyed in a fury of destruction, and it was not hard for Danny to imagine that he was witnessing such a moment. Huge trees fell — their roots ripping and wounding the earth as they tipped to the inexorable power of the wind.

All night the wind and rain continued, and Danny dared not move from the bus shelter, lying on the bench seat, teeth chattering from the cold.

In the morning both wind and cloud had gone. A glaring sun warmed a devastated land. Danny left the bus shelter, blinking at the light like a pup opening his eyes for the first time. The air was clear, as if the rain had removed every impurity.

Water ran in channels on either side of the road, and fallen trees littered the landscape. As Danny walked along the bitumen, he saw roofless houses. Many, whether by sheer luck or superior workmanship remained intact. Few farms, however, would not have to rebuild a shed or barn.

Before he had travelled another mile, Danny came to a river running deep with floodwater – debris showed that the torrent had risen even higher during the night but had dropped to a wide brown expanse – over the bridge and moving fast. Tree-tops protruded above the maelstrom, shaking and waving their resistance to the brown tide.

Half a dozen cars had parked close to the water, Danny guessed that they were waiting to cross. Two men chatted near the water's edge, arms folded and serious.

'That was some storm,' Danny said by way of introduction.

'That wasn't just a storm – Hurricane Hazel. Don't you listen to the radio? She crossed the coast at the Carolinas and come north. They say she's gonna blast her way to Canada. I've lived here all my life and I've never seen anything like it.'

His companion agreed, 'There's never been anything like Hazel.'

A snake nosed his way across the water and slipped into the grassy bank two dozen yards upstream. The freak weather had uprooted and unsettled all living things.

Danny spun around at the tinny horn of a Ford sedan. The driver scowled – a thickset man of around forty years old. A handsome woman of around the same age sat beside him in the passenger seat.

The driver stopped the car, left the engine running and opened his door. He looked out at the spreading floodwater with disgust, as if the weather had caused him personal affront. 'That water's not too deep over the bridge is it?'

No one replied. His voice told of origins somewhere far to the south.

The man shot a glance at Danny and walked to where the water lapped the bitumen road. He gazed at the bridge rail for a minute then addressed the man beside Danny. 'You reckon it's too deep?'

'I think so.'

'Nah, it's under the rail – can't be more than three feet over the bridge – that's not so bad. I think I'll give it a try. I can always reverse out again if I get into trouble.'

Danny looked in surprise. The local man just shook his head. 'I don't know if that's a good idea – she's running pretty fast out in the middle.'

The newcomer didn't reply but stalked back to his car and closed the door. The front passenger looked frightened as the Ford motored forward.

Danny stepped back to let the car pass and had his first view into the back seat, straight into the eyes of a girl a few years younger than himself. Tawny hair and white teeth coloured that first impression.

They locked eyes there on the banks of a flooded waterway, and for a few seconds shared a strange intimacy. The girl was beautiful, and there was solace in her gaze. When she had passed Danny felt the heat of fear in his cheeks. The girl's father was taking her into danger.

'They might well get across,' one bystander said, 'but you never know with these things.'

'How high's the air intake on them Fords?' another asked, 'it all depends on how high that intake is.'

Danny saw a small tree trunk roll along near the middle of the waterway and prayed that such a hazard wouldn't strike the car. He wanted the girl he had seen to reach the other side.

The car entered the water tentatively at first, but once it had moved some twenty yards out and the water only reached the wheel rims the driver seemed to gain confidence. The audience waited. A woman called out, 'The stupid man.'

Danny walked to the water's edge to watch how the river slowly rose up the side panels. Soon the vehicle had ventured almost halfway across and the water was twelve inches over the running board. It was there, however, that the current flowed swiftly, and the car created an obstruction. A wave of water pushed impatiently against it.

The water deepened all at once then, and some of the watchers started to pray out loud. Danny saw the Ford pushed sideways before the tyres gripped again, and he realized that the water grew deeper still.

'She's starting to float,' someone shouted, and Danny saw the car lift. He advanced into the water up to his knees. The Ford's engine screamed but the tires found no purchase.

From there Danny started to run, water sloshing against his legs, dragging him back so his pace never got above the speed a fast walk on land might allow him. When the water reached his waist, he rowed with his arms to speed his progress. People shouted at him to go back.

The motor appeared to have stalled because the car had stopped moving forward. It edged towards the downstream bridge rail rapidly now, bobbing as if it were floating free. It came up hard against the rail and Danny hoped the strong timber beams would keep the car safe. His breath sawed in his throat at the tremendous effort he made to reach the car. He heard splashing behind – others were coming to help.

Danny was just twenty yards short when the rail burst and the car tumbled away down the stream, sinking fast. Screaming in anguish he changed direction, moving for the submerged rail, slipping over, quickly out of his depth, clawing at the water for purchase, trying to keep his head free. Danny had never learned to swim beyond a clumsy dog paddle, but his own life was no longer a consideration.

Half submerged trees flashed past and the car spun in an eddy before plunging on. The rushing stream brought Danny close, and it seemed that he heard a scream above the sound of rushing water. The car was low in the water now, with only the top few inches of window glass visible. When Danny finally reached the stricken vehicle, the glass had gone. He made a desperate lunge for purchase on the sill. He gripped hard, but the car was going down.

Danny snapped his mouth closed just in time, but still he held on, letting the car's weight draw him under. It stopped quickly

– wedged against either the stream floor or a tree branch. He scrabbled with his fingers and found that the window was open enough for him to force his hand in.

Panic and lack of air started to work on Danny, and he would have abandoned the car but for a sudden touch on his fingers from inside the car – living, vital skin.

Danny frantically forced his arms inside. reaching for the window handle – winding it down as fast as he was able. A body came into his arms and he pulled it from the car.

Together they rose toward the surface, kicking through sheer instinct. They burst through, and Danny's head felt as if it might explode with tension. The girl was still in his arms.

Danny could have sobbed with relief as the river carried them away. With the girl held loosely with one arm he grasped at a tree branch and held on with one hand.

'Help them,' she screamed, 'help them, please.' Her eyes had closed, her hair pasted close to the sides of her face. Blood seeped from a red welt near her hairline, and one silver earring had torn partly through the flesh of her ear lobe.

Danny understood despair – he had known it when his mother closed her eyes for the last time, and when they had told him about Matt. He had known it those first nights in Algoa, crying in his cot to a God he believed had turned his back on him forever.

'Please,' Danny said, chest heaving, 'you mustn't panic.' He was afraid of the thick brown water, and his arms and legs already ached with fatigue, but he could not bear the look in her eyes.

'I'm going back for them,' he said, 'stay here and hold on. Someone will come for us in a boat soon.' The girl said nothing but nodded perceptibly.

Danny moved upstream by pulling himself along the treetops, heedless of scratches and tears from sharp vegetation. The ache in his arms became a torment as he reached the area where he judged that the car had gone under, determined to drag the people the girl loved out of the car. He tried to guess how long they must have been under water – one minute? One and a half? He stopped calculating – or he would give up and not make the attempt, for it had been too long.

He dived, but the current brought him to the surface again. He tried opening his eyes, but the water was just a dark brown blur. It was hopeless, he knew it, but tried until he was so exhausted that he could do nothing but let the water carry him down to where the girl clung to the branches.

Her eyes asked the question. Danny shook his head.

'I'm Danny,' he said, 'and we're going to be alright. You wait and see. What's your name?'

Her lips trembled so badly she could not speak, but Danny could read the words from her lips.

'Anne,' she said.

# TWENTY

For more than an hour the small group around the campfire had listened in near silence, but now Tasha burst into tears, covering her face with her hands. Danny went to her, kneeling beside her camp chair and passing his arms around her.

'I'm sorry everyone,' Tasha said through the tears, 'but that's how they met – on a flooded river, and if my father wasn't the man he is then they would never have come together – I'd never have been born.'

Jamie broke the silence. 'We'll take a break,' he said. 'Brew up a cuppa, maybe throw on some johnny-cakes if anyone feels like making them?'

'Good thinking, Sarge,' Ray said, and went off to fetch a flour drum, and some salt. Within a few minutes he had a loaf baking in the camp oven. Wally went for a walk and came back, standing listlessly. Jamie had expected him to complain about listening to the American's story, but it didn't seem to bother him.

By the time they all gathered together again, Tasha had dried her eyes, drinking a mug of coffee sweetened with condensed milk, while Ray's damper was already sending an enticing aroma over the camp.

'Do you want to hear the rest of it?' asked Danny.

Jamie looked around. 'I know that I speak for all of us when I say that we do.'

Danny replenished his tea, and stared into the bush for a while before he started again. The expression on his face was a strange mix of pleasure and pain.

'While Anne was in hospital,' he began, 'I hung around town. I helped the police locate the car and winch it out with the bodies inside the next day. I guess that I was something of a celebrity. Everyone wanted to help me. I got a job in a hardware store, and though Anne went away with relatives for a time, we never stopped writing.' He lowered his head. 'She came back and we were married in 1960.'

Within a few years I started getting into the property game. I read a book by a guy called Bill Levitt, who made a fortune subdividing land near New York, and I had a hunch that the same thing might work around Baltimore. It did – and I started to make some real money.'

# TWENTY-ONE

Through those years, Danny was locked in a war of words – letters, requests, official denials and obfuscation. Generals and politicians on both sides of the Pacific had decided that what happened that night over Korea must never reach the public ear. Spin doctors churned out disinformation and clutter. People slept peacefully in their beds, comforted by the truth they were allowed to hear.

Danny knew in his heart that *they* had tried to do something indescribably evil. The dark wings of that knowledge overshadowed his life, creating a gaping hole that he came to believe was his own sacrifice. To bring it into the light seemed to be the only worthwhile purpose.

The problem is that *they* do not tell the truth. The truth becomes hidden, or something less than absolute. For a long time, the battle seemed lost, but in 1973, when he was thirty-five years old, Danny made his first real progress in discovering what had happened to his brother.

By then he and Anne owned a fine house outside of Baltimore. On a personal front, things were as good as they could be for a man with such deep internal scars. His marriage to Anne was a wonder for which he gave thanks every day. Natasha Jane Carter had arrived five years earlier. A loving relationship, and watching Tasha grow became one salve to the ache in Danny's heart.

Now, however, with funds at his disposal, Danny set out to hire a private detective. Discreet enquiries led him to a man called Tom Wrigley, a solo operator who had no business card, did not advertise his services, yet came with impeccable references, never in writing but whispered in back rooms and businessmen's bars. He was a man with few noticeable features. Everything from nose to hair colour defied any description but 'normal,' or 'average.' His suit looked like any other marching along Constitution Avenue. Only his eyes were, on closer inspection, remarkable – a very dark brown, almost black. Danny always had the uncomfortable feeling that Tom Wrigley could read his thoughts.

After only a month, at the first of their regular briefings, Tom Wrigley brought the sad news that Tony Cassetari had been killed in a car accident in Mexico, in 1958. 'He had been dishonourably discharged from the United States Air Force six months earlier,' Wrigley explained.

Six months went by, then a year. Each week Danny mailed a generous cheque made out to an obscurely named private company and heard very little that he had not already known for years.

Tom Wrigley, seemed, for a while, to be a waste of time and money.

Then, soon after Danny's thirty-fifth birthday, Wrigley made an appointment for an unscheduled meeting. Danny cancelled all his calls and could hardly concentrate until the private detective appeared at the office, closing the office door behind him as he entered.

The detective began to look carefully around the room, checking light fittings and under furniture. Finally, he lifted the telephone handset from its cradle and started unscrewing the cups. He delved inside and lifted a small electronic object. He pulled it hard, so the wires snapped. Danny looked on in amazement. 'What the hell was that?'

'A bug. I also suspect now that you are being followed, at least part of the time. As you can see, your office was bugged, and quite possibly your house too.'

'Who?'

'The same gang who have dogged you in the past. AFOSI. Air Force Office of Special Investigations. They've been watching you for a long time – I can tell by how casual they are. They know your routine.'

Danny pointed at the dead gadget, wires hanging like blood vessels. 'Is that the only one?'

'I think so, but I can't be sure. Let's go for a walk.'


'I have some news,' Wrigley began, as they hit the sidewalk, 'that was confirmed only yesterday.'

'What is it?'

Wrigley stopped to tap a cigarette from a soft pack of camels, lighting the tip with a flaring match and drawing in, 'We have located a crew member from your brother's plane.'

Danny's breath caught in his throat. 'God, really? Where?'

'Columbus, Ohio.' Cigarette in hand, the detective continued walking.

'Alive?'

'Yes, alive.'

Danny stopped walking, almost losing his balance. The news was so unexpected that later he would tell how his heart stopped for at least a minute. 'Who?'

'His name was Samuel Snow. The bombardier, apparently.'

'Sam Snow. God, I knew him. Where on earth did he turn up?'

'Darwin, Australia, of all places. Apparently, he wandered into town in 1952, badly burned and with head injuries. They identified Sam by his dog tag and flew him home.'

Danny stared at Wrigley. 'You must have known about this for some time.'

'I've been hot on the scent for maybe a month, but I like to confirm things before I inform a client.'

'Is it possible that my brother's aircraft made it all the way to Australia? It's a long way from Korea.'

'I've already thought of that. It's 3400 miles from Seoul to Darwin,' Wrigley said, 'and the B50 was an intercontinental bomber. It had a range of over 5500 miles, enough to get from Guam to Korea, then all the way back down to Northern Australia before it would finally run out of fuel.'

Danny was trying to find arguments against the obvious conclusions he wanted to draw. It seemed too big a development to believe. 'The Air Force say that one of their ships found debris to confirm the crash in the East China Sea. How do you explain that?'

Wrigley shrugged, 'It was a war zone. I imagine there was all kinds of debris floating around. People believe what they want to believe.'

They stopped at an intersection, letting a Bedford truck go through before stepping over the gutter and across the bitumen.

Danny shook his head in amazement. 'You've earned your pay,' he said. 'Where do we go from here?'

'Do you want to see Sam Snow?'

'Of course.'

'Then book a flight for both of us. Tomorrow is okay for me. Then we'll shift our focus to the Darwin area. This is a hard case, but I often find that once a hard case starts to crack things happen fast.'


The next day the private detective drove Danny west along Broad Street, Columbus, away from the lofty office buildings into the residential suburbs. They stopped outside a weatherboard house in a quiet street.

'That's the house,' Wrigley said. 'Sam's mother knows we're coming.'

Danny followed behind, waiting while the detective knocked. A woman in her seventies, almost bald apart from fine wisps of white hair on her scalp opened the door. She nodded without enthusiasm and motioned at them to enter without bothering to introduce herself to Danny.

'Come right through,' she said. Danny walked in behind Tom.

The house smelled of illness, age and pork roast. Sam Snow

sat in an armchair, smiling up at Danny. He ignored his visitor's offered hand, just stared vacantly around him. The scars from what must have been dozens of skin grafts covered his bald head and face.

'He was badly burned when they picked him up,' Sam's mother explained. 'The operations went on for years.'

Danny squatted in front of him. 'Hello Sam, do you remember me?'

There was not even a glimmer in response.

'He can't talk,' the woman went on from behind Danny, 'not a word. Oh he mumbles stuff, but it never makes any sense.'

Danny stared, frustration building in his chest. The man in front of him knew everything – knew what had happened to Matt, yet he couldn't speak.

'Please Sam. I just want to know about how you got to Australia.'

No answer.

'What happened Sam? Why were you in Darwin, two years after the crash?'

Sam's mother lifted her teacup to her lips and shook her head slowly. 'You're wasting your breath, honey. The Air Force had him for months, trying to get him to speak. There's nothing inside that head of his. The lights are on, but nobody's home.'

Danny stayed for an hour. At least, he told himself, he now knew that somewhere, somehow, Matt's Superfortress landed. It did not crash in the East China Sea. At least one man walked away from the wreck.

'Thank you, Mrs Snow,' he said finally, 'but we'll be going.'

The private detective followed suit, standing up and patting his trousers, 'We'd better get going.'

As Danny walked back through the house, he noticed a very old Hohner harmonica on the shelf. He stopped and picked it up. There was a charred section on one side.

'Sam had it with him when he was picked up, apparently,' the woman said.

'Incredible,' Danny breathed. 'I'm pretty sure that this was my brother's ... he used to play it all the time.' Danny's mind slipped back through the years. The repertoire wasn't huge – the Daniel Boone theme song, Clementine, and Home on the Range.

'Why don't you take it with you? Sam wouldn't know one way or the other in any case.'

Danny held it in his hand. Then, making a decision, he slipped it back onto the shelf.

'No, it's nice just to know it's still in one piece.'

Thirteen days later a black Continental sedan parked across the front entrance of the office carpark, just as Danny arrived at work. Two men climbed out.

Danny opened the rear door to retrieve his briefcase then approached the visitors. Both wore dark suits, were in their late twenties, and wore sharp sideburn cuts.

'Can I help you?' Danny asked.

The stouter of the two quit leaning on the car and approached Danny.

'Hello Mr Carter?'

Danny nodded, uncomfortable with finding strangers on his lot at the beginning of his day. 'What's your business?'

'Major Temple would like you to grant him a short interview.'

Danny remembered the AFOSI Lieutenant. How could he ever forget him? 'What on earth for?'

'Ask him yourself. He wants to talk to you.'

'Have I got a choice?'

'Of course. You don't have to. But he said that it's very important, and he's waiting nearby, you don't have to go all the way to Washington.'

Danny grimaced. 'Okay, let's see what he wants.' Locking his car, he followed the two men to the vehicle, slipping into the back seat with his briefcase on his lap. Entwined in his heart as the big motor car rumbled down the road into Baltimore, was a burning hatred of Temple, and curiosity at what he might have to say.

The car stopped alongside Druid Hill Park, with its towering oak and elm trees, acres of lawn, and weathered sandstone features. Danny stepped out after the driver and followed him to where two men waited on a park bench alongside the duck pond. One had a briefcase open on the seat. Danny stopped at a distance of a few paces and stood with his hands on his hips.

Temple stood, glaring at him. 'We've met before, but not for a long time.'

Danny studied Temple's face. The man's face had more flesh on it than it had fifteen years earlier. Both first and second fingers on his right hand were yellow from nicotine.

'Thanks for coming Danny,' Temple said, 'short notice and all that, but needs must.'

'I guess I should be grateful you gave me a choice.'

Temple nodded, 'We all have choices, Danny, particularly you. What you have to understand is that your brother is dead.'

'Sam Snow wasn't dead.'

'We believe Sam Snow may have survived, clung to some debris and ended up in Australia. He turned up more than a decade ago. No one else has.'

Danny folded his arms. 'It seems to me that Matt might have steered that plane all the way to Australia. I want to know what happened then. I want to know what you're so afraid of.'

Temple said, 'We know you've hired a detective firm to find information.'

'Of course you do. Because you've been eavesdropping. That's why you picked me up today. Because you know that I know about Sam Snow.'

'Careful with the accusations Danny. You're the one in a situation here.'

'I don't believe I have broken any laws.'

'That's where you are wrong,' Temple said. 'Listen to me carefully. The United States Government has determined that the events surrounding the final mission of aircraft designation B50A serial number 46-006/047 will remain classified. Therefore, any attempt to obtain information will be regarded as a felony. That information, we believe, may be detrimental to the interests of America and her allies if it became public.'

Danny shook his head in disbelief. 'Are you saying that I can no longer make enquiries into my brother's fate?'

'That's exactly right. Call off the investigation you have financed and forget about it. It was all a long time ago.'

'What if I don't obey this instruction?'

Temple tapped the blunt end of his pen against his leg. 'Don't make the mistake of thinking that we can't touch you.'

Danny tried to work through the implications of this information.

Temple half turned, 'I have nothing further to say. Please make arrangements to call off all lines of enquiry.' He slapped Danny good-naturedly on the back. 'Sometimes Uncle Sam and his Good Friends have to keep their secrets.'

The tendons and veins in Danny's forearms stood out like ropes. 'I don't want you guys around my family. I don't want my house bugged. Get out of my life and leave me alone.'

'That's up to you.'

'Why are you trying to make me feel that I'm the one in the wrong here? What are you hiding from me, and why is it so important to you?'

Temple closed the briefcase, stood up and started walking towards a second vehicle, also parked alongside the kerb. Danny stared after him. The anger dissolved into the air, leaving just a vague sense of impotence.

'Excuse me sir.'

Danny turned. It was one of the two men who had driven him to the meeting. 'Yes?'

'We have orders to return you to your office.'

'I'd rather walk.' He turned on the spot and hurried off towards the street.

# TWENTY-TWO

The blue Arafura Sea stole the view on one side of the aircraft, straw-yellow and green woodland the other, punctuated by rocky hills and waterholes. The pilot pointed out the spiralling South Alligator river, so clear that weed beds and logs were visible under the surface. As they descended to spotting height Danny saw crocodiles on the sand banks, sometimes dozens of them basking in the morning sunshine.

So far, the visit to Australia's Northern Territory had been interesting but disappointing. Darwin had a frontier feel, with hardy and enthusiastic inhabitants whose solution to every problem seemed to involve consuming another beer. As one local told him, 'It's not just the taste, or the coldness of it. It's just that when you're pissed you don't give a shit about the heat.'

This was wild country, deep inside of Arnhem Land, where few white men had penetrated, and as they flew south it became still more inaccessible and remote. The imposing sandstone escarpment forced the pilot to climb, over stark ridges and deep-riven gorges channelled through the rock matrix.

Danny had a pair of Zeiss binoculars around his neck. He used the crisp lenses to investigate every strange colour or object. Almost all turned out to be natural for there were no roads or towns here. He had worked on the assumption that an aircraft the size of a Superfortress would be relatively easy to find, but he had not counted on thick tropical forest in the valleys, and grass almost as tall as a man on the plains.

Still the Cessna droned deeper into the wilderness, veering over and around the sandstone fortresses, bedrock of the world's oldest continent.

'We've covered just over a hundred miles since the coast, and we need enough fuel to get back,' the pilot, a reliable looking man of about thirty called Brad King told him. 'Will I turn for home now?'

It seemed unlikely that Matt could have kept the plane flying for much longer. 'Another twenty,' Danny replied, 'then we turn back.'

The country grew even more forbidding, with deep gorges showing blue ribbons of water in the depths. There was scarcely enough clear space to land a helicopter, let alone a plane. Danny plied the binoculars until his eye sockets ached, then leaned back with a sigh, 'This is impossible,' he said.

'Not easy to see a plane wreck that's a decade or two old, especially here,' Brad King replied. 'The only thing I can think of is to use colour-infrared film for an aerial series. It would be a lot easier than trying to pick something out by eye.'

'How does it work?'

'Human eyes can't see the infrared part of the electromagnetic spectrum. Infrared film lets us do that – it cuts through atmospheric haze and gives a crisp image. Your plane wreck should stand out.'

Danny watched a herd of fat black water buffalo, glossy with mud, gallop away through the scrub until they passed from view under the speeding Cessna. 'Okay we'll try a different route north, and if we don't see anything we'll talk again about this infrared stuff.'

The pilot prepared to turn the aircraft around. Danny rubbed his eyes. There was no way he could do this day in and day out, even with help.

The ride back was no more productive than the journey in, and finally the Cessna skidded onto the tarmac of Darwin airport. Within a few minutes Brad King had ushered the American into an untidy office, where books and charts covered almost every available space. A naked bulb hung from a hole in the ceiling. Rifling through the piles, Brad handed across an unusual photograph.

'That's an infrared print,' he said, 'taken at five thousand feet over Victoria River Downs cattle station.' He picked up a pen and used it as a pointer. 'You can see the homestead, and all the outbuildings. Anything metallic shows up easily. The water in the river appears black, trees appear red and the pasture is cyan. The contrast, as you can see, is greatly enhanced.'

Danny nodded, 'I think I'm starting to understand the process. Now, if I give the word to go ahead and take these pictures what would happen?'

'Have a seat.' The pilot moved charts and books off two stools and sat down. 'It all comes down to field of view,' he said. 'I'd have to work out just how many photographs are required at a certain height to cover your area of interest. It might be five hundred or even more, in which case I'd need a week just to get the photographs. Going through them carefully for signs of what we are after would take twice as long. As for cost, I couldn't even begin to guess, but it would be very expensive – thousands.'

Danny was disappointed by the time frame, but it seemed an encouraging way to proceed, and perhaps the only way.

'Can you prepare a quote for me? Time, money and all that?'

'Yes, but I'll have to charge you -- even a good estimate will take time.'

Danny had learned to carry cash. He handed over three hundred dollars. 'Is that enough to get you started?'

Brad King looked up, surprised. 'Plenty. Give me three days, and even then I won't get much sleep.'

Danny passed another fifty. 'Please make it two.'

The pilot laughed, and shrugged, 'Who needs sleep?'


The survey brought a new routine for Danny. In the evenings he would drive to the airport, park under the sprawling fig tree outside Brad King's hangar and make his way inside to discuss the most recent available infrared prints.

Sometimes King was still in the air, and the pilot's offsider, a pimply and slightly overweight teen, would bring Danny a cup of coffee while he waited. Finally, the Cessna would land, and Brad would produce a set of infra-red prints and lay them out on the desk. At first Danny would see a shape and suppose it to be an incomplete segment of the crashed plane and get excited to the point of accusing King of lying, before having a dozen similar shapes pointed out to him.

'Rocks,' Brad explained on the fourth day of the survey, 'rock platforms show up clearly against the surrounding vegetation. The exposed sections of this one just happen to look a little like an aircraft.'

'How can you be so sure?'

'Scale,' the pilot replied, 'if this image represented a real plane it would be six hundred yards long.'

Danny nodded, and sank back into the seat.

'Have you seen anything you regard as hopeful?'

'No, I would have told you if I had. Honestly, there is nothing on the ground we've covered so far worthy of a second look.'

Danny chewed his lip in frustration. 'I have to get home – I have a business to run. I just don't have time for a drawn-out search.'

'Well I'm not going anywhere,' said Brad King. 'I fly over that area all the time. If you make it worth my while I could keep an eye out.'

'You mean a retainer?'

'Something like that.'


Danny, Anne, and the young Tasha flew back to Maryland in 1981. Three months later, Temple recruited three local thugs and sent them to the house.

It was a warning gone wrong. The phone rang just after eleven pm. Danny had fallen asleep on his side; one arm half numb where he had been lying on it. After a moment of disorientation, he reached across to lift it off the cradle. Late night phone calls were never good news and he felt the hollowness in his gut as he answered.

'Hello, who is it?'

The voice was as hard and sharp as four-inch nails. 'You were warned. This is just a taste.'

The hollowness turned to a jolt of adrenalin that made him jump. Anne woke, and switched on the bedside lamp. He looked into her sleepy eyes, trying not to let the panic show.

There was a crash of breaking glass from downstairs. Danny dropped the phone and leapt out of bed in his pyjamas.

'Wait Danny,' Anne said, 'it might be dangerous.'

Danny owned a Smith and Wesson revolver, but it was locked in the safe in his study. He came down the stairs just as the front door broke inwards, and three men wielding baseball bats burst through, separating to smash everything in their path.

'Hey, stop that you sons of—'

The three men wore black balaclavas, long sleeved shirts. The nearest swung to face him, lips and brown teeth obscene in the slit in the woollen head covering. Tight blue jeans stretched over muscular thighs. His belt sported an enormous brass buckle.

These, Danny realised, were not Government agents, but merely local criminals, probably released from the penitentiary in exchange for smashing up his house. He had seen those same kinds of eyes in Jeff City all those years earlier.

'Get back,' the man shrieked, then hit the hall cabinet with a roundhouse swing that pulverised the glass and cleared a shelf of the porcelain nick-nacks that Anne had collected over the years.

Danny led with his shoulder, attempting to force the man off balance, but he reversed the bat, stepped neatly to one side and punched it hard into Danny's kidneys.

'Leave him alone.' Anne screamed from behind.

In later years Danny would remember flashes of her pale blue dressing gown, eyes glazed with protective fury. And the last time their eyes would meet on this earth, there was something else. Blame. That he had brought this calamity upon them.

'No,' Danny screamed at her, 'go back.'

But the eyes in the balaclava had become furious red slits.

The bat was already coming down. Danny watched it connect. The top of Anne's head seemed to compress as if screwed down by a clamp. She fell to the ground.

'Fuck,' the man screamed, pushing Danny aside, then to his companions. 'Let's go. Now.'

Danny was scarcely aware of retreating footsteps, and the scream of tyres as a car accelerated away. He was on his knees, cradling her upper body, her face serene and calm as she had not been in her final moments. The police, when they came, had to prise her out of his arms.


The team of attorneys that Danny assembled had just one instruction. Find the truth, uncover the evil, make them pay; but there was nothing that could be done. The hidden shadow-puppets of the intelligence underworld were too well protected. Officially, Temple did not exist. Denial faced them at every turn.

'I'm sorry, Mr Carter,' the senior partner of the law firm had said, 'but there is no evidence to contradict the official police line that this was a burglary that went too far.'

Telephone records disappeared. Men who should have talked would not. Meaningless lies flowed like handfuls of cheap glitter. The rage grew in Danny's heart.

He was learning that a lie, once begun, can shake the world. The search for Matthew Carter and the truth had stalled. Darwin seemed like a dead end.

Then, in 1989, Brad King mailed across a grainy photograph taken deep inside Arnhem Land. It appeared to show the tail wing of a very large plane. It was enough, in Danny's opinion, to launch an expedition.

By then Danny had some political connections and was able to request help from the Australian Government. Security was the main thing. AFOSI would surely not attempt to interfere when he was under the protection of the Australian government.

Danny was pleased but not surprised when Tasha and her husband of twelve months, Glenn, threw their support behind the enterprise.

'Just try and leave me at home,' his daughter had said with a steely eye, and Glenn just smiled in that quiet way of his. Danny knew he had gained an important ally as well as a son-in-law.

Now, finally, at fifty-three years of age he was close to the truth, and nothing would stop him from finding it.

# TWENTY-THREE

There was a long silence, broken finally by Holly. 'And here we are,' she said.

'Yes,' echoed Jamie, 'I'm more than a little honoured that you've taken us into your confidence so completely.' He coughed awkwardly. 'I'm sorry that I didn't understand; that I was maybe a little insensitive.'

Danny Carter shook his head, 'You weren't to know. Thank you for letting me say my piece.'

'So just to get it straight, that tail fin belongs to your brother's plane.'

'Yes.'

'But you still don't know where he is or what happened to him?'

'No. And I still don't know why my own government tried to shoot him down.'

Jamie stood up and glanced at his watch. They had been sitting, listening, for nearly two hours. 'Okay you blokes, I'm sure you'll agree now that we wouldn't be doing our job if we walked away without exploring all the options. As I said, I'll check with the Colonel, but I'd say that he'll support a decision to continue the search.'

Nico looked down, compressing his chin so the dimple

looked like a crater. 'Yeah, I understand. The only thing is, what about the rivers coming up with this rain.'

'Not much rain overnight. So far so good. But if we're going to check out the gorge itself, we'd better get cracking before the creek rises too much. Ray and I will take Danny, Glenn, Tasha and Holly. We'll carry gear and tucker for two or three nights in the field to be on the safe side. I want the rest of you to stay with the vehicles to keep the skeds and be ready to take us out once we've found what we came for.'

'Or not found,' Mick put in.

'Yeah, that's right. Or not found.'

Mick was still trying to look pissed-off, but there was a hint of pleasure in his eyes. A couple of days just to tinker with the engines, repair punctured tyre tubes, repack wheel bearings, grease ball joints and check oil and fluids was no hassle for Mick. Nico, meanwhile, could pursue his personal fitness regime and keep his mate company at the same time. They'd be happy enough.

'What about me?' Wally asked. 'Can't I go down in the gorge too?'

'No, I want you here with Mick and Nico.'

'Aw come on Sarge, I've never seen that country before—'

Jamie tried to analyse his thought processes. There was really no reason for Wally not to come down with them into the gorge. He just didn't like him was the truth of it and separating him from Ray was smart leadership. 'No sorry. You stay here.'

'You want us to wait right here in this spot Sarge?' Nico, after earlier pushing to head home, was back to his usual loyal self.

Jamie shook his head. 'No, once you've got those wheels changed, I think you should move from here. I noticed a creek with some shallow waterholes about a klick back from here. Go there, and it might be an idea to drive well in, out of sight from the track we came in on. String up some camo netting.'

'You think we should hide in case that Yank chopper comes looking?'

'Just the smart thing to do. We'll be back in a day or two.'

Mick chimed in with a sensible query. 'What about comms between you and us?'

Jamie decided against lugging one of the heavy F3 field sets. 'I'll take a couple of the UHF handhelds we've been using. That'll have to do.'

'Might not get the best reception down in the sandstone, Sarge, UHF is line-of-sight.'

'True, but I can always climb a ridge. I'll call in at 1700 each day we're down there, sound okay to you?'

Mick nodded his assent, once the technical details were sorted out, he was usually happy to go with the flow.

'Everyone satisfied?' Jamie looked around. The little group, apart from Wally, looked positively energised. 'Okay then, break camp, and let's get moving.'

The party was fired with new purpose as they prepared for what might be two days on foot, away from the vehicles. Packing up took less than an hour so Jamie okayed the new direction with Darwin, then helped change the tyres, with Holly also assisting.

As Mick lifted one wheel off the studs, Holly stared into the space behind and into the arch. 'Hey, look at that – not another one of those bugs, is it?'

Mick leaned in to pluck the magnetic device from its place, uncoiling back onto his haunches to examine it in the early morning sunlight.

Jamie swore, 'Yep, that's the same thing alright.'

Mick looked up at him. 'Sarge, if you'd already found one of them you should have thought of checking our RFSV when we arrived.'

'Yeah, I should have. Bloody stupid that I didn't.'

Jamie took the bug, dropped it into the hottest part of the fire and watched it melt into a few metal components with a near personal enmity. He hated making mistakes, especially elementary ones like this. Determinedly he pulled the resultant mess from the flames and ground it to nothing between two rocks.

'Sarge,' observed Ray, 'you making sure to kill that thing real good.'

Finally, with the fire now extinguished and the camp fully packed up, Mick, Nico and Wally drove off to form the new base camp.

'You certain going down in the gorge is a good idea?' Ray asked Jamie as they set off towards the steep game trail that led down into the gorge.

'We'll be fine. Please, let's just give it a chance. My feeling is that if the air search hasn't picked up the remainder of the wreck on the plateau, it must be down there somewhere.'

The trail that wound its way down the escarpment was treacherous, yet they walked downwards in file. The unwieldy packs made it difficult to stay balanced on the loose ground.

On both banks were signs of the coming monsoonal floods that scoured their way down the sides of the gorge each wet season – tufts of grass against exposed roots, logs jammed hard against trees, and drifts of gravel and rounded river rocks. Twist-ed paperbark trees grew where they had found enough earth to gain a foothold, their fibrous roots making a new surface of their own, host in turn to tiny ferns and creepers, a source of delight for Tasha.

Once down, the going was easy, and Jamie chose the eastern bank, still striped with morning shadows. The new environment was enough to keep the party's spirits up. The three younger men carried the lion's share of the gear, and the trek was hard work with heavy packs. Around the first bend they were re-warded with a breathtaking view down two or three kilometres of gorge.

'No sign of a plane,' Jamie said.

'It's okay,' Holly said, 'we'll find it. I know we will.'

'Yeah, I know we will too. Shame it's not a bit easier.'

# TWENTY-FOUR

The day was slow going. They stopped constantly to investigate side-gullies. At other times the way forward was blocked by deep pools or sheer cliffs, and they had no choice but to ascend and skirt around.

An hour before nightfall Jamie estimated that they had covered only about five kilometres. However, realizing that the party had little stomach for more walking, in consultation with Ray he selected a gentle curve where the water gurgled into a gravelly pool, for a campsite. It had a shelf of rocks on one side, with coarse river sand to sleep on. The combination of stone grandeur and water was irresistible.

Once Ray had assured the Americans that they were too far upstream for saltwater crocs to be present, they had scarcely dropped their packs before they were heading for the water. Jamie unloaded his SLR and made sure that Ray did the same before laying the weapons flat on a towel on a niche in the gorge face. This done, he slipped behind a rock to strip off the hot DPCU uniform and slip on his board shorts.

Holly was standing at the water's edge in her swimsuit. Jamie's eyes started at her bare shoulders, tanned with just a hint of the muscles underneath. Then a deep groove down her spine, and just above her buttocks a dimple in the skin on either side.

The prim Ms Jones, he decided as she entered the water, had one of the best bodies he had ever seen in his life.

He let himself drift past the others and into the rapids, sitting on smooth rocks with the water flowing over and around his body. He caught Holly's eye. 'Come over here into the current.'

She dog-paddled over and stood beside him on the bed of smooth rocks, 'This is fun. The water's so warm.'

Holly came almost close enough to touch through the water. She reached down, scooping up handfuls of coarse sand and using them to scrub herself.

'Great spot for a swim,' she said.

'This is what we call a bogey,' Jamie said.

Humour danced in Holly's eyes. 'What?'

'A good wash — we call it a bogey. It's a Territorian thing.'

'Oh okay, great place to have a bogey then.'

'I'm glad I've got a chance to talk to you away from the others. Is Danny Carter's story true?' he asked.

'Jamie. This is not a simple situation, and I don't know everything either, but as far as I know, it's true. Didn't you believe him?'

'Pretty much, yes, but I'm a naturally suspicious type. Besides, he didn't tell us everything. How and why did the plane go down here, for a start?'

'I don't know.'

Jamie glared at her. 'No more bullshit Holly.'

'It's not. That's something we're hoping to find out.'

'If that's the case why would ASIO send you here? And why are the Yanks so interested in an old aircraft.' He didn't say that he had seen the cables, but she must have realised he knew more than he should have. 'Give me something, for God's sake, Holly.'

'There are some heavy-duty secrets at rest, around here somewhere,' she said at last. 'That's why I came along and that's why we can't give up.'

Jamie breathed slowly. 'I'm happy to keep looking, but where the hell can a plane that size be?'

'I don't know.' Holly reached out and took his hand under the water.

The touch was electrifying. Jamie knew they could go back now but he made no move to stand up. Their joined hands moved until they rested on his thigh. His skin dusted with goose bumps, but before he could acknowledge the touch with a word she let go and swam out into the current.

Back up at the fire Danny was sitting on his haunches, and as Jamie approached, the older man stared up at him, eyes enlarged like eggs.

'What's wrong?' Jamie asked.

Danny stood, and walked towards him on unsteady legs, one hand extended. 'That medallion you're wearing, can I see it?'

Jamie looked at Tasha, then back at Danny, 'Sure, what's the problem?' From around his neck Jamie lifted the chain with the medallion hanging from it, then held it out to Danny, who took it in both hands, the chain looped around his wrists.

Tasha came up close and placed a hand on his shoulder. 'Dad, what's wrong?'

Danny ignored her, face red. His white, even teeth were just visible under the curl of his upper lip. 'Where did you get it?'

Jamie's heart hammered in his chest. 'It came from my father.'

The American studied the medallion, both sides, then slipped on his glasses and used the last rays of sunlight to examine it closely.

'Is there a problem?'

Danny seemed to recover. 'It's just unusual. It's from Cleveland, minted in 1946 to celebrate the Sesquicentennial. The figure in the front is General Moses Cleveland. My brother had one of these. I thought you said that your father was from Maine?'

'That's what I've been told,' said Jamie, accepting the medallion back from Danny and slipping it around his neck. 'I only started wearing it all the time about five years ago – bought a chain for it. Now I feel naked without it.'

After an evening meal of rice, with rehydrated beef and vegetables, Jamie said. 'I don't like having to do this, but after last night I think we should stand sentry duty, watch the camp for any intrusion.'

'Good thinking, Sarge,' said Ray.

'Tasha and I will go first if you like,' Glenn said. 'We stay up late, back home, anyway.'

'No worries,' Jamie said. 'I'll take the midnight shift.'

'You shouldn't do it alone,' Holly said. 'I'll go with you.'

Jamie nodded. 'Alright. Then Ray and Danny. I'll wake you mob at about three.'

# TWENTY-FIVE

Later, when Jamie and Holly took their turn, they sat high up on the rock, looking out over the waterway. For a while they didn't talk at all, but their hands touched and gripped, for the second time.

They sat in silence, the gentle touch of their fingers and palms being enough. At another time Jamie would have taken this as a signal and tried to kiss her. On this night the hand holding was special enough.

'You don't smile much,' she said at length. 'Why not?'

Jamie shrugged, 'It's a lot of responsibility, being in charge, maybe I'm just busy doing my job.'

'No there's more to it than that – there's a sadness in you. Something deep.'

'You're not a shrink, Holly. Maybe we should just concentrate on the matter at hand.'

Holly kept at him. 'You're hurting, aren't you? Is it something to do with this trip?'

'Does it matter what we feel? Everyone still has to function. You have to do things. The army keeps me busy. Before that I was a bit messed up.'

'What about now?'

Jamie swallowed and shook his head. 'I just dunno who I am.

I feel that something's happening … something strange and I don't think I like it.'

'I'll be ready to listen,' she said, 'any time you feel like talking. You're not the only one with a past. Not the only one who's known pain. For some of us it's not dramatic or easy to explain. And the best thing we can do is share it, talk about it.'

Jamie realised that outside of his army mates he had met few people he could trust. Holly was one of those people. 'Have you got family?'

'Yes, Mum and Dad live in Goulburn, not far from me, and my sister lives down in Sydney,' Holly said. 'She's married with a kid – my niece – and she and I get on really well. Her name's Marika, she hasn't even started school yet, but she says she wants to be a spy like me when she grows up.'

'She could do worse than be like you,' Jamie said. 'My parents are both dead.'

'I heard you talking about your dad being American.'

'That kind of thing is more common than you'd realised. I know a bloke in Katherine whose dad is one of the LJ Hooker family of New York, and his mum a full Wardaman., Yes, my dad was American, but I never knew him. Mum meant a lot – pretty much everything – to me. She died of cancer, five years ago.'

'I'm sorry.'

'It's not your fault.'

They sat in silence for a while. Then Jamie said, 'I was just wondering, how you got mixed up in this.'

'You mean why I got sent on this mission?'

'Yep.'

'Well, it happened the way these things usually do. My supervisor called me in … I work under the Assistant Director-General of Security Advice and Assessments. He told me that an American man by the name of Danny Carter had located a section of a major air wreck from way back in the Korean War. I hadn't heard anything on the media, but I was naturally interested, especially when I was told that his brother was the pilot. Anyway, I was given the file and told to do some digging.'

'All in a day's work,' smiled Jamie.

'Not really,' said Holly. 'This was off-beat stuff, even for us. My first step was to verify that the alleged brother had, in fact, existed. Anyway, the American Battle Monuments Commission maintains records of all US servicemen killed in military conflicts since the Civil War. They faxed through what they had. I learned that Matthew Carter was born on the 24th of September, 1928, in Cleveland Ohio. The records confirmed that he was a captain in the US Air Force, 43rd Bombardment Squadron. He was listed as missing, presumed dead, in December 1950. The location was given as the East China Sea.

'The record went on to say that Captain Carter was the pilot of a Boeing B50a Superfortress that encountered a storm north of Taiwan. The aircraft went down with all crew, and debris found in the area confirmed the loss. Captain Carter and his crew were apparently en route to base from a mission in North Korea.

Jamie shook his head in wonder. 'But he didn't go down north of Taiwan. How the hell did he get that plane all the way to the Northern Territory, and why?'

'That, of course, was what I tried to find out. I searched all the databases. The 43rd, as Danny told you, was based at Davis-Monthan field in Tucson. The strange thing was that they were around during the Korean War years, but according to publicly accessible records, they never officially left Arizona. They never went anywhere near Korea. It didn't make sense. Matthew Carter is listed as dying in the Korean War theatre, but he was not supposed to be there. I had to go deeper.

'I needed paper records – the physical unit archives, and my boss agreed. I flew across to the States, to the National Personnel Records Center in St Louis. The archives covered a range of dates from the 43rd Bombardment Wing's activation on November 3, 1947 through to late 1950. I was mainly interested in the Morning Reports, or Musters – a daily accounting of each member of the unit. They covered only exceptions – personnel not present, and the reason for their absence, whether it be death, sickness or transfer. Returning personnel were noted also. Official orders from the Strategic Air Command formed a large proportion of the archives. Other documents included award and medal recommendations, official commendations for the unit, and equipment allocations.'

'How do you remember all this stuff?' Jamie asked.

'I don't know. Just a trick of the trade I guess.'

Holly did not complain when Jamie's arm gently encircled her back. 'I'm not boring you?' she asked.

'Not in the slightest. Please go on.'

'The unit was, I learned, established as the 43rd Bombardment Wing, Very Heavy, in November 3, 1947. Originally the Wing was equipped with World War Two vintage B29 bombers but in January 1949 took delivery of the spanking new Boeing B50a Superfortress. The 43rd became specialists in aerial refuelling using KC29 tankers. By 1950 they were made up of four bomb squadrons and three refuelling squadrons.

'It was by going through the Morning Reports – the most boring part of all – that I finally hit pay dirt. August 21, 1950. One group of names caught my attention – Captain Matthew Carter, Lieutenant Evan Gray, Staff Sergeant Charles Pearce, Sergeant Samuel Snow, Staff Sergeant Burleigh Connor and six others.' She paused, 'See I can't remember everything – crew for one aircraft. It was the annotation after the list that told the story: deployed to Andersen Air Base, Guam, via Site Baker, Killeen Base.' Holly stopped, 'Do you know what Site Baker was?'

'No, I don't,' said Jamie.

'It was one of several stockpile locations the US Air Force kept at the time – for nuclear weapons.'

'Jesus Christ,' Jamie breathed.

'That's what my boss said. And I imagine that our illustrious Prime Minister, Bob Hawke said something similar when he heard. So, a few days later, a Hercules transport carried me north from Canberra to Darwin, there to join the RFSVs that would carry Danny Carter to the crash site.'

'That's when you met me,' said Jamie, and he realised that despite the gravity of what she had told him, he was smiling.

They said nothing for a long time, just enjoyed the warmth of each other's presence, under the vast tableaux of stars high overhead.

The next day, with Ray leading, they followed the riverbed, occasionally crossing sides when the waterway backed up against one side of the gorge. Sometimes the walls narrowed to just twenty or thirty paces across and it became necessary to climb then descend again.

Light rain came and went, washing this world of stone clean. Jamie moved automatically, keeping an eye on Ray. They were just coming up to another kink in the gorge when Jamie saw Ray stop, then signal a halt with four fingers and thumb extended. He followed this by raising his hand above his eyes. Loosely translated the sign sequence meant, 'Rest here for five minutes, I want to check something out.'

Jamie called to Holly and the others. 'Take a pew for a bit, Ray's found something.'

The rest of the party lifted packs from their shoulders and sat on the rocks, waiting while Ray left his gear, and walked to the northern side of the gorge. There he started to climb. Jamie pulled the binoculars from his pack and studied the ledge that Ray was heading for. It was dark with shadows, almost hidden by vegetation, but even so, with the help of the lens, Jamie could see ochre shapes on the stone walls, well above the flood levels. More stone art – a full gallery.

Ray was a capable climber, but even so it took him ten minutes or so to get close to the ledge, and again Jamie could hear the soft sounds of his singing floating on the breeze. Yella added the occasional sharp bark. He had climbed as far as he could, but remained far below his owner, and was giving voice to his displeasure.

'What's Ray doing?' Danny asked.

Without turning Jamie said, 'He's singing.'

'Do you think we could go up there too?' Tasha asked.

'If he wanted us to, he would have said. No, best to leave him alone. He might take a while, if you want to get a bite to eat.'

The singing stopped, and through the binoculars Jamie could see Ray squatting in front of the ledge now, immaculately still.

The painting was long, slug-shaped, with a bulbous white head filled with white spots. It was unusual, like nothing Jamie had seen before.

The sun came out through a chink in the clouds. It was almost instantly hotter, steam rising from the rocks. Holly offered a dry Vita-wheat biscuit smeared with peanut butter and Jamie took it gratefully, washing it down with a pannikin of water taken straight from the stream.

'Another one?'

'Yes please.'

'Hardly gourmet fare—' she smiled.

'I wouldn't know gourmet food if I tripped over it. This is fine, better than C-Ration biscuits any day.'

Ray returned after a while, climbing down and approaching the group with a grave expression on his face.

Jamie went to meet him. 'What did you see up there?'

Ray squatted, staring at the ground. Jamie knew his mate well. When the music has died inside, his eyes go dull, and the muscles of his jaw slacken so his lips don't quite join.

'So, what's the story?' Jamie asked.

'We have talked about Bolung before today, right Sarge?'

'Yes, I know about him.'

Bolung, the snake, was one of the important creator beings from most of the Indigenous nations in the region. Bula was the other.

'Bolung left his picture up there.' Ray pointed up at the cliffs, then further down the gorge. 'He sleeps in the pools, down in the gorge, and we aren't allowed to disturb him. That's what my grandfather warned me about. We should go back now.'

'Ray, I respect your reasons, but we've got a job to do. We can't just turn around.'

'We got no choice, Sarge.'

Ray stood up slowly, then walked back to where he had left his pack and rifle, shouldered them and turned back the way they had come. That was it, he just started walking back, and the rest of them watched, dumbfounded. Glenn and Tasha had taken off their boots and socks, and were sitting on a rock in the water with their feet submerged to the ankles, staring.

Danny stood up, 'What's going on?'

Ray wheeled an arm. 'Come on, you mob. Back this way.'

'You can go back,' Danny said, 'but I'm not.' There was a pugnacious look in his face that Jamie had not seen before.

Jamie called out. 'Ray, stop right there, that's an order. I'm on your side but we need to talk.'

Ray slowly walked back, stopping a few paces short of Jamie. He pointed down into the gorge. 'Bad country, sickness country. Go there and wake up Bolung ... bad things happen.'

Jamie turned to the party of Americans. 'Look, this is awkward, but we have to be respectful of Ray's beliefs. This is significant country for him.'

Tasha was standing now, still in her bare feet, looking down along the gorge. 'Hey wait,' she said. 'I can see something, just a little way down the gorge.'

'What is it?

'It looks like mist ... but at this time of day?'

Jamie took the binoculars from his pack and climbed to the highest of several nearby boulders. He stared through the crystal-clear Zeiss lenses down the gorge.

Clouds had been building in the north for the past hour or so, but the light was still good.

'Jesus,' Jamie said.

'What?'

'It does appear to be mist. Here, have a look.'

Jamie handed the binoculars to Danny, who had come up beside him. 'That's spray rising from a waterfall, it has to be.'

Tasha said, 'Hey, surely the most likely place to find the plane would be a deep pool where it's lying hidden. Waterfalls almost always have deep pools below them – at least they do where I come from.'

Jamie looked at Ray. 'That's only half a click down from here. Can we go that far, do you think?' Ray looked pained, and Jamie pressed the advantage. 'We can move silently, you know that.'

Ray shook his head slowly, looking pointedly at Danny, Holly, Tasha and Glenn. They were the problem, and both of them knew it. The kind of self-discipline needed to move without noise through the wilderness comes from long familiarity, understanding of the various signals, and training. The visitors from Maryland did not have that, and nor could Jamie and Ray leave them here alone.

Jamie threw up his arms. 'I'm sorry then guys. This is Ray's country, if he doesn't want us to go down there, then we won't.'

Danny said nothing, just sat on the rock with his head on his hands, looking down, as if he were ready to crack.

Jamie caught Glenn's eyes. They had turned a paler shade of blue. Even so, it was a surprise when he burst out, 'Are you fucking kidding me?'

Tasha grabbed his hand, but her husband shook it away, standing in his bare feet. 'Look you guys, Danny has been waiting for this day for forty years – travelled around the world – spent hundreds of thousands of dollars – and now, possibly within a mile of more wreckage that may well give us some or all of the answers you're going to pull out on the basis of a stone age superstition?'

Jamie raised his chin. 'Too right I will. You're only walking on this ground because Ray and his grandfather are allowing you to.'

'But that's complete bullshit.'

'Will you just sit down so we can talk about this reasonably?'

Tasha turned on him. 'Jamie's right Glenn, you're being an insensitive twat.'

'Maybe I am, but can't you see how crazy this is?'

Ray muttered something in Kriol.

'What did he say?' Holly asked.

Jamie grimaced. 'That he understands the need, but that if we go down there only bad things will come of it.'

Danny folded his arms over his chest. 'Glenn's right. I'm not stopping here. Sorry Jamie, you can take out that rifle and shoot me if you have to. That's the only way you'll stop me.'

Glenn said, 'Jamie, you and Ray can stay here, and after we have a look we'll come back. Then if we wake up this Bolung or whatever his name is, he will come after us, not you and Ray.'

Ray shook his head sadly. 'You don't understand, brus.'

'Whatever.' Glenn stood up and shouldered his pack. 'Sorry guys, but I'm going down with Danny to check out that waterfall. Y'all can stay here if you want.'

Finally, Ray stood up. 'No.'

'Are you going to stop us?'

'You gonna walk down there shouting and angry, that's a bad thing. We all go, just that little way, no further, and we do it my way. We walk softly, talk softly. Whisper all the time. No yelling, no fights. You understand?'

Jamie could feel Ray tearing. He lived in two worlds, and occasionally they conflicted. 'You sure you want to do this?'

'It's better, yes. But we tread softly.'

The clouds that had been building passed before the sun, and the day darkened considerably.

Even Glenn settled into this new mode of walking, treading lightly on the spine of the earth, and it was not so hard to believe that mythical creatures slept in the cracks and hollows of black water and musty air.

The sandstone gorge closed in, and it seemed to Jamie that the shades were darker, the stone platforms more polished and prone to weird shapes where they had weathered. Even the stream itself appeared to be more viscous and dark. Ray peered in all directions.

Tasha moved freely, the Nikon in constant use, capturing curved and sculptured sweeps of stone that resembled men, buildings, and otherworldly shapes that Jamie could not name.

The gorge narrowed again, and the rising mist of spray appeared just ahead. Jamie heard the rumble of the waterfall before the drop opened in front of him, at which point he edged along until he could see down the falls – brown-tinged water pouring off the cliff. Over millions of years it had scoured the sandstone below into a pool, now about eighty metres by sixty in extent.

Holly showed no fear at the giddying drop, pointing down at the pool with one slender arm. 'Do you think the fuselage could have ended up in there?'

Jamie chewed his lip reflectively. 'It's possible, there's enough space to hide it. Let's get down there and have a good look around.' He turned to Ray, who had walked behind them. 'What if we set up camp down there, no further than that?'

Ray inclined his head. Jamie had never seen his mate so stricken, and Yella stayed glued to the right leg of his master, as if sensing his unease.

Tasha reached out and took her father's hand. 'Are you okay?' she asked.

'No, but we're close to Matt. I can feel it at last.'

# TWENTY-SIX

From that point onwards Jamie led the way, skirting the sheer face of the falls, locating an easier path that rambled along on one side, so well used by animals so that the trail was plain, difficult at times, but not impossible. The pool was out of sight for much of the descent, but finally, rounding a bend, he pushed aside the hanging leaves of a rambling smilax vine to reveal a stretch of white sand, surrounded by verdant green pandanus fronds, blue water and yellow stone.

It was a dark place, where the sun must rarely penetrate, neat as a garden, with water still dripping from leaves to earth, legacy of the last shower. Jamie paused, a strange little dart of emotion in his heart – the feeling of having been here before – that this was somehow familiar.

'You right there?' Holly whispered.

'Yeah fine. It's just beautiful.'

And it was. Together they walked on to a beach-like clearing alongside the pool, the sand swept clean by bristles of rising water each wet season. The others came up at their own pace, each with their own emotions. The feeling of invasion was lying heavily on Jamie, and he avoided Ray's eyes.

'Okay you lot,' he said softly. 'We'll camp here. Choose your spot and we'll get some firewood together.'

'So, what's the plan?' Danny asked.

'It's too dark to see underwater with all that cloud. I'll wait until tomorrow, hopefully we'll get a bit of sun and I'll go for a free dive. Even in the dirty water it won't take long to work out if the wreck is in there.'

The overhang provided shelter from the rain, and they set up camp on the sand underneath. Dry driftwood provided fuel for a fire, and Jamie found a shallow niche in the rock wall where he laid their SLRs on a towel.

Later, while Ray used a hand line to catch three fat grunter, with their glossy scales the colour of brown coal, from the pool, they sat in silence, watching rainbow bee-eaters swoop and play over the pool, bright droplets of water falling in the afternoon light as they dipped beaks in the reflective surface.

Holly had been standing, staring at the waterfall. When Jamie came up beside her, she pointed. 'I think it might be possible to walk behind the waterfall,' she said. 'Look. You can see moss on the rocks behind the white water.'

Jamie looked, and saw what she meant. 'We should check it out.'

Danny stood up slowly, then Tasha and Glenn, leaving only Ray at the camp with his dog.

Holly was right – a narrow passage led to a wide ledge behind the falls – a beautiful place curtained by water. Eerie light fell on mossy grey, brown and yellow rocks and patches of delicate ferns. Jamie led the way across the space, mindful of the slippery, damp rocks beneath his feet.

Tasha knelt at a patch of herb like plants. 'God, I bet some of these haven't even been classified.' She glanced at Jamie. 'Ray's not happy, is he?'

'No, but what can we do? And at least he made the decision to come down here himself. I would never have forced him. Right now we've got a high-stakes situation going on to the southwest of here. A mining company wants to dig up a place called Coronation Hill. But the Jawoyn people believe that a major myth-figure called Bula has his final resting place there

– real bad sickness country. Years earlier they mined some uranium on the same site, in the face of protests from the Traditional Owners. There was an outbreak of whooping cough that killed dozens, and the locals believed that it was because Bula had been disturbed. There's a lot of shit going down on both sides of the argument and it still hasn't been resolved.'

Tasha looked around to check that her husband wasn't close enough to hear. 'Sorry Glenn was being a prick about it.'

Jamie shrugged. 'He forced the issue, and I guess that served a purpose.'

They walked to the other side and found that the ledge continued after the waterfall, giving access to the pool's far bank. There was no sand on this side, just an expanse of scattered dark rocks of all sizes.

Jamie swept his eyes upwards to a feather of water tumbling from the high cliffs across from them. 'Another small waterfall,' he said, pointing it out. 'Must be a side-creek. Let's take a look.'

Crossing those stones took time – some looked solid but slid when they committed their weight to them. Holly, with Tasha at her side, pulled ahead, and reached the tiny waterfall first.

Jamie watched as Holly bent over and advanced, so the water tumbled onto the back of her head. She lifted her wet face, smiling, tossing her hair. Tasha joined her, the two women soaking wet and laughing, but Jamie was looking at the cliff face adjacent to the streaming water. Four to five metres up a narrow crack – a chimney in climbing parlance – started, making the face climbable almost to the summit.

Glenn, who had arrived at a sedate pace with Danny, held a hand out and let the water impact on his skin. 'This is surreal.'

'There's a way up,' Jamie said, 'I can see it.' He moved to the most logical place to attempt a climb, straining upwards until his neck hurt. His eyes fixed on a strange projection from the rock. Reaching upwards, his hand curled around a dull but strong rolled aluminium spike that had been driven into the rock, almost invisible from below. Jamie looked down and found the next, at waist height.

'You see it, Danny? Pitons. They're bloody climbing pitons.'

Danny's face had shaken off the pasty fatigue of an hour earlier. 'Oh God, you're right. Do you realise what this means? Matt and the crew must have made them.'

Jamie hung all his weight off the piton, testing it, surprised when it accepted him without any give. 'The pool has to be the priority,' he said, 'but there must be a reason for this.'

Danny was shaking with excitement. 'This is how Matt and the others climbed out of the gorge.'

'Or into it,' Jamie grunted. 'We shouldn't jump to conclusions. Either way, I'm going up for a look.'

'That might be dangerous without ropes,' Holly warned.

'Try and stop me.' Jamie threw a glance at Glenn, who shook his head.

'Sorry dude, I'll have a go at most things, but climbing sheer fucking cliffs isn't my thing.'

Jamie started off nervously, trembling in the back of his knees as the pitons took his full weight. They were, in all likelihood, almost forty years old. They held his weight easily, however, helping him into the 'chimney,' where he wedged himself inside and started to work his way upwards.

It took two or three minutes of hard climbing to reach the cliff top, at which point he turned his attention to the stream itself, scarcely flowing, emerging from thick bush to become that tiny waterfall.

'Hey you,' came a call. It was Holly, arriving up and over the edge. She looked red and a little frightened, face shiny with sweat, yet there was pleasure in her eyes at her achievement as she brushed away his offer of a helping hand.

'You okay?'

'Can't say that I enjoyed it, but I'm fine.'

'I'm the same, but I have to say, going down will be harder.'

'I don't like going down,' Holly said.

The words had been hanging in the air for a few seconds before Jamie saw colour fill her cheeks, and he understood the double entendre.

Holly coloured, 'Oh, you know what I meant—'

'Yeah, I know. There's a long way around if you'd prefer.'

'So, where does this stream go?' she asked.

'I'm not sure, but it's worth checking out.'

'You want to go a little way now?'

'No, let's investigate the pool first. Then we'll follow up on this.'

'Cool.' Holly cocked her head at an angle. 'Long way 'round?'

Jamie pointed, 'Back up, wade across the top of the waterfall, then down the way we arrived earlier.'

Holly smiled with relief. 'Sounds good to me.'

At sunset Jamie went down to the water with the smell of roasting fish strong in his nostrils.

The pool and its surrounds were tranquil. Tiny ripples spilled out across the water as a dark, nuggety rock wallaby drank on the other side. Deep green pandanus and imposing cliffs formed a backdrop at the far edge of the pool. An archer fish stuck his snout up near the edge and fired a globule of water high up into the air, bringing down a flying ant, swishing his tail swiftly to swim across and wolf it down.

Jamie took off his shirt and waded into the water, sand coarse between his toes until he reached a rock platform that dropped off into deep water. Bending his knees, he launched himself into the depths, shivering at the cold but quickly driving his right arm overhead to begin a fast freestyle.

He kept it up all the way to the opposite side, slowing before he touched stone, then held on to the slick surface with one hand for a moment, loving the dank smell of the water and the roar of the falls sending foam speckled water towards him. Finally, he wiped the water from his eyes and face, then turned and swam back.

Thinking about how he would approach diving the pool the next day, he climbed the sandy beach, and dabbed at his face with a towel. Not bothering with a shirt, Jamie lifted the medallion from where he had left it and slipped it over his neck. Danny was sitting near the fire on a rock, staring at it. His eyes were like lenses, focussing on the medallion and seeming to ignore everything else.

Jamie caught Danny's eye, seeing how he immediately looked away. Jamie remembered his reaction when he'd first seen it.

'My medallion,' he said finally. 'It means something to you, doesn't it?'

The American's voice was deadpan. 'My brother Matt had one exactly the same. He used to carry it for luck.'

Jamie stopped dead, made a sound through his nose.

'Can I have a look please?'

Jamie lifted the leather thong back over his head, swung the medallion like a pendulum for a moment then passed it into Dany's waiting hand. The older man took his glasses from his top pocket, extracted them from the case and perched them on his nose before examining the medallion minutely.

'You said your father left it to you. Where did he get it from?'

'I don't know where it came from originally. My mother passed it on to me when I was about ten.' Jamie's voice caught. 'It's the only thing I have from him.'

The others stopped what they were doing, and gathered in a silent cluster, listening and watching. Glenn cleared his throat, 'Danny, surely plenty of these got made. It can't be the same medallion.'

Danny passed it onto Tasha. 'Maybe you're right, Glenn. Maybe it's not the same one. But I do know one thing for sure, whoever owned it must have been in Cleveland in 1946. Like we were.'

Tasha took the medallion from her father's hand and walked a few steps away, chasing the sun, now retreating quickly to a final corner. She held it up to the last golden rays, so it glowed like fire.

'How did your father die?' she asked Jamie.

'He was living at a boarding house in Darwin. He and my mother weren't married when they got together. There was a fire. Six people were killed, and my father was one of them.'

'That's awful,' breathed Tasha.

Even Glenn hung his head and muttered, 'I'm sorry.'

'But what if,' Tasha suggested, 'Uncle Matt accidentally lost the medallion somewhere – maybe in Darwin – and Jamie's dad had found it before he died?'

'I guess that's possible,' Jamie conceded.

'Or stolen it,' joked Glenn.'

'It's also possible,' Tasha went on, shooting her husband a sharp glance. 'That they knew each other.'

A shiver went through Jamie's body, starting in his feet and bringing the hairs erect on his legs, body, arms and the back of his neck. Just a tiny portion of those deep roots of the past were being exposed, and he wasn't sure that he was enjoying the sensation.

They ate with their fingers, picking through the bones as night slowly fell around them. In deference to Ray, and the brooding presence they all felt here, there was no singing, and no jokes. Later, when Yella was busy crunching away at the charred fish bones, the clouds parted, and a glorious full moon shone milky light on stone and water.

Jamie pushed in the burning sticks in the fire and waited until the camp was quiet. Finally, calling in at his pack for his spongebag, Jamie walked to the bank to clean his teeth, and had almost finished when a yellow torch beam left the campsite and approached him.

'It's just me,' Holly said.

'Hi, I was wondering where you'd got to. What's up?'

'I was thinking that you and I are going to be on picquet duty in an hour. It's hardly worth going to sleep. It must be beautiful behind the waterfall now that the moon's out.'

'I guess it would be.' Jamie looked back towards the camp. Danny was probably snoring by now, and Ray had been in his swag for some time.

'Do you want to have a look?' she went on.

'Might as well.'

Holly held the torch for both of them, the beam seeking out small footholds all the way to the ledge, then behind the waterfall. Jamie stopped about half-way, easing down so he was sitting on the damp rocks, waiting while she settled beside him.

The flashlight flicked off, and it took a second for his eyes to adjust. The moon sat suspended behind the falling water, trans-forming it into a curtain of liquid diamonds. Jamie felt the goose bumps rise on his arms and the back of his neck.

Holly clutched at his arm. 'I've never seen anything so beau-tiful,' she said.

'Neither have I,' Jamie said, conscious of her touch.

'I feel insignificant here,' she said suddenly, 'as if I have only a small role in the scheme of things.' The moonlight, reflected off the jewelled cascade, danced in Holly's eyes.

'Me too.'

Holly moved closer, her shoulder just behind his so he could feel her breast against his bicep.

The touch was electrifying. Jamie knew they could go back now but he made no move to stand up. Their joined hands rest-ed on her thigh. His skin was dusted with goose bumps.

'What do you want from life?' she asked. 'Is it just to be a soldier?'

'I want to do my bit, in whatever form that takes. Then may-be a few acres on my mother's country, with a winding little creek with deep pools and a few fish. And a little house, where I can grow veggies and be part of the land. That's my dream I guess, pretty simple, really.'

'Not simple. It sounds perfect.'

'What about you?'

'I don't know yet. Like you, I've got a part to play in the world. I'll go where it takes me.'

Jamie saw that the moonlight shone on her face. Her eyes gathered light, then half closed with her chin tilted high to bring her lips closer to his. He had never seen anything quite so thrill-ing. Her quizzical, beautiful smile was both a question and an answer. He ran one hand around the back of her neck. Her hair was the softest thing he had ever touched. They stayed like that for a moment, before she moved her head back, looked him full in the eye then moved her lips over his.

Jamie was unsure at first where the boundaries were. It was she who opened up and drew him in deeper. Warmth and wet-ness. Irresistible explosions of the senses. Even this wasn't enough for him, and it was a relief, a shiver of thanksgiving when she stood and slipped out of her clothes. Her body was lean and spare, with small breasts and a dark V of hair at the base of her abdomen.

She squatted over him, brought down his shorts, lifted his shirt, kissed along his collarbone, then lowered herself onto him, soothing and passionate at first, slowly building in urgency.

Up until then he hadn't noticed them sliding closer to the falling curtain of water, but tiny droplets misted over them. Her body grew slick like an eel, and his hands slid over her, never holding in one place. He felt the skin of her thighs dimple with the force of downward pressure she was exerting on him, and the deep heat where their bodies joined. He tasted salt in her lips and ran his tongue over her neck and shoulders as if the moisture would sustain the moment forever.

Later. Always. Every day of his life. Jamie would remember that night behind the waterfall as one of the few times in his life he had forgotten every source of pain and been truly, deliriously happy.

# TWENTY-SEVEN

Ray had scarcely slept since they had entered Bolung's country, but now he was even more on edge than he had been on previous nights. Something was stirring in the lands of his ancestors.

When Jamie tagged him for picquet duty he sat up from his bedroll, 'Don't wake Danny, Sarge. He needs the sleep. I'll be right – in any case – I've got Yella to keep me company.'

Standing, he fetched his rifle from the niche and walked to the path, climbing the gorge sides in the moonlight on silent feet. Finally, at the summit, his eyes were drawn to the eastern sky. At first it was merely the crescent moon and bright stars that drew his eyes, the magic dust of the galaxies.

But then Ray saw something that made him shiver – dark shapes gliding down from the stratosphere. Shadows momentarily blocking out the moon, moving slowly. Ray counted ten of them. To the military part of his mind they could only be one thing, HAHO parachutists, drifting in with the night. To the brain that belonged to his country and ancestors they were part of something much older.

More than troubled by what he saw, he reached for the earth with each hand, delving into the soil itself, feeling sharp quartzite drive under his nails. The earth was his parent, and he knew that he had done a bad thing by bringing Danny Carter and his family down here. Bolung did not sleep easy, but with one eye open and one ear tuned to the land of his creation. Bolung was waking, and he was angry. The manifestation of that anger could resolve in unimaginable ways.

Ray shivered from the tips of his toenails to his hair, and when Yella came close he fondled his ears. As the last of the dark shapes merged with the earth to the north the first heavy drop of rain fell. Then another. Within a minute the rain had become a deluge, falling in sheets and running down Ray's hair, onto his nose and bare back.

He began to shiver with cold, and he knew he should go back down to the camp. He could not see more than a few yards around him in any case.

Terrible things were coming, and it seemed like there was nothing he could do to stop them.


The rain woke them all, forcing them to carry their bedding in close under the cliff edge for shelter. It started out as a deluge, then grew heavier still, and in all the hours since it had not let up, not even for a minute.

Jamie stirred to Ray's gentle but insistent voice. He wore no shirt and was obviously cold. He held a tin mug of coffee in one hand and passed it to Jamie.

'Here Sarge,' take it.

'What's up?' Jamie croaked.

'Bad things, I think. Just when I was on guard duty, I'm pretty sure I saw some parachutists come in. Never heard an aircraft so they must have been HAHO.'

Jamie's brow creased with thought. HAHO was an acronym meaning high altitude high opening. The aircraft could drop the paratroopers far from the target, each of whom would then use their altitude to steer their chutes long distances, even fifty or sixty kilometres. It was technique used for silent infiltrations by Special Forces troops.

'Sounds unlikely, are you sure?'

'Yep, I'm pretty sure. But who the hell are they?'

Jamie took a long sip of his coffee. It wasn't as hot as he liked it. Everything seemed cooler with the rain. 'Most likely Canberra has sent in some SAS to keep an eye on us. I bet they hate this fucking weather.' He caught Ray's eye. 'I don't even mind if they have sent in some backup, brus. Though this is a complicated fuckin' situation: of course, they should have warned us.'

'What if it's not SAS?' Ray said. 'What if it's … someone else?'

'For fuck's sake brus, don't even think like that.'


Later, as soon as his breakfast had settled, Jamie stood poised at the pool edge, wearing only a pair of yellow board shorts, staring out into the deep water. The waterfall was flowing with, it seemed, twice the volume of the previous day. Ray was sitting on the stone platform beside him, Tasha and Holly flapping their bare feet in the water. The rain still fell steadily, and they were all streaming wet from their hair to their feet.

'You wanted a sunny day,' Holly said.

'Yeah, strike that one off the wish list. Not only that, but the one thing we need more than any other and we don't have it – diving gear. I'll have a go at free diving, we used to train for it, but the problem is crap visibility. Bare eyes don't see too well under the surface, and the water's dirty enough as it is.'

Tasha had that frustrated look on her face. 'You can't like, make goggles of some sort, out of a pair of dad's glasses or maybe a pair of sunnies?'

'I'm not sure how we could seal them – but it's an idea.'

Ray held both hands like goggles to his eyes, then faked a cough.

It took Jamie a moment to catch on, then. 'Gas mask? Good thinking.' Then to Holly. 'He's not just a pretty face, that bloke.' The NORFORCE RFSVs each carried a set of British Avon full-face masks in canvas bags. Jamie imagined that they'd be easy enough to seal. 'Just a shame we didn't bring one with us.'

Ray lifted one hand like a school kid volunteering to empty the wastepaper basket. 'I'll get one Sarge. Won't take long if I walk along the tops of the ridges.'

Jamie thought about it, walking along the top would be much

quicker, cutting through the bends and twists of the gorge. Few people could move cross country like Ray. 'It's worth a try, but maybe take one of the UHF units – wrapped in plastic so it doesn't get wet – then call Mick when you get to the top and get him to meet you half-way. That'd save an hour or two. And tell him to get you a tube of silicone as well.'

Jamie walked back to camp with Ray and took the radio out of his pack. 'Here, take this.'

Ray took the unit and walked away, up to the top of the waterfall, rock hopping his way across then disappearing from view. Jamie thought that he had looked relieved to be getting out of the place. Yet he was back in under three hours, carrying a gas mask in its canvas carrying case, and a tube of silicon in the other, complete with caulking gun.

The rubber Avon M50 full face mask had good seals and a huge Perspex viewing area. Sitting out of the rain, working on a spread shirt, Jamie removed the filter cartridges, packed the spaces with wads of silicone then put it all aside to dry. Ray sat a few metres away, watching him work.

'How are the boys going up there?' Jamie asked.

'Maybe a bit bored from sitting on their arses. Nico's made himself a chin-up bar and all.'

Jamie sensed that Ray wasn't happy, and when the others had wandered away, he asked him straight out. 'What's wrong?'

'Boss, they reckon Wally's gone off and they dunno where he is. He took his rifle too.'

'I'll skin him alive,' Jamie hissed. 'What's he playing at?'

'Mick wants you to call him on the radio. When I told them about those parachutes they nearly freaked out.'

'Okay, sure. I'll have a dive then climb up high enough to transmit.'

When the silicone had more or less dried, Jamie stripped down to his shorts and stood at the edge of the pool with the contraption in hand.

'Are you sure there are no crocodiles in there?' Tasha asked.

'Definitely freshies – the smaller ones, but they won't hurt me. I checked out the slides before I swam across last night. There are no salties here.'

'Slides?'

'You see the marks where their bellies drag over the sand when they get in and out of the water to sunbake or whatever? We call them slides.' Jamie pointed to a sand drift across the other side of the channel. 'See there?'

'Oh yes, wow. And you're still going in?'

'Yep.'

The water was cool as Jamie picked his way off the rock shelf. Goosebumps quickly populated the skin of his chest. The depth dropped off rapidly at the end of the shelf.

Jamie stopped with the water lapping at his navel, then spat in the makeshift mask and rinsed it with a dollop of water. Then, turning one last time to look at them he pushed forward into the water. Within a few strokes the bottom disappeared. It was deeper than he'd thought, he saw, churned by the maelstrom of water and stone that would come down the falls in the wet season.

The mask did not leak. The soft rubber seals on those Avon masks were faultless. One benefit of some, but not all, military equipment is that it is made to work, not manufactured to a price like so much of what sells in stores.

Jamie changed actions, moving out to the middle of the pool in an easy breaststroke. There, treading water, he began hyper-ventilating, breathing in deeply, then exhaling completely, over and over again. Jamie continued this process for a couple of minutes before rolling over onto his front and into a duck dive, using his arms and powerful kicks to drive him deeper into the water, into a brown nether world. It was colder down under the surface, locking up his chest.

Strangely, as he descended, the water cleared somewhat, and he realised that the new runoff water had not yet fully mingled with the remnants of the clear dry season pool water.

Visibility changed from being so dirty that he was scarcely able to see his hand in front of his face, to the equivalent of his own body length. A school of bony bream flashed before his eyes, then finally the bottom, but by then Jamie was fighting his natural buoyancy. His descent slowed, and he attempted to swim parallel to the bottom.

From this position, just a couple of metres above the bed, he kicked along as far as he could before he was forced to ascend and breathe again. Over five or more dives he attempted to complete a reasonable cross section of the pool.

By then it was obvious that there was no aircraft fuselage in the pool. It was just too big an object to have disappeared so completely. There was, however, something unusual amongst the natural pattern of rock, sunken logs and gravel on the pool floor. The exhaustion from this kind of diving is cumulative, however, and Jamie knew that he would soon need to return to the bank for a rest.

In one last effort, using his final reserves of air Jamie kicked hard for the bottom, and there he saw what looked like piles of irregular dinner plates thrown en masse from a shelf. The desire to breathe was too strong to investigate further, and Jamie struck out for the surface, finally breaking through, lungs on fire before he opened his mouth and sucked in the first great breath of air.

The rain was now so heavy that he was forced to raise one hand across from his nose so he could breathe without ingesting rain. The pool looked strange, hemmed in, rain falling like darts of disturbed light.

Tasha and Danny were on the bank together as he breast-stroked closer, their faces twisted with concern. Holly stood above them, hands on her hips, and Glenn waist deep in the water.

Jamie reached the shallow water and sat, his breathing quickly returning to normal. 'How could you stay down so long?' Holly called. 'You frightened the life out of us.'

Jamie held his finger to his lips, reminding her to keep her voice down. 'Sorry, but I know what I'm doing.'

Danny leaned forward from the edge expectantly. 'Did you see anything?'

'I can say categorically that there is no intact air frame in this pool, but there's something unusual down there.'

'So, what's the next move?' Holly asked, whispering this time.

'I just need to upgrade my equipment.' Jamie dug around in the knee-deep water for a suitable sized rock, finding one around the size of his head and lifting it in both hands.

'What's that for?'

'I'm going to use it to get down to the bottom fast. This pool is way deeper than I expected. Can someone find me a good-sized lump of driftwood I can float it out on?'

Holly climbed back towards the campsite and returned with a flattened section of dried-up, bleached wood, half the size of a surfboard. She stepped into the water and floated it out to him.

'Perfect. Thanks.' Jamie said, though the rock would not balance on the driftwood and he had to hold it in place. This done he turned and started paddling back to where he had last surfaced. Again, he hyperventilated for about a minute before gripping the stone in both hands, pushing the log aside, and taking a final deep breath.

The stone took him down fast. His feet hit the bottom of the pool, but he did not release the stone. It seemed to weigh very little down here. His ears hurt, but because of the mask design Jamie had no way of reaching his nose and equalising the pressure. Putting up with the pain in his head he started to look around.

The murky landscape at the bottom of the pool was not what he had expected. It looked like a subaqueous junk yard, for he had landed adjacent to a huge pile of cut aluminium plates, and scattered girders.

The metal sections were from one to two square metres in size, all with jagged edges, many stacked ten or more deep. Fish had found havens and caverns in the spaces in between, and a hefty barramundi shot out and disappeared into the furthest reaches of the pool, with powerful strokes of its broad tail.

Jamie tried walking, but the stone he carried was so perfectly weighted that the easiest way to move was to take giant moon-walker-like jumps. Ascending the scrap pile Jamie soon saw the extent of this wasteland. In many places it was overlaid by gravel, stones, and sunken timber, but as far as he could see or travel in any direction, the litter of scrap aluminium and rusted iron continued. Jamie selected the most portable example he could find, and pulled it from the floor of the pool.

At the end of his wind, Jamie dropped the stone and rose to the surface. He did not speak until he had reached the edge. Looking at Danny Carter's face Jamie reaffirmed the significance of this moment.

'Did you find it?' Danny asked.

Jamie lifted the grimy and corroded aluminium sheet. 'Yes. But it doesn't look the way you'd think.'

# TWENTY-EIGHT

Squatting down on the rocks overlooking the pool, Jamie watched while Danny turned the flat aluminium sheet with its rough edges over and over in his hands.

'So, there are hundreds of these in the pool?' Danny asked.

'More. Tens of thousands. Someone cut the plane up into tiny pieces. They didn't want it to be found, that's for sure.'

Danny put down the sheet and lowered himself into to a sitting position. He pointed over at the pitons. 'My guess is that Matt's plane crashed up there somewhere beyond the cliff – further east than we were looking. My brother and his crew knew that the USAF would be searching for them. They knew that they had to hide the crash site. They cut up the plane and brought all the pieces here. They could have just chucked them down and climbed after them via the pitons to place them in the pool. Easier than burying them, I guess.'

'Why would they do that,' Jamie breathed. 'You must be right though. There's no other explanation. And that's why the old man said it had disappeared.' He had a sick feeling deep in his gut. This was somehow momentous, much more vital than simply some hidden pieces of aluminium. He glared at Holly. 'Why was the USAF after them? Why would they break up the fuselage of one of the biggest warplanes ever built? It must have taken years. Why? What were they afraid of?'

Danny's voice was deadpan. 'You tell him, Holly.'

Holly sighed deeply, as if recognising that this revelation could not be delayed any further. 'Sorry for not telling you before. I don't know all the answers, not yet, but as I said, we do know that this plane visited a designated nuclear stockpile, called Site Baker, before it flew out to the Pacific. It's therefore possible – in fact likely – that this plane was carrying a fully armed Mark IV plutonium bomb when it came down here.'

Jamie's eyes rolled skywards. 'I guess I didn't really think this through. What the hell is a Mark IV plutonium bomb?'

Holly wiped the water from around her eyes with her fingers. 'Pretty much identical to the "Fat Man" bomb that was dropped on Nagasaki, just many times more powerful and with a few safety improvements.

'Surely this wasn't an operational mission.'

Danny's eyes were dull as he looked down at the fragment. 'We still don't know for sure, but I do know that Matt and his crew took off from Andersen Base on Guam, en route to Korea, with that weapon on board.'

'Why break the plane up like this?'

'Anecdotally at least, it seems that the United States Government had already tried to kill them once. I expect that if we examine more of those plates, we'll find damage from machine gun and cannon fire. Matt knew they'd try again – so they had to hide the plane.'

Jamie knew there were no answers to the questions that kept forming in his mind, but still he kept shooting them out. 'Why did their own government try to kill them?'

Holly answered, 'I'm still not sure. But something happened.'

Danny broke in, 'As I told you before I had a private detective with some highly placed contacts. But I already knew that they were hiding something of moment. I also knew that the 43rd were designated carriers. I researched the whole situation, over the years. I learned that in 1950 General Macarthur ordered nine Mark IV nuclear capsules to be transported to the Far-East theatre, and that he proposed the idea of dropping thirty or more bombs across the neck of Manchuria to create a radioactive wasteland through which China could not invade Korea. In another interesting coincidence, Macarthur was relieved of his command just a few months after Matt's death. He was replaced by General Ridgeway.

Holly was surprised by that. 'So, it's possible that this situation cost the career of a general?'

Jamie, shirtless as he was, was feeling the cold, crossing his arms in front of his chest. 'Between the three of us we should be able to put this together. Come on Holly, give us everything you know, it's pissing down rain, and we need to get out before the rivers rise. I have to try to put together some kind of freaking idea of what the hell has gone on here.'

Holly's body language changed from argumentative to contemplative, with the rain running down over her hair and face. 'The transfer of nukes to the Korean theatre is consistent with what we already know about it. Macarthur was keeping nuclear equipped planes in the air over the Far East twenty-four hours a day – these were the days before nuclear submarines, and the ballistic missile arsenal was still small – so there were certainly plenty of "fat man" type bombs around.'

Jamie glanced at Danny, 'Please don't take this the wrong way, but is it possible that the Russians are involved?'

'My brother was not a traitor – don't think that for a moment. Whatever he did, it was for the right reasons. He loved his country.'

They sat in silence for a moment, while Holly made a rope of her hair and squeezed the water from it. 'If there's a nuke, then where is it? Surely they wouldn't have cut it up and put it in the pool as well.'

'No, it must be somewhere else.' Jamie stared for a moment, then cleared his throat. 'Either way that's about as far as we can go. We're not equipped to deal with something of this magnitude. We need to call in some help and get the hell out of here. It sounds like we have some visitors – some men parachuted into the area last night.'

'Who?'

'My guess is that they're paras or SAS, someone in Canberra keeping an eye on the situation. I can find out, when I get on the radio.' He paused. 'I need to report in.'

Danny's face turned ashen. 'Not yet, give me time to follow the trail up those pitons.'

Jamie raised both hands to his eyes and massaged the closed lids gently. 'I know what you're saying, and I understand what you've been through, but this is beyond our capabilities now, and you're too emotionally involved. Maybe I am too.' He pointed to the jagged piece of aluminium. 'The wreckage I just saw in the bottom of the pool constitutes new evidence, and I have to report it. We are way out of our depth. I'm going to climb up to the top of the gorge and use the radio.'

'Please, give us time to find out before you call your people in. They'll lock us out, both of us—' Danny's voice was heavy with significance.

'I'm sorry Danny. Whatever else I am, I'm a soldier first and foremost. I have a job to do and I won't turn my back on it.'

Hampered by the rain it took Ray and Jamie ten minutes to climb back up above the waterfall. The flow was still increasing, churning down in a maelstrom of white-tipped brown water into the pool. A steep climb took them to the summit, from which vantage point they could see squall lines of rain marching across the wilderness in squadrons.

Ray found a comfortable perch and sat fondling Yella's wet ears.

'So, more people are gonna come here?' he asked. 'Maybe the Colonel and all that mob?'

'I don't know Ray, but the remains of a USAF bomber are in that pool. Maybe there's a nuke hidden somewhere nearby. We have to call it in. Then we have to get back to the vehicles and hit the road so we can cross the creeks before they flood.'

Jamie scrambled up a boulder that had been cleaved by time and the weather into geometric perfection. The world was changing all around him, the truths he had grown up with were crumbling away. Yet new horizons had appeared in the distance

– new histories – new possibilities.

Standing, bare chest wet, covered in goose bumps, Jamie lifted the UHF handset, and pressed the transmit button.

'Green Base this is Green Leader, over.'

Jamie repeated the call several times before Mick's voice crackled through. 'Sarge, thank God you're back onto us … there's something going on.'

'Yeah, there's plenty going on. Listen. I want you to call the Colonel and tell him that we have now located the remnants of the aircraft. Now wait for it … I'm told that it was carrying a plutonium bomb – forty years old, but Christ alone knows where it is and how dangerous the fucking thing must be.'

'Yeah, listen Sarge, it's all over the news. This is becoming some kind of international incident. The Colonel wants to talk to you right now. You'd better get back here.'

'Not yet. Call him for me, tell him that what we need for a start is to get the civilians out. Then we need a SCUBA team, maybe a nuclear expert, and at least a platoon strength force to guard them. We have reports of HAHO parachutists coming down last night, but they haven't made contact and I don't even know for sure that they're ours. Also tell him also that the rain is pissing down and I dunno how long we've got before the pool is inaccessible.'

'Yeah okay, hold tight while I call them.'

Ten minutes elapsed before the handset crackled. 'Sarge, this is Mick, over.'

'Go ahead.'

'I've talked to the Colonel. He rogers all that, and says that he's getting personnel together and will airlift them in. Experts need to be flown up from Canberra, meaning a delay – maybe forty-eight hours. Orders are to secure the site. Brus, listen to this. According to the Colonel the Yanks are maybe going to stick their paws into this. There's that carrier still in the area – I've never heard the Colonel so rattled. If those parachutists are there you have to keep them out of the site, they're probably Americans.'

'Forty-eight hours, shit. But yeah, okay, Ray and I will babysit the pool until they get here. I'll climb back up here at 1300 so you can report in, sound fair?'

'Understood. Talk then.'

'This is our patch. No one, not even the fucking Yanks, can push us around here.'

# TWENTY-NINE

Danny Carter had been living on nerves for days, and now the bare edges of the wires were frizzling away. He knew that Jamie McKinnon's radio call would bring officialdom down on the area. He would not, he had decided, be diverted from his course. He knew deep in his gut that the smaller waterfall and its line of pitons was the key to the truth.

Holly and Glenn were sitting, talking in the shelter along the rock ledge. Tasha was hanging bright T-shirts and white underwear on a cord strung between two trees out of the rain, deep under the overhang. Jamie and Ray had climbed the gorge to use the radio.

No one noticed Danny shoulder his rucksack, and walk away, passing behind the curtain of falling water to the other side of the pool. He placed one hand, then his foot on the first piton, and eased his weight onto it. The feeling that he was following in Matt's footsteps manifested itself in his trembling limbs and nervous sweat. He looked back towards the camp.

Equal measures of fury and love simmered together in his heart. Love for the brother who filled his world. Fury at those who had taken the woman who was fated to be his – who had filled the empty spaces in his soul.

*They killed Anne, as well as Matt. They forced me to spend four years of my life in a prison cell. All to protect a secret that I am now close to finding. I will not wait for them to come.*

He started to climb, knees trembling, anxious to reach the top before Tasha, Glenn or Holly looked up and saw him. Once inside the chimney he felt surprisingly safe, with hard cool stone on three sides. Even so, he had to stop and rest several times, forcing himself not to look down, only out across the ethereal landscape of falling rain, stone and water.

*They ran and left her shattered body on the carpet of my home.*

At the cliff top the chimney merged into an undercut stream bank, and Danny stopped to rest against the curved stone faces. The feeling of being alone and away from the others was strangely liberating. This last part of the journey would be his alone, and that was fitting. A little boy in the body of a man, looking for the big brother he loved.

Danny dropped to his knees and drank earthy water from the brown rushing stream just before the banks became shallow and he found himself on the edge of the woodland that lined the gorge on both sides. It was an alien landscape to him – grey termite mounds as tall as his shoulder, austere trees, and earth only just starting to bloom green with new grass.

*I am a broken man, and there is only the truth left.*

He turned away from the cliff and faced the scrub. Getting lost in the heavy rain was a real possibility, but he didn't care. Matt had come this way. Forty years earlier his brother had climbed in this place. The pitons indicated that he had done so many times.

The main fuselage of the B50 must have crashed up here somewhere, above the gorge. Matt and the others had cut it to pieces and dropped those bits deep into the pool below the waterfall so they would be safe. It seemed like an enormous task, but they were intelligent men – engineers, pilots, technicians. The giant bombers had comprehensive tools on board. Such a thing was within their capabilities.

As for why, that was easy. These men were being hunted and they knew it.

Danny walked for perhaps half an hour, following the twisting bed of that stream. He came to an enormous but scarred ghost gum tree on the creek bank that grew at an angle closer to the horizontal than the vertical. The trunk had been mangled by some long ago impact. Nearby, in the grass lay the remains of a perished rubber wheel, far too big for any regular land vehicle.

Paperbark trees began to close in, blocking out the sunlight and leaving an eerie darkness. There were stone walls on each side, creating a deeply hidden valley. Danny passed springs that bubbled from cracks in the rock and gathered into narrow but deep pools. Bird calls. Flashes of colour from blooms he had not seen in other parts of the bush.

Again, he drank from the stream, in the shade of tall, leafy trees. The ground was moist from the spring, giving rise to cycads and rushes. He knew that Tasha would love this place. He would bring her and the others here later, he decided. Danny sat down on a cool rock in the shade, gathering strength, aware of the power in this place. Power that resonated out of the shadows and folds. Life and death, time without end.

The feeling that he was not alone came gradually, and when he looked up, he saw the old man, Ray's grandfather, standing beside one of the trees. He was wearing the same baggy old jeans and checked shirt with stains and tears in the fabric. His skin was so dark it took on an almost bluish sheen, his whiskers shockingly white apart from where they had yellowed around his lips from nicotine.

Danny narrowed his eyes, 'How long have you been watching me?'

The stub of a hand rolled cigarette danced on the old man's lips as he spoke, protected from the rain by a broad brimmed cattleman's hat. 'Ha, long time.'

'How did you know who I was when I met you back at the camp two days ago?'

'Cos you look like that man who been here long time back. I seen you first time and say to myself, them two bala might be brothers.'

'Who are you talking about?'

'Long time ago, that aeroplane come from the sky and crash

right about here.' The old man pointed into the scrub and his voice lowered into a conspiratorial whisper. 'I creep, creep, through the bush and watch. Your brother and three other bala, they work like ants, take the plane into bits. So that big-bala plane not here no more. It disappear jes' like I said.'

'Why didn't you tell us the plane was all cut up in the pool?'

The old man shrugged as if that were inconsequential. 'Gone, like I said.'

'What happened to my brother? All my life, I've been looking.'

'He just work alla time. Never stop. He an' the other white fellers live in a cave, like ants, and come out, work work all day. Cut up steel and put it away.'

'The plane was really here?'

'Yeah, that's right. Just over there. Big, broken down bird. I used to come here and watch sometimes. Every day they go back to where plane was and cut it up.'

'How did they transport all the material?'

'When that wet season come they float it down the little creek on raft. Over and over again until – all gone. That plane was like a bird – it had an egg.' The old man's eyes widened with wonderment at this word. 'Big iron egg, very heavy, and they drag that away, using logs like wheels – rollers underneath. They take that egg to the cave.' The old man shook his head. 'Clever buggers – your brother and his mates.'

'This cave. Is it far away?'

'No, close by.'

'Can you take me there?'

'Yeah, follow me. Not far.' The old man started to walk away. Despite his age, he moved faster than Danny, flowing over the contours of the land, so that the American had to work hard to keep up.

With the old man as a guide, Danny's eyes were truly opened, walking around the fringes of the stone ledges carved by millennia of wind and water. Smooth weathered waves of stone, jagged only where pieces had broken away and fallen.

They reached a grass clearing between two encircling arms of stone. On the ground, laid out in a neat row, were a series of sandstone slabs, irregularly shaped, but unmistakeably tomb-stones. Eight graves. Danny fell to his knees and traced the names, carved into the faces, filled with lichens and dark moulds.

The names were a roll call of Matt's aircrew. The names of men he had met on Saturday night beer parties, where they sung the unit song and spilled beer on the floorboards and pro-fessed their comradeship and love for their country. Singing the unit song, open throated, full bore so the walls rumbled.

*Men of the 43rd*
*half-man, half-bird.*
*Foes of freedom,*
*we'll smash asunder.*
*Down below they'll,*
*Hear our thunder.*

Danny went from one to the other, remembering. Connor, Johnson, McKenzie, Lord, Gray …

Matt was not there. He, at least, had been one of the men who dug these graves. Tears fell from Danny's eyes and onto the earth. The journey was consuming him, body and soul. He was filled with a power that was more than just earth, stone and sky.

As Ray's grandfather stood and started to lead him away, Danny knew that here, near the end of the journey, he was on a boat spiralling out of control down a wild river. He had no choice but to hold on and see where the journey might take him.

# THIRTY

Jamie was on his way back down to the pool when he saw Tasha hurrying to meet him, her brow creased into a frown. 'Have you seen Dad?' she asked.

'No, isn't he here somewhere?'

'If he was, I wouldn't be asking, would I?'

Jamie walked with her back to the overhangs alongside the cliff, where Holly was sorting out her gear, and Glenn whittling away at a lump of stinkwood with his pocketknife.

'You haven't seen Danny, by any chance?' Jamie asked.

Holly sat up, face reddening. 'Why? What's happened?'

'We don't know where he is,' Tasha said.

Glenn's knife blade continued to peel strips from the timber. It looked like he was trying to sculpt a face. 'I haven't seen Danny for at least an hour, and he didn't say a word about going anywhere. Has he taken anything with him?'

'His rucksack isn't here.'

'Why would he just wander off like that?'

Tasha folded his arms across her chest and her eyes bored into him, 'Maybe because someone has called in an army, and nuclear experts, and dad wants to discover things for himself. Maybe he's sick of governments, and armies, ruining his life.'

'Hang on a minute. This is not my fault, Tasha,' Jamie said.

'My responsibility is for the safety of everyone here, and if your father had been more forthcoming about the contents of that aircraft, I would have gone about this outing very differently.'

The young woman's face blazed with fury, and that anger made her look so much like her father Jamie almost did a double take. He hadn't seen her like this. 'Have you any idea what our family has been through? He's lost his wife. I lost my mother …'

Holly did something surprising. She stood up and took Jamie's hand in front of the others and squeezed it hard. It was a declaration. Real allies now. More than allies. 'Arguing about this isn't going to help find Danny. Let's start looking.'

With Tasha leading the way, they walked together out towards the pool, onto the rock platform in the rain.

'He wouldn't have gone swimming, would he?' Holly asked.

'No.' Tasha was adamant. 'You've seen him – he knows he can't swim and stays right near the edge.'

They wandered on, and Jamie called to Ray who was keeping a lookout above the waterfall. 'Hey Ray, come and give us a hand. Danny's missing.'

Ray glared at him, as if to remonstrate with Jamie for raising his voice, but he must have heard the worry in his voice because he started picking his way down the rocks in that long-legged smooth gait of his.

Jamie was scanning the area, hoping to see Danny sitting on a rock, or just wandering maybe. As his eyes swivelled downstream something caught his attention. It looked like a scrap of dark olive fabric, a scarcely detectable movement that might have been a branch in the breeze – except that there was no wind.

'What is it?' Tasha asked.

'I don't think we're alone.' Jamie was thinking quickly. They were out from the overhang. His SLR was fifty metres away. They were unarmed and exposed.

'Head back towards the campsite,' he said to the others. 'I'm right behind you.'

The instruction came too late. Two figures, both armed, appeared at the top of the waterfall, and more emerged from the path that led down to their camp. They moved quickly towards

Jamie's party, stepping from the undergrowth near the top of the cliff, cutting them off. First in line was an armed man in camouflage fatigues, then Wally with his SLR.

'What the hell are you doing back here?' Jamie spat. 'And who are these people?'

Wally just grinned insanely and twitched his trigger finger visibly. 'Just some friends of mine, McKinnon.'

The soldiers were Americans, Jamie could see that right off. They wore no badges or insignia, but they carried M16 rifles. Their headgear was identical to those Jamie had seen on Americans during the 'Kangaroo' joint exercises that had been going on for the previous decade or so.

Jamie was conscious that he was standing in a pair of yellow board shorts as more of them arrived, some coming down from above the waterfall, a smaller group from downstream. The operational brain of his was already counting men and weapons, picking out an older man dressed in fatigues as the ranking officer. He carried no rifle, just a sidearm buckled in a webbing belt around his waist.

'Just who the hell are you and by whose authority are you here?' Jamie demanded, but a set of fatigues and a pair of boots has an effect on a man – he stands taller. Now, shirtless, barefoot and unarmed, Jamie knew himself to be at a disadvantage.

'I'm not going to dick around here, son. My name is Major Elliott Temple and I'm looking for certain property that belongs to the United States Government.'

'This is Australian soil and you have no right—'

Jamie didn't see the nod that must have precipitated the attack, but Wally stepped forward and jabbed the rifle barrel deep into the muscles of Jamie's stomach, driving into his flesh like a blunt knife. Jamie doubled over, eyes wide with surprise and pain.

'I've been looking forward to doing that,' said Wally.

Even when confronted with weapons Jamie had doubted there would be a physical element to this incursion. He had thought it much more likely that the situation might become a minor stand-off, where they exchanged information and perhaps, after a few radio conversations with Canberra and Washington, he might have allowed the Americans to examine the floor of the pool.

Yella, meanwhile, had left his patch of dry dust right up against the cliff, out of the rain. He had occupied this niche for most of the previous twenty-four hours, but the arrival of the new group in the gorge piqued his interest. He crept towards one of the men, sniffing as he went.

Jamie glared at Wally. 'I never thought I'd see the day that a man of mine would turn.'

'I never turned, Sarge. I'd been working for a pittance for Mister Brad King the flash pilot for many years when this good man here made my acquaintance and offered me money to keep my eyes and ears open. He offered me even more to join up with you damn greenskins. Worst coupla months of my life.'

'I knew you were trouble, right from the start,' said Jamie. 'But it all makes sense, Danny reckoned that he knew you from somewhere. That was you who let down our tyres and knocked me out, wasn't it?'

Wally smiled. 'Of course it was. You were so easy to take out. You fell for my fat lazy bastard act, but Major Temple here flew me over to the States for a few little courses – unarmed combat was one of them. I haven't lost a fight at the Vic Hotel since.'

'Whatever you say, turning on your comrades is a dog act,' spat Jamie.

'I just told you. I was *never* on your side. I don't like any of you, black, white or ...' He pointed down at Yella who was creeping towards him. He kicked out at the animal and the dog snapped at his leg, Wally tried again, lashing out with his foot. The dog scampered off a few paces and stopped, growling.

Wally raised the SLR, aimed at the dog and fired. At close range the 7.62mm projectile opened up Yella's abdomen like a machete. The cliffs and hard stone compounded the sound of the gunshot, a deafening roar at close range.

Streaked with blood and leaking entrails into the wet rock, Yella tried to run on already dying legs, while Ray walked towards the stricken animal, blundering steps, mouth open with grief.

'You bastards,' Jamie heard his own voice boom across the cliffs, as if disconnected from his body. 'For the love of God, at least finish him.'

'Let him suffer,' Wally said. 'I hate that mongrel dog. Skinny-arsed prick of a thing.'

Yella was still trying to struggle out of a pool of his own guts as Ray gathered him up in his arms. Ray turned to look at Jamie, then back upstream to where Bolung had left his image on the stone walls. The look was heavy with meaning. It clearly said: I warned you that terrible things would happen.

Jamie's feeling of guilt was sudden and complete, but with it came a flood of anger so powerful it made him shake. 'You'll pay for that,' he promised, glaring at Wally.

Temple gave a short, sharp laugh, then. 'There's no point standing around talking. Where's Danny Carter?'

It was Tasha who answered, hands on hips, eyes blazing. 'He's gone,' she said. 'The further away from you the better.'

'I know who you are,' Temple said. 'The daughter, Natasha, isn't that right?'

'I know who you are too,' she hissed back. 'You killed my mother.'

'That's not technically correct, but it'll do, given the circumstances.'

The American leader's attention had been diverted from Ray, who picked up the bloody dog in his arms, and turned away, fat tears rolling down his cheeks, chest swelling with the force of each inward breath as he walked away downstream.

One of the armed men called out, 'He's walking away. Should I stop him?'

Wally shook his head. 'Nah. Ray's a typical blackfella. He'll just go walkabout for a week or two. Forget about him.'

Temple inclined his head. 'Let him go then. Concentrate on searching this shithole. In the water and out.' Then, to Wally. 'Get those people up out of the way and watch them, we've got work to do.'

'Orright, you heard him,' said Wally. 'Back up under the overhang.'

But when Jamie tried to head for the campsite the armed man shook his head. 'No way, not there where you've got weapons hidden away and all that. Further along.'

The dry area was not so wide here, and they were forced to spread out under the cliff, sitting on the sand. Wally took up position just out of the rain, standing, the SLR clamped under one elbow while he rolled a smoke.

Jamie was watching the Americans fan out around the pool. A couple went through the campsite, finding and unloading the two SLRs, throwing the bolts into the pool and rendering them useless before heaving them off into the bush.

Two others opened carry bags and removed masks, snorkels and fins.

At least they're prepared, Jamie thought wryly. He turned to Holly. 'Stay strong. This is temporary – a quick operation, and they can't afford to hurt us – they're our allies.'

She turned on him. 'If I need you to patronise me, I'll ask, okay? Same goes for the SITREP – I can work the basics out for myself.'

Jamie knew enough not to take umbrage at this outburst. He knew that people react differently to stress. 'I'm sorry,' he said. 'This is my fault. Ray said he saw parachutists coming in – I just would never have dreamed that they weren't ours.'

The fire in Holly's eyes subsided a little. 'Same here. There's going to be hell to pay for this, politically speaking.'

When Jamie looked to see how the others were faring, he saw that Glenn was holding Tasha's hand fiercely.

'Are you two alright?' Jamie asked. Glenn nodded back, but it was a dumb question, Jamie realised, the distress they were feeling was palpable.

Wally finished his cigarette, walked across and stubbed it out on the cliff face.

'I hear tobacco's expensive in prison,' Jamie said to him. 'You might have to cut down.'

Wally stepped back and smirked. 'I'm not going to any fucking gaol, mate. You see, I'm making a tidy pile of cash outta this lark. I'll be sitting back on a beach somewhere, drinking Crownies and laughing at you.'

'You're lucky,' Jamie said, 'that they outlawed the death penalty. They used to hang people for treason.'

Wally lifted the rifle. 'Shut the fuck up or I'll put a hole in you.'

'Major Temple wouldn't like it if you did.'

'Well I'd just tell him the gun went off accidental, won't I.'

Jamie caught Holly's eye. She shook her head, a signal for him to stop needling.

The warning was unnecessary, as a commotion started across the pool, when one of the searching Americans discovered the pitons leading up the cliff. Temple walked across and studied them carefully before sending one man up to investigate.

Jamie watched for a bit then said, 'Hey Wally, I'm freezing, brus. Can I get a shirt from my pack?'

Wally scoffed, 'And bring back a knife to stick between my ribs? No bloody fear. You stay like that while I can see what you're carrying.' He sniggered to himself and dropped his eyes to Jamie's crotch. 'And it ain't much, I can see that.'

The divers, meanwhile, had brought a number of aluminium plates from the pool, which they piled on the rocks. After a long discussion with Temple they towelled off and dressed in their fatigues. The scout came back from the cliff top and more talk followed. Gear was collected. It was clear they intended to start moving out.

Major Temple bustled around. He ran a tight outfit. Jamie had been trying to work out whether the American unit were Special Forces or Intelligence, and had decided on the latter. They were a mixed bag, all great with their weapons, but they were spooks not real soldiers. Finally, when the major walked towards his little band of captives Jamie got a good look at him, revising his age-estimate upwards to at least sixty, on the cusp of retirement age.

Temple squatted in front of him, took off his hat and wiped his eyes. 'You're Sergeant Jamie McKinnon?'

'You're telling the story.'

'As a fellow military man, I bear you no ill-will, but you've gotten yourself caught up in something far more important than any of us. When you are cognisant of what's at stake, you'll understand better why we have to take strong measures here today.'

'All I can say is that you better run fast and hard if you want to get out of this country before my regiment catches up with you.'

Jamie would never forget the sneer on Temple's face. The sheer stinking superiority complex. 'I know they're on the way. We intercepted your radio messages, but hell, do you really think we're afraid of a few bush boys in Land Rovers?'

A round of chuckles from the Yanks came next, and Jamie heard Crocodile Dundee mentioned a couple of times. They'd all seen the movie, of course.

Like a performer entertaining the crowd, Temple went on, 'Fifty minutes flight time from here is a nuclear-powered aircraft carrier called the USS *Carl Vinson*. That one ship can unleash more hell than your entire piss-ant country. Just bear that in mind.'

Jamie said nothing, as the AFOSI major stood again, turning his back on him, and calling two of the chucklers. 'Get up, all of you.'

Jamie stood up. 'Where are you taking us?'

'None of your business.'

'We've seen too much, haven't we?' Tasha was screaming out. 'You're going to kill us, aren't you?'

'Shut that woman up,' Temple ordered, and a hand clamped over Tasha's mouth, staying there until she was short of breath, and had to bend over for air. Glenn looked like he was going to explode, and started forward, but another man bent his arm behind his back and twisted until his face turned beetroot red.

Jamie was reminded what a well-practiced suite of dirty tricks can do to even a big, strong man like Glenn.

'Okay guys,' shouted Major Temple, 'we know that an Aussie contingent is on their way in, we need to move it. Like now.'

Responding to the prods and browbeating of the guards, Glenn and Tasha started moving.

Holly shouted. 'You are making a big mistake.'

'We know who you are too, Miss ASIO. Shut up, for God's sake, or we'll gag you. Get moving, now!' He shoved her in the back, and she staggered, barely keeping her feet.

Jamie stopped still. 'I need a shirt, and boots. If we're out after dark, I'll freeze.'

The American major nodded at Wally. 'Take him to get a shirt.'

A smirk. 'Let the bastard freeze.'

The major's eyes hardened. 'I said take him to get a shirt but watch him like a hawk.'

'Come on then,' Wally said, waving the barrel of his rifle. 'You've got ten seconds.'

Jamie walked in front, conscious of the feeling of having a firearm trained on his back. It wasn't a pleasant sensation as he picked his way along the sand between patches of turkey bush and rocks.

Finally, he came to the place where his pack hung from the stub of a wattle branch under the overhang. His boots were there also, tied by the laces. Jamie reached up for the pack.

'No way,' Wally said. 'Fuck knows what you've got in there. I'll find your shirt for you; you just get your boots on. Temple's in a hurry, and he don't like waiting at the best of times.'

Jamie watched while Wally cradled the rifle in one hand and lifted down the 'Nam pack with the other. Sitting in on a rock ledge he fumbled with the buckles.

Jamie untied the laces that joined his boots. 'Any dry socks in there, brus?'

Wally turned and snarled at him. 'Fuck the socks. Just put your boots on. I was told to let you get a shirt and boots. That's all.'

Shrugging his shoulders Jamie leaned down and slipped on first one boot then the other. Adjacent to his right foot was a stone about the size of his right hand. He made a show of tightening and tying his laces.

'Where the hell is this freaking shirt?' Wally said, obviously frustrated.

'Bottom pouch, brus.'

Jamie deliberately kept his voice friendly while the other man struggled with the buckles one-handed. He knew that time was short, at any moment Temple, now out of sight, might send a man over to check.

Then, red faced with impatience Wally made a fatal mistake. He laid the rifle down on the rock ledge so he could use both hands to unfasten the pack. Jamie had finished tying his laces but was still bent over, fiddling with the right one. He recognised the moment when Wally found the shirt and was absorbed in dragging it out.

Jamie seized the rock in his right hand. In the same moment he lurched forward and swung the stone. Wally saw it coming, eyes wide, and raised the hand that held the shirt as if to ward off the blow. It was coming too fast, however, and the rock struck him hard in the side of the head.

Wally crumpled to the ground without a sound. Jamie worked fast, taking the shirt from the other man's unconscious hands and buttoning it on. Then he slipped his pack over his shoulders and grabbed the SLR from the rock platform.

Still screened from the others Jamie started to run, through the vines and upwards on that path around the waterfall to the higher ground. He was half-way up when he heard shouting and gunshots.

At the top he turned one last time to see two of the Americans following, then headed up out of the watercourse and into the scrub.

# THIRTY-ONE

YOU KNOW IT WELL.YOU LIVED IN THAT LAND. YOU
LEARNED OF ITS HARSH GIFTS. AND EVEN NOW, FAR
AWAY, YOU REMEMBER WHAT IT WAS LIKE.

YOU WAKE IN THE DARKNESS. THIS IS YOUR PEN-
ANCE, THESE HOURS OF NOTHING.

LYING RIGID YOUR HANDS CURL AS IF THEY HOLD
THE CONTROLS STILL. THAT MACHINE YOU LOVED HAD
FOUR ENGINES. YOU TRY TO RECAPTURE THE FEEL-
ING OF POWER - BALANCING SIXTY TONNES OF GROSS
WEIGHT HIGH ABOVE THE GROUND.

IN JANUARY 1949, YOU PICK UP YOUR NEW COMMAND
- A BRAND NEW B50A SUPERFORTRESS FROM THE BOE-
ING FACTORY IN WICHITA. THE GUYS THERE PAINT
THE BROWN BEAR YOU WANT JUST AFT OF THE COCK-
PIT BUBBLE. THEY SLAP YOUR BACK AND CLAP AS
YOU MOUNT THE COCKPIT FOR THE FIRST TIME.

YOUR ORDERS ARE TO FLY THE B50 TO DAVIS-MON-
THAN IN ARIZONA, WHERE YOU WILL BE BASED, BUT
FIRST A THREE DAY DIVERSION TO GRIFFISS, UP-

STATE NEW YORK, WHERE THE LATEST RADAR SYSTEMS WILL BE FITTED.

THE WINDS ARE STRONG, BLOWING FROM THE SOUTH EAST AND YOU LET THE WINGS WAGGLE MARGIN-ALLY AS YOU GLIDE THE BOMBER IN, FEELING YOUR WAY WITH THE LANDING GEAR, UNTIL FINALLY THEY TOUCH WITH A GENTLE HISS FOLLOWED BY A COUPLE OF APPRECIATIVE COMMENTS FROM THE CREW.

YOU ARE PROUD OF THE WAY YOU LAND THE PLANE. YOUR SKILL IS ONE OF THE REASONS YOU HAVE JUST BECOME THE YOUNGEST CAPTAIN OF A FOUR-ENGINED BOMBER IN THE UNITED STATES AIR FORCE.

IN THOSE DAYS OF DOWN TIME, YOU AND TWO OTH-ERS TAKE THE MIDNIGHT TRAIN TO NEW YORK CITY, SWIGGING WHISKEY FROM HIP FLASKS, BEGINNING A HEADLONG TOUR OF THE CITY'S ATTRACTIONS, SMART IN YOUR UNIFORMS, FLIRTING WITH WIVES AND OF-FICE GIRLS ON LUNCH BREAKS.

AT THE TOP OF THE EMPIRE STATE BUILDING, YOU AND SAM SNOW POSE FOR PHOTOS AGAINST THE BACK-DROP OF NEW YORK. YOU ARE SO SIMILAR, SAME HEIGHT AND BOTH SO BLUE-EYED HANDSOME IN YOUR UNIFORMS THAT STRANGERS LOVE TO TAKE PHOTOS OF YOU. YET YOU WISH DANNY COULD BE WITH YOU LIKE YOU ALWAYS DO WHEN SOMETHING GOOD HAPPENS AND YOU CAN'T BEAR FOR HIM TO MISS OUT.

BY LATE AFTERNOON YOU'RE DOWNING BEER IN MID-TOWN MANHATTAN. BY NINE YOU EAT AT THE FAMOUS CARNEGIE DELI ON 7TH STREET. BY ELEVEN YOU'VE MET THREE SECRETARIAL WORKERS FROM A POOL IN THE CITY. YOU SIT TOGETHER AT A WINE BAR, DRINKING CALIFORNIAN SHIRAZ THAT YOU PRIVATE-LY HATE. EVAN GRAY LEAVES WITH THE BLONDE. SAM

FALLS ASLEEP. THE OTHER TWO WOMEN LEAVE, AND YOU'RE DETERMINED TO FINISH YOUR GLASS.

TWO WELL-DRESSED MEN WALK INTO THE BAR, TAKING THE ADJACENT BOOTH. ONE OF THE ACCENTS YOU RECOGNISE AS AUSTRALIAN, THE OTHER SOUTHERN AMERICAN. WHEN THE WAITER COMES, THEY FUSS OVER THE CHOICE OF WINE. THE TWO MEN ARE FROM ANOTHER WORLD TO YOU, OBVIOUS FROM THE SOPHISTICATED VOCABULARY THEY USE, AND THE CUT OF THEIR SUITS.

'WHEN I WAS IN LONDON—' ONE OF THEM SAYS.

'FROM WHAT THE SECRETARY GENERAL WAS SAYING YESTERDAY—'

THE TWO MEN, IT SEEMS, WORK FOR THE UNITED NATIONS.

WHEN THE BOTTLE IS HALF EMPTY, THEY TALK ABOUT AMERICAN POVERTY. HOW A TINY PERCENTAGE OF THE POPULATION CONTROLS THE WEALTH. HOW BANKS AND INDUSTRIALISTS CONSPIRE TO KEEP THE WORKING-CLASS POOR.

YOU HAD LIVED IN A POORHOUSE. YOU HAD LISTENED TO THE STORIES. YOU FELT SOMETHING FILLING INSIDE YOUR HEART AS THEY TALKED.

'YOU'RE RIGHT,' YOU BURST OUT.

THEY STARE AT YOU AS IF YOU ARE AN ALIEN. PART AFFRONTED THAT YOU HAVE BEEN LISTENING IN, PART AMUSED.

'GO ON, YOUNG FELLOW,' ONE OF THEM SAYS.

YOU TRY TO GET THE WORDS OUT. 'I MEAN, I'M SORRY FOR LISTENING IN BUT—' YOU SILENTLY CURSE THE ALCOHOL IN YOUR SYSTEM, TRIPPING YOUR TONGUE AND SLOWING YOUR MIND. 'I KINDA GREW UP IN A

POORHOUSE, SO I KNOW ABOUT THIS.'

THE AUSTRALIAN CALLS YOU OVER. 'COME HERE AND SIT WITH US. IT LOOKS LIKE YOUR FRIEND WILL BE FINE THERE BY HIMSELF.'

YOU BRING YOUR GLASS. 'DON'T JUDGE SAM TOO HARSHLY, YOU GUYS. HE'S MY BUDDY – AND WE WERE ON A TRAIN ALL LAST NIGHT AND KINDA DRINKING A BIT.'

'YOU'RE YOUNG, THAT'S UNDERSTANDABLE. MY NAME IS DR IAN MILNER, AND THIS IS MY FRIEND ERIC T. PRICE.'

'YOU'RE AN AUSSIE?' YOU ASK.

'THAT'S CORRECT. I'M HERE AS A REPRESENTATIVE OF MY GOVERNMENT.'

'I'M A TEXAN,' ERIC SAYS, AND TO YOU THAT'S ALMOST AS INTERESTING AND EXOTIC AS BEING AUS-TRALIAN.

'ANYWAY,' MILNER SAYS, 'I'M INTERESTED IN WHAT YOU HAVE TO SAY ABOUT AMERICAN SOCIETY AS YOU EXPERIENCED IT. YOU LIVED IN A POORHOUSE?'

'THAT'S CORRECT.'

'TELL US ABOUT IT.'

YOU START TALKING, AND AN HOUR TICKS BY. YOU KNOW ALL THE STORIES BY HEART – STOREKEEPERS ON WHOM THE BANKS HAD FORECLOSED, FARMERS WHO LOST THEIR LAND. MANY HAD BEEN RIPPED OFF BY THE SYSTEM IN THE WORST POSSIBLE MANNER, SOME OF THEM REPEATEDLY. THE OTHER MEN DO NOT IN-TERRUPT, EXCEPT FOR AN OCCASIONAL CLARIFICA-TION.

WHEN YOU FINISH ERIC CLAPS SOFTLY. 'THANK YOU. FEW PEOPLE COULD HAVE STATED THE PLIGHT OF THE

AMERICAN UNDERCLASS SO SUCCINCTLY.'

DR MILNER JOINS IN. 'DO YOU THINK WE REQUIRE ANOTHER BOTTLE, ERIC? NO MORE FOR YOU? NO PROBLEM, I HAVE HALF A GLASS AND I WILL DRIP-FEED MYSELF ON THAT. NOW MATTHEW, MY FRIEND ERIC AND I BELIEVE THAT THE KIND OF PEOPLE YOU ARE TALKING ABOUT ARE THE VICTIMS OF AN UNFAIR AND UNJUST SYSTEM THAT REWARDS THE RICH AND POWERFUL AND PUNISHES THE WORKER. I TAKE IT THAT YOU'RE A PILOT?'

YOU TELL THEM THAT YOU FLY A HEAVY BOMBER, A B50 SUPERFORTRESS AND THAT SOON YOU WILL BE GOING TO KOREA.

DR MILNER LOOKS AT YOU WITH VERY WISE EYES. 'IF EVER YOU NEED A REFUGE. IF EVER YOU NEED TO RUN, THE TOP END OF AUSTRALIA IS RIDDLED WITH WORLD WAR TWO AIRSTRIPS MADE FOR B29S. GO THERE AND YOU WILL BE SAFE.'

# THIRTY-TWO

The old man said nothing as he led Danny into a place where towers of stone rose on all sides like medieval castles, turrets rearing high and trees waving in the breeze. Somewhere in the distance a crow cawed, but all Danny could hear was the breath in his lungs, and flies buzzing around his face in ceaseless clouds.

Years in the building and property development game had taught Danny that places that have been lived in feel different. Now, Danny could sense past lives as he approached a deep chasm in the stone face, with the old man leading the way. He could feel them in the air itself. As if snatches of human spirits stay in the landscapes they inhabit.

He stepped into a dark entrance in the stone. A smell of bats invaded his senses, including his skin, like a sticky coating he couldn't remove. The floor of the cavern alternated between hard stone and loose sand.

The old man led the way inside. Danny stopped dead. Every nerve came alive, taut as a guitar string. He did not have to be told that Matt had been in this place. He could almost hear the notes of his harmonica echo. Camptown Races and Home on the Range, played slow and mournful. Danny heard it as if he were again four years old on the poorhouse steps, the same songs

Matt had played after they buried their mother, surrounded by a ragtag group of churchgoers, filled with pity at the lonely boys, but lacking the means to assist them.

The cavern was vast inside compared to the narrow entrance, with light emanating from an opening somewhere up high on the walls. The stone itself varied in colour from sand to bloody red to black where soot from hearth fires had darkened the ceiling.

Around a central fireplace of hearthstones and an iron tripod were the remnants of iron aircraft seats. Near one wall was a clotted mess of paper that must have once been the pages of a magazine. A ruined comic book sat on a stone that had been rolled up to serve as a table.

Other 'furniture' had been fashioned from corroded metal. Shelves from bent aluminium. Glass bottles with the remains of tallow and wicks sat here and there – makeshift lanterns – along with animal bones.

Danny looked up to see the old man motioning to him with his hands, indicating a side passage off the main cavern.

'You want to see the egg, brus? In here.'

Danny could almost feel Matt's breath on his shoulders as they walked down a narrow chasm to a smaller chamber. The object that dominated that area was as long as a small car and about half the width – bulbous in shape, if not quite as egg-like as the old man had made him believe. It had been stripped of its fins and some of the casing. Even so, it was instantly recognisable to Danny, almost indistinguishable from the "Fat Man" plutonium bomb that had vaporised Nagasaki in 1945, yet far more powerful.

The two and a half tonnes of TNT that once acted as a precursor was stacked on a platform nearby, with only the mass of electrics and physical components still inside. On a smaller platform sat an aluminium box that contained what could only be the removable core.

This is what Matt died for, Danny breathed. And he understood at that moment what his brother had done all those years ago.

# THIRTY-THREE

Hurrying downstream, Jamie was thankful for the boots on his feet and the shirt that gave him warmth, though he still wore the yellow board shorts he had dived the pool in. At first, he could hear the Americans following and he threaded his way expertly through the scrub to lose them. In the rain they had little chance of tracking him, even if they had the skills, and he soon left them behind.

Taking a wide arc around the waterfall, he passed the pool at a distance of some eight hundred metres before meeting the creek again downstream. Once there he scoured the banks, walking until he saw a sign, just two pebbles piled on one another. Jamie recognised the signal; it was one he and Ray had used before. It had been placed parallel to a side gully emptying brown water into the stream, and Jamie headed towards it without hesitation.

He did not look for tracks, Ray would have walked through the churning brown water to hide his sign. Jamie did the same, heedless of his boots filling with water as he walked upstream in the water, the country altering into some heavier woodland, a thick lancewood scrub with a few milkwood trees near the gully itself. It was at the relatively dry base of one of these trees that he found Ray.

'Hey Jamie, for fuck's sake brus. You took your time?' Ray

ran his eyes up Jamie from head to toe. 'The Colonel would be pissed off if he seen you running around in yer yellow board shorts brus.'

Ray had taken off his shirt and fashioned it into a sling. Inside was the bloodied body of his dog.

'Is Yella … dead?' asked Jamie.

'Yeah, he's dead brus; poor bugger.'

'Then we need to lay him to rest now and go get Mick and Nico. Fuck knows where Wally has gone.'

'We've got no shovel. I'll carry him until we get there, then bury him proper way.'

'I'm sorry mate,' said Jamie.

'Yeah, me too.'


It was late afternoon when they reached base camp, and Mick's voice was a pleasant boom as Ray and Jamie approached. 'Thank Christ you two are okay.'

Jamie linked hands with Mick, then clasped thumbs in the local handshake before dropping into a chair and accepting the full canvas water canteen that had been hanging from the bull-bar of the nearest of the two immaculate RFSVs. The camp had been strung with camouflage netting, with green tarps hanging above the vehicles to keep off the rain.

Nico was wide-eyed at the sight of Jamie in board shorts, shirt, and boots. And Ray all bloodied with the dead dog cradled on his chest. 'Fuck, what's happened?'

'A lot. First thing I need to do is get on that radio and update Darwin – and can someone help Ray bury poor Yella.'

'What happened to him?'

'Wally shot the poor little bugger. He's working with the Yanks. Now stop staring and let's go. Bury the dog and start kitting up, we've got a job to do.'

Jamie opened the front door of the LandCruiser and tuned the vehicle's AM radio to the only available station, ABC National, turning it up so the men outside could hear. Then, delving in his kitbag he found a towel and dry fatigues.

*The United States has been forced to defend what has been called an 'undisclosed incident' during the Korean War. President George HW Bush, addressing congress this morning, stated unequivocally that reports of the finding of at least part of a downed delivery aircraft in Australia's Northern Territory are fabrications.*

*In local developments the Australian Minister of Defence has denied an eminent Australian physicist's claim that the Lucas Heights reactor was originally built in order to supply enriched uranium for a home-grown nuclear program, and that several prime ministers, including Menzies and the ill-fated Harold Holt, had secret programs to secure nuclear weapons for our nation.*

Having towelled himself dry and dressing quickly, enjoying the feel of dry cotton against his skin, Jamie pulled on socks and his spare boots. Ready now, he switched off the AM radio and lifted the VHF mike. The transmission was answered by a warrant officer on duty in the barracks comms room. The colonel was out in the loading area getting things ready.

'You reckon it's important enough to go grab him, Sergeant?'

'Yeah, I reckon.'

When the Colonel came on the line, he was breathing hard. 'What's going on, Jamie?'

'Shit's coming down that you will not believe in a million years.'

'I know that, and we're getting ready now. Have you heard the news?'

'Yeah, but it's worse even than you think.'

Lineham listened in silence. Then, 'Arnhem Troop has every available man on the way by road from Nhulunbuy. Three Hueys are en route to the barracks now, and they'll load up and be down there ASAP. I'm coming personally. This is important; do not let the American party leave the area.'

Jamie put the mike back on the hook and briefed Mick and Nico while they drank tea and geared up. 'This is huge,' he said. 'It might even be the end of the ANZUS alliance if things get any further out of hand.'

'Who cares?' Mick said. 'We saved the Yanks' arses in World War Two, and we don't need them now.'

Jamie shook his head, 'I love you Mick, but a few thousand

historians might not agree with what you just said.'

'Especially the American ones,' Nico said. 'But come on, let's get moving.'

Jamie had never seen the young Greek so energised. The prospect of real action had put a glint in his eyes.

'You feeling alright now Sarge?' Ray asked.

Jamie nodded. Three cups of tea and copious slugs of water had him fully hydrated, at least. The desire to find Holly and stop an injustice did the rest. Meantime, the radio droned on.

*The President of the United States has strongly denied reports that an attempt was made to deliver a nuclear weapon on a North Korean city during the 1950-53 war. A spokesperson for the North Korean government has expressed deep concern that such a mission, aborted or not, may have taken place. He stated that in view of the fact that the Korean War has not, technically, ended, his country would find America's stance on their own nuclear program as hypocritical, and provocative, especially given that the peace accord was finally signed in Kaesong, the apparent target of the nuclear strike, making an attempt to destroy it highly symbolic.*

*Reports are that Kim Il-Sung has ordered the movement of five divisions of troops to sites alongside the border with South Korea and ordered his country onto a war footing. He has also halted all talks aimed at developing a shared industrial park at Kaesong.*

Jamie stopped dead, listening. It made sense, of course. Perhaps the only thing that made sense.

The newsreader crossed to the voice of an Australian academic from the National University in Canberra, while the four men pulled on waterproof ponchos over their fatigues.

*Three dead men, Macarthur, Eisenhower, and Truman are the only ones who know how close the United States went to us-ing nuclear weapons in Korea. The historical record leads us to suspect that they went very close indeed.*

Ray shovelled the last few spade loads of dirt over Yella's grave and changed into dry clothes, loaded a spare rifle and stood ready near the vehicles. He jabbed a finger towards the radio. 'That's history, they're talking about Sarge. You and me, and Mick and Nico, we have to worry about right now.'

'Yes, you're right. Time to concentrate. You up for this, boys?'

'Shit yeah,' said Nico, and the others nodded.

'Right,' Jamie said, 'we form a foot patrol and we go in. Right now. Live ammunition. This is for real.'

# THIRTY-FOUR

As it grew dark outside Danny sat near the fire that Ray's grandfather had lit in the cavern and closed his eyes. At least it was dry in that ancient space while the rain hammered down outside. Nodding off, head lolling to one side, he dreamed that he was back in their backyard in Tucson. Matt was pitching the ball, firing it hard with his strong right arm, the paling fence as a backdrop. Danny dreamed of swinging the bat, the ball glancing off the top edge and spinning high, both of them watching it fall against the Arizona sky, then landing neatly into Matt's glove.

'Gotcha,' he said.

It was as if Danny could feel Matt's hand warm on his shoulder, the healthy sweat and cologne smell of him. 'Let's go downtown and grab a burger. They'll send a car for me about four, and I've got packing to do.'

'I don't want you to go.'

Matt kneeling, eyes dark with sadness. 'I don't want to go either, sorry buddy.'

'You'll be back, though. Promise me.'

'Of course. I promise.'

The sky darkened, and Danny's next vision was of an aircraft droning on over storm clouds dappled with moonlight. A dark iron object filled the bomb bay, finned at one end and bulbous at the other, spewed out by an evolutionary process that began with a stone shaped into a knife. A symbol not so much of warfare, but of a race intent on self-destruction.

The thought woke Danny momentarily, and he opened his eyes to see the old man sitting cross legged on the other side of the blaze. He was far from relaxed, rigidly upright, head stockstill. The air itself was pregnant with anticipation. That thing in the side passage was too powerful a presence.

A lifetime of being harried had given Danny a sense of how close they were at any given time. His senses were in overdrive, screaming at him to run or hide, yet he knew that there was no point in doing either. Not now.

He closed his eyes, forcing himself to relax and sleep again. All the years of looking, and now, in this silent special place he had found a different kind of memory.

# THIRTY-FIVE

The hotel suite was lit by the street lights on Commonwealth Avenue, glowing through the white net curtains. The balcony door was ajar, and the curtains moved with it.

The honourable member for Wills, Robert James Lee Hawke, Prime Minister of Australia and her territories, woke to a light tap on the door. The bedside clock said just after five am. Far too early for him to be disturbed. Wondering if the knock was a mistake, he started composing an angry riposte. Only two men knew where he was, and they knew better than to tap on his door at this time of the morning.

Still in his pyjamas he slipped out of bed and opened the door as far as the security chain would allow. The face of his principal private secretary, Dennis Richardson, appeared in the dim corridor lights.

'What's going on Dennis? It's still bloody dark in case you haven't noticed.'

'I'm so sorry sir ... there's a situation. The US Secretary of State has arrived in the country, he's at the American embassy right now with their Ambassador, and he wants an audience with you ASAP.'

'Holy shit, that's just what I need.' Hawke did not have to be told that this was a serious matter, James Alexander Baker did not fly into countries in the dead of night without good reason. 'Give me five minutes.'

'Of course.'

Hawke closed the door and went to the shower, came back out and dressed in a crisp blue shirt straight from the wrapper, tie and jacket.

He leaned down and kissed the sleeping woman on the cheek.

'Something's come up Blanche, I have to go.'

She sat up suddenly. 'Will you be back for breakfast?'

'No, sorry love.'

They both enjoyed the leisurely breakfasts here. It was a secret pleasure.

'I'm disappointed too, love. Go back to sleep and I'll call you when I can.'


Rather than heading for the main entrance of the grand new Parliament House, the white Holden Statesman rolled silently into the PM's private courtyard adjacent to his office in the Ministerial Wing, on the ground floor of the building.

Hawke's mind was busy as Dennis ushered him towards the private access door. He could think of only two reasons for an unheralded visit from the Secretary. One was Iraq, of course. Yet the deadline for the expiry of UN Security Council Resolution 678 – demanding that Saddam Hussein pull his troops out of Kuwait – was still a couple of weeks away. Hawke had already promised an Australian involvement in the international force – indeed two frigates and a supply ship were already enforcing sanctions in the Persian Gulf.

The only other possibility was this antique USAF bomber situation up north. The international media had latched onto the story and were trotting out conspiracy theories so fast it was hard to keep up. Baker's arrival had to be related to that. It was the only thing that made sense.

As Hawke entered the meeting room adjoining his office the door opened and he was joined by two more staffers, then Robert Ray, the Defence Minister. All were quiet and watchful from the early wake-up.

Even as staff came and went, preparing for the meeting, there were other things on Hawke's mind, and he dealt with attempts at conversation with monosyllable replies. Never far from his thoughts was that treacherous bastard Paul Keating going public with his leadership ambitions at the Press Club's Christmas address. Also, at the edge of his conscious thought was regret at leaving Blanche, when he could have curled up with her for another few hours.

One of the staffers opened the door to his office and switched on the light. It smelled of waxy polish and new paint. The room was tastefully furnished with solid timber furniture, and the walls displayed some of the most famous artworks in the country – a Brett Whitely, a Ken Done and a Tom Roberts – all originals. Australian Prime Ministers are permitted to take their pick from the National Gallery and Hawke had enlisted Blanche's help to make his choice for the new office.

Hawke settled himself at the desk and arranged himself with writing paper, pens, while a young woman in catering whites carried in bottled water, glasses, and a plate of packaged sandwiches.

'Piss that off will you,' Hawke ordered, 'and bring us a pot of coffee. Nice and strong. Mr Baker likes his black, and the Ambassador white with one – cubes if you can rustle one up. There's a good lass.'

Hawke had time to finish one cup and pour the next before Dennis ushered in the Secretary of State, with the ambassador, Melvin F. Sembler following close behind. Hawke rose and shook first one hand and then another. 'Good to see you again, James. Mel, early start today?'

Hawke knew the ambassador well, of course, he had been around for a couple of years, and they met at one function or another once or twice a month.

Even so, throughout the introductions, Hawke had hardly taken his eyes off James Baker. Power has a smell and a sound. It was evident in his walk, the suit, the carefully slicked back hair and the ferociously alert eyes. He was one of the administration's most experienced operators – one of the most powerful men in the world.

The two men were not so crass as to get straight down to business, but sat down, chatting over the coffee.

'How's your wife? Hazel isn't it?' Baker asked.

'Uh, yeah she's very well. Good as gold.'

'The kids?'

Hawke inclined his head; they were all grown up and living their own lives now. None of James A Baker's business, really. They moved on to small talk on Iraq for a while before Hawke looked at his watch pointedly. The gesture clearly meant – you got me here at a crazy hour of the morning, now what's it all about?

The Secretary of State cleared his throat. 'For more than a century the relationship between our two countries has been one of the highest order. We have fought two world wars, along with Vietnam and Korea together. Yet it seems that we have a situation that delves into the heart of the trusted relationship between our nations.'

Hawke cleared his throat, he had just the faintest taste of acid in the back of his throat and wished he had sent Dennis out for some Quick-Eze. 'I have no idea what you're talking about. Can we back up a little?'

'I won't insult you by going over the basics – I'm sure you are well aware that the wreck of one of our Superfortresses has been located in the north of your country. News media have been speculating about the possibility of a nuclear cargo and an attempt to drop it on Kaesong. This is extremely counterproductive, as now we have North Korea on full alert. Your troops are accompanying three of our nationals towards the site – without any consultation I might add.'

The tingle of bile in Hawke's throat now felt like a flood. 'Well, uh, I'd like to thank you for bringing this to our attention and must hasten to reassure you that the Commonwealth of Australia regards the United States as our most important friend in the international community.'

There was no answering nod from the Secretary of State, no

warmth in his eye. The disaster was certain, his expression said, it was only trying to limit the extent of it.

Baker pushed his glasses off his nose and rubbed the spot where they sat. 'We've had no choice but to take steps to recover our property. We have a team of men at the site. They are armed and authorised to take any action necessary to return our plane and anything that might have been on it.'

Hawke slowly nodded. He was a good, instinctive, politician. He knew when to roll over, when to shed a tear when the electorate wanted it. But he also knew that sometimes, in politics and life, big balls are required. 'You've got sixty seconds,' he said, 'to explain what you just said about America having a team of men within our borders that I don't know about.'

# THIRTY-SIX

When a soft early morning light filtered through the entrance to the cavern, Danny opened his eyes to see the old man stand up and melt away through some hidden exit in the crannies and nooks at the rear.

The armed Americans came in silently. One moment they weren't there, the next they slipped in like shadows, flashlights glowing, rifles at their shoulders, sighting down their weapons as if they were extensions of their bodies. Two covered Danny until he could see directly into the wrong end of the scopes, the lenses throwing strange purple hues in the firelight.

One carried a Geiger counter, and it hissed with white noise as it neared the passage. 'It's here, Major. It has to be.'

Temple walked in like a general taking possession of a city, head tilting while his eyes moved from makeshift furniture to walls. When he had finished his exploration, he approached Danny almost casually. 'You found this place first, I guess that's one to you.'

'I knew you were coming. I could smell the stench of you.'

Men were spreading out through the cavern and filing into the side passage that led to the weapon's resting place.

'Hey, Major, you'd better get in here.'

Temple followed the others into the narrow passage, then

came back moments later, bustling orders at a signaller. 'Have you got an antenna raised for that outside yet?'

'Yes sir.'

'Then raise me the *Carl Vinson*.'

When the signaller was ready, he handed over the mike to Major Temple, who spoke loudly into it. 'CVN70 Gold Eagle this is Cub Leader we need chopper extraction for us and our cargo. I repeat, chopper extraction required ASAP. Our location is one-four-point-one-zero-four-niner-eight, one-three-four-point-eight-three-eight-zero-nine.'

'Sir,' the radio crackled back. 'I need to confirm that you are ordering us to enter Australian airspace in force.'

'Precisely. Now get those fly boys in the air – unless you want to be responsible for a nuclear weapon falling into the hands of a foreign power.'

'They're our allies, sir.'

'I've been around a lot longer than you have, son. They're our allies today, who knows if they will be tomorrow.'

When the call was over Temple came over to Danny, unscrewed an aluminium water canteen and said, 'You understand that I can't let you live, don't you?'

'What's a few more deaths? You have enough blood on your hands already.'

'You want me to tell you how your brother died?'

Danny wanted to know, wanted closure, yet the truth would be final. He knew it would hurt. He inclined his head, 'Yes, you son-of-a-bitch. I want to know.'

Temple grinned. 'We found him and the others, in Darwin, in the late fifties. Him and two other survivors. They were living in a boarding house under false names. An infernal place. We watched them for a while, found out what we could. One of them – Sam Snow, as you already know, had head injuries from the crash and couldn't function, but the other two were working jobs, trying to get money together for passage back home.

'I poured gasoline on that building. I knew how fast it would burn. I heard your brother scream, Danny. I did it myself. Some things you can't ask junior operatives to do.' Temple paused to take a long drink from a water canteen. 'The local fire brigade managed to save Sam Snow's life. Of course, his head injuries from the crash meant he could tell the world nothing. We tried to get him to talk, but there was nothing upstairs. Enlisted the best shrinks in the United States to work on him – we were looking for the crash site as hard as you were. Our bad luck that he couldn't tell us, but your brother was dead, shame you won't live to visit his grave. It's still there, in Darwin. Gardens Road Cemetery, under the name he was using – McKinnon I think it was.'

Danny gasped for air. The scene in the cavern was becoming surreal. Two men in protective gear produced a thin lead-infused sheet that would make the nuclear weapon safer to handle. Others were dragging the huge casing and its contents into the main passage, one tough metre at a time. Shirts off and muscled backs and arms slick with sweat, they manhandled it towards the cavern entrance.

'You murdered them all – my brother, the others, and a bunch of innocent people who happened to be living there?'

Temple's jaw clenched tight. 'It was necessary. I'll be judged in heaven.'

Danny's rage, contained for so many years, was building like explosives in an iron vessel. Yet now was not the time to release that fury. In a voice shaking with contained emotion he whispered, 'No you won't. You'll be judged in hell, damn you.'

Temple turned and pointed at Danny. 'Get him outside with the others.'

One of the soldiers pulled Danny to his feet, then pushed him out through the entrance and into the rain, across a clearing to where a tarp had been crudely strung between three saplings. Tasha, Glenn and Holly were sitting in a group, and Wally stood over them, menacing them with the rifle, his bandaged head looking very sore indeed. A flashlight wedged in the juncture of tree trunk and branch lit the area.

The soldier shoved Danny in with the others. Tasha moved close to him and drew an arm around her shoulders. Her face was scratched and filthy, her skin white with fear and pain. 'Thank God you're alright.'

Danny stared into her eyes, unable to hold her close like he wanted to. 'I'm okay.'

Wally was standing, smoking at the far edge of the tarp, watching the Americans drag out the massive casing.

Danny was also watching, rage building in his heart at that thing – that evil thing in a casing of steel. Built by men who misguidedly believed that it could make world a better place.

Ray, at point, led the patrol back to where the stream flowed over the cliff near the larger waterfall, then tracked the formation of intruders upstream, using moonlight and a small torch to illuminate the signs left by the armed party.

Dawn arrived just as they entered the eerie stone country. Finally, they heard voices and smelled smoke. Jamie used hand signals to order the patrol to surround the area. He checked that he had a cartridge up the spout, standing around the corner of a boulder, then called Mick and the field set over.

Using the binoculars, Jamie studied the clearing. The sight of not just Holly, but Danny Glenn and Tasha under guard made his blood boil. He lifted the radio handset. 'Base, this is Green Patrol Three Leader. We have surrounded a small force of hostile gunmen. They have a large munitions device that we suspect is a legacy nuclear weapon, and some prisoners. What is your ETA, over?'

'Thirty minutes. We expect that they will attempt to take the device and all personnel out by chopper.'

Jamie ended the transmission, then turned to the others. 'Okay. There are six men with M16s in position, one with an SLR. That's one hell of a lot of firepower. If we try to run in on them, they'll take us apart.' Again, he lifted the unit to his eyes. 'We also have the four captives under that tarp. Any suggestions as to what we are we going to do now?'

'They're obviously waiting for a chopper pick-up,' Nico said. 'We could shoot at the helo when it comes in.'

'Yeah,' Mick said. 'What if they bring in a gunship? A Cobra maybe. Besides, those choppers are armoured.'

'So,' Nico said, 'you think we should do nothing, then brus?'

Mick wiped the sweat from his forehead with the back of his hand. 'Gunship or no gunship, I think you're right. We should wait until they try to load that nuke into the chopper then start shooting – make sure they never get it away.'

Ray ejected his magazine then slammed it back in. He nodded seriously. 'Good thinking brus. They're not taking that thing anywhere.'

# THIRTY-SEVEN

Flight time from Larrakeyah barracks was ninety minutes. The three Hueys were part of an ageing fleet, some of which had seen service back in Vietnam, but as Lieutenant Colonel Stacey Lineham, strapped into the mid-cabin bench seat, well knew, they were still the best utility rotary wing aircraft in the world.

The pilot's voice came through the headset comms. 'Hey Colonel, better get up here and take a look at this.'

Lineham threw off his belt and leaned into the flight deck, to where the co-pilot was pointing at the radar screen. Three red blips, westbound from the Gulf of Carpentaria.

'What are they?'

'Choppers. Judging from their course they're inbound from the USS *Carl Vinson*. Yanks, and they're in our airspace.'

'Pass me the mike.'

First, using a secure comms channel he called through to Tindal Base.

'This is Lineham. I want you to patch a message through to Canberra.'

'Wait five sir.'

Lineham waited impatiently, looking through the Plexiglas at the cinnamon-dark landscape below, lagoons and river channels shining in the moonlight, cutting through like kidneys and intestines.

'We have a connection, sir. The Prime Minister has the American Ambassador and Secretary of State in the building.'

'Thank you, please tell the Prime Minister that there's an American force heading our way by air, in addition to men on the ground. Presumably inbound from the USS *Carl Vinson*.'

Another pause then. 'Affirmative, I'm assured that diplomatic negotiations are underway. Meantime, Prime Minister Bob Hawke requests that you raise those forces on an open channel and demand they turn back.'

'Roger.'

Lineham reached out and changed channel to VHF 121.5 MHz, which the Americans would surely be monitoring. He lifted the mike again.

'US Navy helicopters, this is Colonel Stacey Lineham of the Australian North West Mobile Force. You have made an unauthorised entry into our air space. I am formally advising you to turn around immediately.'

The answer came back. 'This is officer commanding chopper detail USAF, and it's me telling you what the score is. Back off. We only want what's ours, and nobody will get hurt.'

'Negative. I say again. Turn around and leave our airspace or I will conclude that this is a hostile act and respond appropriately.'

'Listen you Aussie son-of-a-bitch. I'm in a Seahawk Mark III state-of-the-art chopper, another two are following behind me. I'm equipped with four AGM114 Hellfire missiles, Mark 54 torpedoes and two M134 miniguns. Suggest you get out of our way.'

Lineham felt a tingling sensation in the base of his spine, 'Well we've got something called the ANZAC spirit. Ever heard of it?'

'No, what the fuck is that?'

'Come any closer and you'll find out, I promise you.'

# THIRTY-EIGHT

Staring down from the Huey, Colonel Lineham could see a hanging pall of red smoke, obviously the loading zone for the choppers.

This was a game, not of cat and mouse, but a chessboard of high stakes, where a wrong move could see men killed, ambassadors recalled, and potentially even alliances torn up. Alliances vital to an Australia isolated geographically and surrounded by powerful neighbours.

Lineham also understood why the Americans were working so hard to protect their interests. They were spooked by the spectre of a new war on the Korean Peninsula. The irrational Korean leadership would need little encouragement to unleash one of the world's largest land armies.

It was a fuck-up, pure and simple, one that had drawn on for forty years, and Lineham knew that only he and his men could stop that fuck-up from turning into disaster. Just a kilometre away, the American choppers were in visual range. Like black insects hurtling towards him. One was a giant Sikorsky Skycrane.

The radio came to life. Canberra: 'Do not engage. I repeat, do not engage. The American Secretary of State has issued orders that any operations on the Australian mainland must immediately cease.'

'Okay, but those Seahawks are still coming,' Lineham almost screamed into the radio, 'and they're about to attempt to evacuate their people, and whatever that freaking bomb is.'

'Orders take time to trickle down the chain of command, but those orders have been issued.'

Lineham switched channels. 'US Navy Seahawks. Your government has ordered you to leave this airspace immediately.'

No response.

He slammed the mike down and realised that his entire body was sheathed in the hottest sweat of his life.

Down below, from the dark fringes of the clearing, Danny stared at the sky. He saw the Navy Seahawks and the huge Sikorsky. He knew those birds had the capacity to take a huge payload. In just minutes they would swallow up the nuke in its broken-down casing and take it away.

That would be the end. Temple and the evidence of his crimes would fly away, leaving yet another trail of destruction behind him. He would come off scot-free with God alone knew how many killings.

Danny knew that he could not let Temple get away with the murder of his brother, his wife, and the mucking over of lies with more lies, more acts of vengeance, pointless killings that would start the cycle all over again.

He could not let Tasha suffer for this. Sometimes, he decided, a man has to tell the world that he won't be pushed one more inch.

Tasha tugged at his arm. 'No, dad. Settle down, please.'

The three choppers were on their way down, Danny could see US Navy markings on them. Rain and mud flew everywhere.

Wally, their guard, had his face down, protecting it from the maelstrom, and the SLR held loosely in his arms. With surprising speed for a middle-aged man Danny started forwards, snatched the rifle from Wally's arms and loped into the clearing.

Raising the weapon to shoot from the hip he stared running towards Temple, roaring into the slipstream in an expression of his own rage. Rage that had flared and glowed and flamed for forty years.

You son of a bitch. I can't let you get away.

Finally, the AFOSI major turned, staring at the oncoming man. In his face, for the first time since Danny had known him, was fear. Raw naked fear.

Danny fired, one, twice, the gunshots loud even over the clatter of the helicopters. The rifle jumped in his hands from the recoil.

Other rifles barked, maybe more than one. Something struck Danny a glancing blow in the side. He ignored it, still charging towards the man who had dogged him for so long.

Then something needle-sharp struck Danny in the chest, like a pin into a cushion. Finally, he fell, and he felt something trickle down his back. He was not aware that a bullet had entered his chest and severed a number of coronary veins at the base of his heart.

Temple's face, inches from Danny's, was like some macabre stained-glass window. Blood in crazed lines crisscrossing his face.

*He's dead*, Danny said to himself. *It's over.*


A strange thing happened. The US Navy choppers that had been about to land, instead merely hovered above the ground, dropping a ladder on which the American servicemen clambered up and away. The last two men helped winch Major Temple's body up on a stretcher.

Then, leaving the bulbous nuclear weapon in the clearing, they abruptly rose again, disappearing higher into the sky and away towards the east. The men from NORFORCE were taking control. Australian Army Hueys settled to the ground nearby.

Danny lived long enough to see Tasha stroking the hair back from his forehead, and Australian soldiers running from the choppers.

Danny lived long enough to be moved to a stretcher, and bags of plasma attached to a rear vision mirror while a frantic medic tried to save his life.

Danny lived long enough to see his daughter one more time,

kneeling at his side, and holding his hand. He had time to re-member things too. Miss Sullivan. Tony Cassetari. Suzanne and her brownies. Gentle Frank. The people who had moved in and out of his life.

'I love you dad.' Tasha said.

Jamie, Holly, Ray and Nico. All of them were there, as chop-pers came and went.

Then, in the final moments, Danny clasped hands with Jamie McKinnon.

'You,' he breathed, 'are Matt's son. My nephew.'

'What?'

'Please, just think about it. You're thirty-two years old, so you were born when, 1958?'

'Yep. But it can't be—'

'Your father was an American, living in Darwin in a board-ing house with seemingly no history. Temple told me how he burned it down.'

Jamie felt every muscle in his body tense up. 'My father was a businessman from Maine – tractors, agriculture, things like that.'

'The USAF were looking for him, he would have had a cover story. You said his name was McKinnon?'

'That's right.'

'Matt took that name and I know where he got it from. I knew a Joel McKinnon in Tucson – he was a businessman who used to take the lady we boarded with out to dinner sometimes. You want to know what he did for a living?'

Jamie guessed even before Danny said a word.

'He had a David Brown machinery franchise on the Ajo road.'

Jamie raised his arms to either side, feeling the rain run down his underarms. 'No. That's not right. It can't be.'

'I knew in my heart as soon as I met you. You look like him, but not only that, you have the same soul, the same gentle but adventurous soul. Sam Snow had burns, and they'd assumed that they had been inflicted in the plane crash, but what if he was burned in a boarding house fire. The same one that killed Matt.'

Jamie pressed both hands to his temples.

'You are Matt's son,' Danny said. 'I understand now what he

did, and the world needs to know.'

Danny Carter's head fell to one side when he died.

# THIRTY-NINE

There were no newspaper headlines, but quiet DSO medals were arranged for the NORFORCE men. Desperate political negotiations meant the beginning of a new cover-up. ASIO took over the Australian end, sweeping truth under the carpet like crumbs from a banquet for which no one had appetite.

Three months later a RAAF C130 carried a mystery cargo from RAAF Base Darwin to Edwards Air Force Base in California. The news was not released, but there was speculation in all the major newspapers that the flight was carrying the missing nuclear weapon. Wally copped five years on conspiracy charges.

Danny Carter's body was carried by air across the sea so he could lie at peace in the soil of his homeland. Jamie did not go over for the funeral. It was a difficult time and he was full of conflicted emotions. With Danny's body they buried a Rothmans cigarette tin filled with ageing letters and photographs.

Earlier, after their evacuation from that tragic clearing in the wilderness, Jamie spent a precious weekend in Darwin with Holly, enjoying views across the Esplanade to the glittering harbour. The air was filled with smells of tropical seas and frangipanis.

Glenn and Tasha were there too, in the same hotel, but scarcely left their room for seventy-two hours. It seemed to Jamie that he had never seen two people more in love. Even in public they could scarcely keep their hands off each other.

Tasha had changed. When Jamie first met her, she had the air of a frightened little bird. Now the strength was showing, and she had taken control. The first sign of a new life was an indicator strip turning pink, and an anxious visit to a local doctor for confirmation.

Glenn grinned when he told Jamie. 'So, I wasn't shooting blanks, after all.'

On the first night Jamie and Holly sat on a bench overlooking Bicentennial Park and the harbour, hands entwined on his lap. Both were quiet, listening to flying foxes arguing in the trees and breathing in the warm vibrancy of the air.

'I'd love you to stay up here with me,' Jamie said. 'If you can—'

Holly shook her head. 'No Jamie, I love my job. I care about you more than anyone I've ever met, but I just can't drop everything for a man. Would you quit NORFORCE and move to Canberra for me?'

Jamie looked down guiltily. He knew he couldn't leave this life. Not yet. It was his anchor. It had saved him.

Holly squeezed his hand. 'You wouldn't like those frosty Canberra mornings, anyway.'

They made love that night in silence. The act lasted a long time, and they didn't talk afterwards.

The impediments to their relationship were immense. Neither wanted to make the parting worse. The next day there was no more hand holding, no little kisses. Both were preparing themselves for life alone.

'I'll come and visit you,' Holly said, before she went down the tube to the waiting Ansett 727, bound for Canberra.

'You bloody well better.'

Thereafter they began an extraordinary correspondence. By mail and telephone at first, and later, as electronic forms of communication replaced the old, they heard from each other almost weekly. Once or twice a year they met up in Cairns or Broome, for a breathless holiday, but they were busy people and they got on with their lives.

All this time, an undercurrent of excitement held Jamie tight in its grip. Was his father the pilot of a giant bomber that now lay broken into a thousand pieces under the water? A man who had carried one of the most destructive weapons in history? Was it even possible, did it fit the facts, the timeline of his life? Strangely, it did. And most of all, he thought about the things Danny had said about Matthew Carter. His face, his smile. His soul. It was ridiculous, yet it all made sense.

Was there a growing feeling of exultation in his heart? Yes. The excitement of knowing one more of those tree-roots that had been hidden deep underground.

# FORTY

There were milestones over the years. Signposts in the journey as Jamie passed from youth to middle age. Nico copped a fatal bullet wound to the chest in Kazuan province, Afghanistan, in 2003. By then he was a commissioned officer in the 2nd Regiment, SAS, leading his company out of danger after being encircled by a gang of Taliban militia.

When Nico's body arrived in Darwin, Jamie was part of the guard-of-honour that lined the tarmac. Afterwards, the Greek community poured into the Orthodox Church in Cavanagh Street and dedicated the life of their son, brother and nephew to their new country, acknowledging with pride the warrior spirit that drove him.

Jamie had learned that when someone you care about dies, it's your responsibility to carry them in your heart, bear them on your shoulders. It not only keeps them with you, but it makes you stronger.

Mick found employment as a diesel mechanic at the mines, working his way doing FIFO to a house at Fannie Bay and a collection of muscle cars including an original Holden Monaro.

Ray went home to Bulman Community. No one could budge him, not even the Colonel. Jamie drove out to see him a few times. His old mate seemed happy enough, sitting on the riverbank, the nylon line from his hand caster between his fingers, a fire smoking beside him close enough that he could throw the catfish and black bream he pulled from the river straight onto the coals.

Ray's days as a greenskin were over. He never tendered his resignation. He just never went back. Jamie missed him, and the dog as well, just a bit.

Jamie took early retirement in 2007, not yet fifty. In between bouts of employment in the security industry he went fishing, travelled a little, trekked through gorges in the country that called him back with its siren song every time he went away. Yet there remained a heaviness in his soul. Unfinished business. He suspected that we all have a purpose; that each of us is here for something. Discovering exactly what is the trick. Some people are lucky enough to follow the right path early, for most of us it's a tortured road, studded with disasters and regret.

Danny Carter's dying words became a mantra in Jamie's brain, an antidote for the confusion and pain, a chance to know his past.

Even so, for some years Jamie left the past alone. It was too raw, and too much pain had been caused. Yet the idea of making things up to the world, of leaving it a better place grew and grew.

He bought fifty acres on a creek near Adelaide River, with a spur of red stone in the middle and a spartan donga just below it. The deeper waterholes held a few barra, especially after the wet. The fishing calmed and soothed him, gave him a sense of connection.

Yet, strangely, there was something missing. The dream was not complete.

The idea that he was in a unique position to research Matthew Carter's story came to him in 2009. Holly encouraged him by email and letter. It seemed to both of them that in the process, Jamie might discover his own identity.

Years earlier Jamie had visited Gardens Road Cemetery, and thus located the last resting place of the man he had always been told was his father, Joel McKinnon. After obtaining permission to have the man's remains exhumed, Jamie had DNA samples taken by a forensic pathology lab in Darwin, along with a physical examination of the skeleton.

At a final consultation in a white lab that smelled of formalin and floor polish, the pathologist shook her head and passed across a printed form. 'Sorry to tell you, but this man was not your father. No relation, in fact.'

Jamie didn't know what to feel. Unburdened, yet hollow. He had come to believe that his ancestry was part of the story. Integral to it, even. Had Danny got it wrong?

'There's more,' said the doctor. 'The skeletal remains showed evidence of a severe traumatic brain injury to the cerebral cortex, incurred by a massive blow to the upper part of the skull.'

'That must have happened during the fire. A falling beam maybe?'

'No, not at all. There was bone growth over the scar. The injury happened a year or two before his death. It was a devastating injury. He would not have been functional in any way.'

The implications of this revelation kept Jamie occupied for months. Listless and unable to think of anything else, Holly became his long-distance agony aunt as Jamie worked on putting the story together, calling or emailing her almost every day.

The identity of the man in the grave became an obsession. The boarding house fire of 1957 had been newsworthy so there was, at least, a trail to follow. The internet made searching for information easy.

The best source was the Australian Trove online database. Jamie spent hours trolling through newspaper articles. There was only one major paper covering the Darwin region in the late fifties: the NT News had begun its unbroken seventy year run in print. The Northern Standard, mouthpiece of the trade unions, had folded a few years earlier.

The laptop display crisp and shiny, Jamie checked every edition, some of the facsimiles clearer than others. He was surprised how dated the newspaper pages looked, and ancient headlines of forgotten world events scrolled past or tickled little memories from deep in his subconscious.

The main article appeared on Thursday, July 27, 1957. The headline was, BOARDING HOUSE CARNAGE. The photograph was of the ruins of a building, people standing around the fringes or sorting through the debris.

Darwin residents were shocked to hear fire engines racing to the site of one of the city's most popular and enduring guest houses. Six bodies and one badly burned survivor have been recovered by fire and ambulance services, but more grisly finds have not been ruled out as further debris is cleared.

The fire started a little after two am and spread quickly throughout the wooden structure. At this stage police are not treating the fire as suspicious, but any Territorians with information as to the origins of the blaze are urged to come forward.

The photo that accompanied the article showed the bodies lined up on a concrete surface. A car park perhaps.

Forensic details have identified the dead from military ID tags and dental records: Joel McKinnon, John Smith, Ellen Carter, Rose-May Clifton …

The faces had been blanked out.

Jamie printed out the article and fired an email off to the editor asking if it was possible that they had an original of the shot without the faces removed.

The reply came back twenty-four hours later in a cheery tone, saying that the editor had assigned his office assistant the task of finding it in the newspaper archives, and that if available it would soon be scanned and on its way.

The next day Jamie had scans of not just that one photo, but six other shots of the corpses. The names had been scrawled on the back, also scanned and sent through. Jamie sent back his thanks then started going through the prints with a magnifying glass.

His hand started to shake when he saw it.

Yet Jamie was still not prepared to accept what his eyes were telling him. He made careful comparisons with crew photos he had obtained through Tasha Carter. The dead man was Sam Snow. The man buried at the Gardens Road Cemetery was Sam

Snow.

The questions came thick and fast. If that was true, then who the hell had Danny Carter visited in Columbus, Ohio, way back in the seventies?

Jamie could scarcely breathe as he groped for the phone to call Holly. When she came on the line his voice was shaky.

'Have you got time for a trip to America?' he asked.

# FORTY-ONE

Defences fell like Greek columns as Jamie stepped out of the car and zipped his jacket tight to exclude the cold Ohio wind, flecked with powdery snow. Glenn got out of the driver's seat and leaned on the car. 'Good luck guys, I'll be waiting out here when you're done.'

The aged-care facility consisted of three long brick buildings connected by covered walkways. The grounds were perfectly groomed, bare trees pointing ageless branches skyward, snow only just covering the last of the fallen leaves.

Jamie held the door for Holly and Tasha who joined hands as they left the car.

'Are you ready?' Holly asked.

'I think so,' Jamie said.

Yet how does a man of my age prepare to meet his father?

Together they crossed a paved courtyard, passing through an automatic door into reception. The interior was clean and business like. A nurse passed by; clipboard held to her chest.

Jamie stopped just short of the counter. 'We'd like to see Samuel Snow.'

'Certainly sir, are you expected?'

Jamie spoke then, 'No'.

'You know he can't speak?'

'Yes.'

The nurse stood. 'Would you like me to take you to him?'

Jamie felt a tear slide off his chin and drip to the mauve carpet. 'Yes please.'

The woman shouted to someone in the recesses of the office to take her place and hurried out through a connecting door. She gestured at one of the corridors that led off from reception. 'Come this way,' she said.

Doors, numbered in ascending order, passed by. Jamie had never been a nervous type, but his hands, hanging by his sides, were shaking as they walked. His life was changing, and he knew it. Not subtly, but irrevocably.

They passed a common room, where a wall-mounted television was broadcasting the news. Barack Obama had recently become the President of the United States. An appreciative audience sat back in padded chairs and absorbed the drama. Just a few turned to look at the visitors. A grim-faced old woman tottered by in the other direction, leaning on an aluminium walking frame.

Finally, the nurse stopped in front of a door and knocked. Jamie found himself praying, his lips moving but no sound coming from them. The nurse pushed the door open. A man sat on a soft leather chair. A game of American football was playing on the television.

'I can't work it out,' the nurse said. 'He can't say a word — there's nothing upstairs at all — but he loves watching the Redskins play. He's a miracle, really.' She touched Jamie's shoulder. 'I'll leave you to it.'

Jamie walked inside and locked eyes with the man. His skin was disfigured with ancient scar tissue. He looked every day of his eighty-seven years.

'Hello, my name is Jamie McKinnon. I've come a long way to see you.'

The face registered no change or acknowledgement.

Jamie went on, 'I know you're not Sam Snow. He's dead.'

A look of unbridled fear came into those rheumy blue eyes. But Jamie saw something else. The calculated cunning of a man

246

who still hopes that the game is not up.

'Please,' Jamie said. 'Talk to me. The man who hunted you is dead. The terrible thing that you stashed in the cave has been taken away and dismantled.' Jamie saw the relief in the old man's eyes. He could not hide that. 'You're Matthew Carter, aren't you?'

The lips began to move, but then clamped shut again. For fifty years he had acted out a part. Played it with consummate skill because the penalty for discovery was death. How could he change in an instant?

'It's safe now. They won't touch you; I promise.' Jamie placed one arm around Tasha's shoulder. 'This woman is your niece. Danny's daughter.'

Jamie looked into the burned, scarred face, and saw the first tears running. Matt Carter made a noise like grinding earth as he dragged air deep into his lungs.

Then, finally, Jamie lifted the medallion from around his neck and held it out close to his face. 'Do you remember this?'

The head nodded slowly.

Jamie choked up. 'I think I'm ... your son.'

Now it was his turn to break.


Matt Carter did not talk straight away. He took Tasha in his arms, then Jamie. Finally, however, after a long drink from the glass of water on the bedside, the old man formed words. His voice creaked like a door that hadn't been opened for a long time.

'Where's Danny?'

'I'm sorry. He's dead.'

'How?'

Jamie hesitated. 'There was a tragedy. He was shot. I'll tell you the whole story soon − I'm not going anywhere for a few days.'

They waited while the old man covered his scarred face with his hands. Minutes passed before he spoke again.

'Your mother was the only woman I ever loved. Is she still alive?'

Jamie shook his head slowly. 'No. I'm sorry.'

Matthew Carter opened his arms again. For a moment, there

was no body, only two souls, wide open. Father and son.

'There are so many things I need to know,' Jamie said. 'Why did you cut the plane up?'

'Because otherwise it would have been found. We stayed near the crash site for years, until we had removed every trace.'

'Why not the tail section?'

'It was well hidden. We let it be.'

Jamie lowered his eyes. 'What happened then?"

'We walked to Darwin – a local man guided us part of the way, but still it took us more than a month just to walk there. We took rooms in a boarding house and tried to blend in – tried to earn enough money doing odd jobs around the place to pay for our passage home. After a while we knew that they were onto us. We knew what secret service types looked like, but I was in love with your mother, and in no hurry to leave. I wanted to write to you, but I knew that they'd be watching you and I couldn't do it without letting them know my location. I just prayed that you were safe.'

'But then they came one night. Early in the morning, we woke, smelling the gasoline fumes as they set fire to the boarding house. I was the only survivor among our crew, though I had terrible burns. I'd already swapped dog tags with Sam Snow, thinking it might be handy. The AFOSI men identified me as Sam, who had lost his mind in the crash.

'After the fire, they interrogated me for months, in a cell at Fort Bragg. I taught myself not to speak or react to them. Finally, they took me back to Sam's mother. After only a couple of hours she was sure I wasn't Sam, but before long we had a bond. We decided to continue to pretend to the world that I'd lost my mind and couldn't speak. Just to be safe. It became a habit, my defence against the terrible things I had seen. I believed right up to today, that it was my only chance of staying alive.'

Tasha spoke, 'You sat in front of dad. You said nothing.'

'That was the one of the hardest days of my life. The man who came with Danny was a private investigator. He might well have passed information to AFOSI. If I gave myself away, I knew what they would do to both of us. I knew that as soon as Danny became involved, he'd become a target. Knowing he was safe was the most important thing in the world to me. It warmed my heart to see that he was successful. I wept when he had gone. Sitting there without taking him in my arms was the most heart-breaking thing I've ever had to do, but it was the only way I had to protect him.'

'They killed my mother,' Tasha said. 'Then dad as well, in the end.'

Matt touched her hand, 'I'm so sorry that what I did brought pain to you and our family. I was so afraid for Danny. I knew what lengths they would go to.'

'Please,' Jamie said finally. 'Tell us what happened that night in the air.'

'Of course, you need that. But let me tell you that it was worth it.' Matt said. 'Not for Danny, or me, or you. But for the people of Kaesong, it was worth it – millions of people who woke and went about their business of the day, not knowing how close they came to a terrible death – a fireball that would have scorched a twenty-mile circle of humanity.'

Jamie's mouth fell open, 'Your mission was operational?' he asked. 'You were sent to drop a damn nuke on a Korean city?'

'Yes. It was a critical stage of the war. Our 2nd and 25th divisions were in disarray along with the entire 8th army. Four Chinese armies had the 1st Marines pinned down at the Chosin reservoir.'

There was a knock on the door, and the nurse appeared. 'I thought I heard someone crying, is everything okay?'

Matthew Carter, who had not spoken publicly for almost forty years, looked up at the nurse. 'For Christ's sake Mary, leave us alone, we're busy.'

Her eyes flew open in shock, then backed away, closed the door, and ran to tell the other nurses.

When she had gone the old man leaned forwards from his bed. 'They loaded us up with a nuke at Site Baker, then sent us out to the Pacific on November 29. Macarthur himself briefed us at Andersen – the target was Kaesong, with Sariwon the secondary if weather conditions weren't suitable for visual bomb delivery.' Matt shook his head. 'Christ, how can I even begin to tell you how we felt – we'd talked about such a mission a thousand times – read what happened to those guys from Bock's Car and Enola Gay. Suicide. Depression.

'It was hot there in Guam, and the sweat ran off us in waves. We took our positions in the aircraft at 1500 hours, and I had a last look at the met sheet just in case it might help to bail us out. There was a storm north of Formosa but nothing else happening.'

# FORTY-TWO

ON THE APRON AT ANDERSEN BASE, YOU TURN THE
IGNITION AND PRESS THE STARTER AND BOOSTER
COIL BUTTONS.

GENERAL MACARTHUR'S VOICE ECHOES IN YOUR EARS:
'YOU WILL PROCEED TO THE PRIMARY TARGET, KAE-
SONG, NORTH KOREA, AND YOU WILL DROP THE SPEC-
IFIED MUNITIONS ON THE CITY …'

YOUR HANDS SHAKE AND YOUR HEAD POUNDS AT THIS
MOST STUPENDOUS MISTAKE. YOU HAD BELIEVED THAT
YOU WOULD BE FLYING HARMLESS CIRCUITS OVER
EAST ASIA BUT NOW THEY ARE TELLING YOU THAT
YOU ARE GOING TO DROP THIS TERRIBLE THING ON
A REAL CITY.

DESPITE YOUR FEAR, TRAINING TAKES OVER. YOU
OPEN ALL FOUR ENGINES UP TO TWELVE HUNDRED
RPM BEFORE CHECKING THE OIL AND COOLANT TEM-
PERATURES. THE FLOOR THROBS AND VIBRATES WITH
THE MASSIVE CENTRIFUGAL FORCE PRODUCED BY THE
PROPS.

FINALLY, YOU TAXI DOWN THE RUNWAY, CONDUCTING THE FINAL CHECKS AS YOU GO – BRAKES, TRIM, AIR INTAKES, FUEL, FLAPS AND SUPERCHARGERS. YOU OPEN THE THROTTLES SLOWLY.

YOU LOOK ACROSS AT YOUR CO-PILOT. 'THIS IS IT,' YOU SAY.

THE B50 SURGES TO TAKE-OFF SPEED. THE HUGE FLAPS LIFT THE HEAVILY LADEN AIRCRAFT INTO THE SKY, CLIMBING STEADILY AND LEVELLING OFF AT TWENTY THOUSAND FEET.

IT ALL SEEMS AS ROUTINE AS A TRAINING FLIGHT, BUT YOU THINK TO YOURSELF THAT DROPPING DUMMY WARHEADS ON SAGUARO CACTI IN ARIZONA IS HARD TO COMPARE WITH VAPORIZING CITIES. YOUR EYES FLICK OVER THE GAUGES, ALERT TO ANY IRREGULAR-ITY THAT MIGHT PUT YOUR AIRCRAFT IN DANGER. AS YOU BANK YOU SEE ONE OF THE FOUR B29 FOR-TRESSES THAT WILL ACCOMPANY YOU ON THE MISSION ACCELERATE DOWN THE TARMAC. SOME WILL TAKE PHOTOGRAPHS AND OTHERS MEASURE THE BLAST.

'THREE HOURS TO TARGET.' THE VOICE COMES THROUGH THE HEADPHONES FROM CHARLIE PEARCE, THE NAVIGATOR.

THE KB29 TANKER – A CONVERTED B26 BOMBER – WAITS ON STATION WITH THE LIGHTS OF MOKPO SPRINKLED ON THE DARK LAND BELOW. REFUELLING IS NOT STRICTLY NECESSARY, BUT NOTHING ON A NUCLEAR MISSION IS LEFT TO CHANCE. THE B-50 COULD DELIVER ITS CARGO AND STILL HAVE THE RANGE TO FLY ALL THE WAY TO BASES IN WESTERN EUROPE IF IT HAD TO.

THE REFUELLING OPERATION TAKES TWENTY MINUTES FROM START TO FINISH AND AS THE TANKER DIS-

APPEARS TO THE EAST YOU FEEL A SURGE OF PURE DESPAIR – THERE IS NOTHING LEFT TO DO NOW BUT FLY IN AND LAUNCH.

'ONE HOUR TO TARGET.'

GENERAL MACARTHUR RADIOS THROUGH A MESSAGE OF ENCOURAGEMENT, HIS VOICE SHAKY AND EMOTIONAL. HE TALKS OF DUTY, AND HONOUR, AND A PLACE IN HISTORY. 'THERE'LL BE A DISTINGUISHED SER-VICE MEDAL IN THIS FOR EVERY MAN ABOARD,' HE SAYS. GENERAL GODEBSKI IS NEXT ON THE AIR-WAVES, TELLING YOU WHAT AN IMPORTANT THING YOU ARE DOING FOR YOUR COUNTRY.

YET AS THE PLANE DRONES NORTHWARDS YOU WONDER WHY YOU WOULD DESERVE A MEDAL. YOU ARE NOT FIGHTING SOLDIERS – YOU ARE ABOUT TO KILL HUN-DREDS OF THOUSANDS OF UNSUSPECTING MEN, WOMEN AND CHILDREN IN THEIR BEDS. YOU TRY TO THINK OF HOW MANY LIVES ENDING THE KOREAN WAR MIGHT SAVE – MACARTHUR MADE A BIG DEAL OUT OF THAT – BUT YOU KEEP THINKING OF THE FATHERS AND MOTH-ERS, SISTERS AND BROTHERS THAT YOU WILL HAVE TO KILL IN THE PROCESS.

YOU INITIATE THE CLIMB THAT WILL TAKE YOU TO YOUR DROP ALTITUDE OF 30700 FEET, WATCHING THE COOLANT TEMPERATURES CAREFULLY AS YOU DO SO.

'FIVE MINUTES TO TARGET.'

'IFI INSERTED,' CALLS SAM SNOW. YOU KNOW THAT THE IFI IS THE NUCLEAR CORE THAT FULLY ARMS THE BULBOUS MONSTER IN THE BOMB HOLD.

NO MORE JOKES – THE HEADPHONES THAT CARRIED HARMLESS BANTER FOR THE TWO YEARS YOU'VE BEEN TOGETHER FALL SILENT. YOU SEE THAT EVAN GRAY HAS HIS SCAPULA IN ONE HAND, MOVING HIS LIPS

IN PRAYER.

'SHOULD HAVE TARGET VISUAL,' PEARCE SAYS FROM HIS CUBICLE BEHIND YOU.

YOU LOOK DOWN THROUGH THE PLEXIGLAS BUBBLE. DESPITE THE LATE HOUR THE LIGHTS OF THE CITY STILL SHINE LIKE STARS. PEOPLE ARE DOWN THERE SLEEPING, OR PERHAPS MAKING LOVE – DOING THINGS THAT PEOPLE DO IN THE DARK NIGHT HOURS.

YOU REACH INTO YOUR HEART, INTO SOMETHING BE-YOND RELIGION OR IDEOLOGY. SIMPLE HUMANITY. CONSCIENCE.

'TARGET CONFIRMED KAESONG.' SAYS THE RADIO.

YOU FLICK A SWITCH. 'VICTOR ECHO X-RAY. WE ARE OVER TARGET. WEATHER CLEAR. HEIGHT THREE-ZERO-SEVEN-OH-OH.' YOU ARE SURPRISED TO FEEL A DROP OF SWEAT RUN DOWN YOUR FACE AND DRIP OFF YOUR CHIN.

THE VOICE FROM GUAM COMES THROUGH AGAIN, 'PRO-CEED.'

YOUR HAND SHAKES SO BADLY YOU CAN BARELY HOLD THE YOKE. YOU ARE ALMOST OVER THE CITY CENTRE.

SAM SNOW'S VOICE IS COLD AND WORKMANLIKE THROUGH THE HEADPHONES: 'HOLD HER STEADY, SKIPPER ... RIGHT TEN DEGREES, STEADY ... LEFT FIVE ... CAMERAS ON AND TRACKING TARGET.'

YOU TURN TO GRAY, KNOWING IT'S TIME TO GIVE THE ORDER, THAT IT CAN'T BE DELAYED ANY LON-GER. AS AIRCRAFT COMMANDER IT IS YOUR ORDER TO GIVE – YOURS ALONE – AND QUESTIONS OF MORALITY MUST PLAY NO PART.

'MAY GOD FORGIVE US,' SAYS EVAN GRAY.

CHARLIE PEARCE BREAKS IN, 'LET'S GO SKIPPER.

WE'VE GOT JUST THIRTY SECONDS LEFT OVER THE TARGET.'

YOU SAY NOTHING. YOU ARE THINKING OF DANNY. SWEAT HAS RUN INTO YOUR EYES AND BLURRED YOUR VISION.

AN IMAGE COMES INTO YOUR MIND. YOUR MOTHER – SOFT AND WARM – HOW HAPPY YOU ONCE WERE IN THAT EMBRACE. AGAIN, HER WORDS CAME BACK TO YOU. IT HAD MEANT SO MUCH TO YOU, HAD GUIDED YOU SO MANY TIMES.

IF YOU'RE NOT SURE WHAT TO DO, IF YOU DON'T KNOW WHAT'S RIGHT, JUST CLOSE YOUR EYES AND FEEL IT FROM INSIDE, ALL THE WAY FROM YOUR TOES TO YOUR HEART. LISTEN TO WHAT THAT IN-NER VOICE TELLS YOU. IT KNOWS, EVERY TIME. SOMETIMES THE RIGHT WAY IS HARD, SOMETIMES IT MIGHT EVEN MEAN HURTING SOMEONE CLOSE TO YOU …

YOU FORCE YOUR EYELIDS DOWN. YOU BLOCK OUT THE SOUND OF THE ENGINES, THE ROAR OF THE SLIP-STREAM AS THE GIANT BOMBER HURTLES THROUGH TIME AND SPACE. YOU BLOCK OUT THE COMMS THAT BUZZ THROUGH YOUR HEADPHONES.

THEY HAVE DONE THEIR BEST TO INDOCTRINATE YOU. THEY HAVE SAT YOU IN ROOMS WHILE AN URBANE MA-JOR TELLS YOU THAT SOMETIMES IN WAR, THE END JUSTIFIES THE MEANS. THEY HAVE TRIED TO DEHU-MANISE THESE PEOPLE OF ASIA. TRIED TO TELL YOU THAT THEY ARE NOT LIKE AMERICANS. THEY HAVE TAUGHT YOU THAT FOR MOST PEOPLE, DEATH WILL BE INSTANT, WITHOUT PAIN. THAT YOU ARE THE SURGEON, REMOVING CANCERS FROM THE WORLD. YOU KNOW IT IS A LIE.

'FOR CHRIST'S SAKE,' PEARCE AGAIN, 'DO IT NOW

OR WE'LL HAVE TO MAKE ANOTHER RUN.'

YOU KNOW WHAT YOU MUST DO, AND HOW TO DO IT SO THAT THE BLAME WILL BE YOURS ALONE. THAT THE REST OF THE CREW WILL NEVER BE IMPLICATED.

YOU RISE AS FAR AS IS POSSIBLE IN YOUR SEAT, AND SLIP YOUR COLT .45 FROM ITS HOLSTER, AND POINT THE BARREL TO COVER THE CO-PILOT AND THE CUBICLES TO THE REAR – RADAR, NAVIGATOR, RADIO. 'LISTEN UP,' YOU SAY INTO THE INTERCOM, 'I AM COUNTERMANDING OUR ORDERS. BOMB AIMER, SECURE THE MUNITIONS. REMOVE THE IFI. WE ARE TURNING BACK AND THERE WILL BE NO RELEASE. I AM ARMED AND WILL SHOOT ANY MAN WHO DISOBEYS.'

THE PLANE ROCKS AS GRAY LETS GO OF THE CONTROLS IN SHOCK.

PEARCE SHOUTS, 'YOU CRAZY SON-OF-A-BITCH. DISOBEYING AN ORDER FROM GENERAL MACARTHUR? YOU WANT TO SPEND YOUR LIFE IN A PRISON CELL?'

'I'LL LIVE WITH THAT. NAVIGATOR PLEASE SET A COURSE FOR ANDERSEN FIELD.'

YOU BANK FIFTEEN DEGREES TO STARBOARD, A WIDE 'RATE ONE' TURN THAT WILL BRING THE PLANE BACK ONTO A HEADING THE WAY IT HAD COME.

UNTIL THE SABRES CAME YOU PLANNED TO FLY BACK TO ANDERSEN FIELD AND LAND, GIVE YOURSELF UP, TAKE FULL RESPONSIBILITY AND LET THE OTHERS GO FREE. ONCE THE SABRES ATTACK YOU REALISE THAT THEY CANNOT LET YOU LIVE – A PLANE CARRYING A LIVE NUKE WITH UNKNOWN INTENTIONS IS TOO DANGEROUS.

THAT'S WHEN YOU FLY INTO THE STORM, THE AIRCRAFT SO BADLY DAMAGED THAT IT SHOULD NOT HAVE

STAYED ALOFT BY ANY RULE OF AERODYNAMICS.

YET YOU REMEMBER WHAT DR IAN MILNER HAD TOLD YOU, AND YOU STEER THE PLANE SOUTHWARDS. COUNTLESS HOURS LATER YOU CROSS THE ARNHEM LAND COAST TWENTY NAUTICAL MILES EAST OF MANINGRIDA, BURNING THE LAST VAPOUR FROM THE FUEL TANKS, DRONING ON INTO THE INTERIOR, LOSING ALTITUDE, CASTING A WINGED MOON SHADOW ON THE CHASM THAT WOUND LIKE A SCAR THROUGH THE WILDERNESS BELOW.

YOU HAVE NO TIME TO SEEK OUT AN AIRSTRIP. YOUR LANDING GEAR DROPS CLEAR OF THE FRAME, SNAPPING AS IT HITS THE TREES. THE AIRFRAME BOUNCES, THEN SETTLES AGAIN. ONE TURNING PROPELLER THRASHES THROUGH BRANCHES AND LEAVES AS SIXTY THOUSAND KILOGRAMS OF ALUMINIUM AND STEEL MEETS STONE AND WOOD. BIRDS SCATTER. NIGHT CREATURES SQUEAL THEIR DISTRESS AND SCURRY FOR SAFETY.

FINALLY, THE FRAME STOPS, LEAVING ONLY SILENCE AND SCORCHED EARTH.

IN THAT WORLD OF STONE VALLEYS, YOU AND THE OTHER SURVIVORS WORK LIKE SLAVES, BURYING THE DEAD AND SETTING UP CAMP IN THAT VALLEY WHILE YOU STASH THE BOMB. WITH JUST THREE FIT MEN IT IS THE WORK OF YEARS. SAM SNOW HAS LOST HIS MIND, AND YOU HAVE TO LOOK AFTER HIM IN EVERY WAY.

EVERY MINUTE OF YOUR LIFE YOU KNOW THAT YOU DID THE RIGHT THING. THE CONSEQUENCES HAVE BEEN TERRIBLE, BUT IT WAS AN ACT OF COURAGE, HEROISM AND SACRIFICE.

# FORTY-THREE

After a week in Ohio, Jamie spent three days with Holly in New York. She was almost fifty by then, yet there was a new wisdom to her that he was falling in love with all over again. Her career, from what he knew of it, had been frantic – no marriage or children or house with picket fence for her – and he could see in her eyes that she was burned out.

Holly had lived in Geneva and London, spent months working out of Baghdad's Green Zone, not knowing if her next step would be her last. In what was often called a man's world she had proved herself over and over. Too many times, and a world-weariness filled her eyes.

On Jamie's last night in New York they went to dinner at one of the city's classier restaurants, overlooking the Hudson with its endless river traffic. They had spent the day touring monuments and architecture that screamed greatness to the world. Yet Jamie was learning that greatness is something proven, not proclaimed, and sometimes it is not even visible.

'So, you've met your father,' she said. 'What now?'

'I'll fly across to see him regularly. He's not well – his heart is bad.'

'What about work, you've left the army, but you're still a fit man?'

'I'm going to write my father's story down, but I'll need a few weeks thinking time first. I might fly home. I miss it. You'd love it Holly … when you're out on the river just as the sun rises behind the ridge. How it glows! It really does.'

Jamie wanted to explain to her how the river, the wild places, were calling him again. That it wasn't just the fish, but a deep connection to the planet, to the food web, that many people were losing. It was something necessary to him.

Holly's eyes reflected the lights on the lake. 'Sounds wonderful. I wish I could be there.'

'You could come too,' he said, 'if you wanted. You've been promising me a visit for years.'

The words hung in the air. She looked away.

# FORTY-FOUR

Engrossed in his work, Jamie was on the front verandah, with a new blue heeler pup at his feet. It was a crazy little thing, full of mischief from dawn to dusk. When it slept, however, it went out like a light. The manuscript was almost finished, and he was reworking a couple of paragraphs when he heard the car engine. He stood up. It was a Ford Falcon taxi. It seemed ridiculous. No one would catch a cab all the way out here.

Jamie looked down at the dog and said, 'Who the hell is that?'

The taxi pulled up, and with a jolt of excitement he recognised the slim figure who lifted a pair of compact suitcases and a tube of fishing rods from the boot, dropping them onto the dust of the drive while she paid the driver.

Jamie sat the laptop down on the desk and went down to meet her.

'God Holly, it's so good to see you. How long can you spare?' he asked her.

'How about the rest of my life?'

'You mean it?'

'I've resigned, I'm finished,' she said. 'I've given most of my life in service. Now it's time for me, and you.'

Jamie watched as she unzipped one of the two suitcases,

delved inside, then tugged out a towel. 'Now where's that creek you were telling me about,' she asked. 'I'm dying for a bogey.'

He smiled. 'I can't wait to show you.'

'No crocs?'

'Only small ones. Nothing that will bother a big, tough ASIO spy.'

'Ex-ASIO spy,' she corrected, then leaned up and kissed him lightly on the lips.


AND IN TIME, YOUR STORY ENDS IN A HOSPITAL. AN ALARM SOUNDS. MEDICAL STAFF CONVERGE, SHOES RUNNING, LOUD ON LINOLEUM CORRIDORS. LYING ON YOUR BACK, CLUTCHING AT YOUR CHEST, YOU FIGHT YOUR LAST FIGHT AGAINST THE BLOCKED ARTERY AND SUBSEQUENT CARDIAC ARREST THAT IS FAST DRAWING LIFE FROM YOUR BODY.

A NURSE CHECKS FOR A HEARTBEAT AND BEGINS CPR, WORKING IN TANDEM WITH ANOTHER WHO ARRIVES SECONDS LATER. SOMEONE WHEELS IN A DEFIBRIL-LATOR AND PREPARES IT FOR USE.

YOU ARE MY FATHER, AND I AM PROUD OF EVERY-THING YOU DID AND EVERYTHING YOU ARE. I HAVE BEEN AT YOUR SIDE NEAR THE END, AND I HOLD YOUR HAND WHILE THEY TRY TO KEEP YOU BACK FROM THE BRINK.

DESPITE THEIR EFFORTS, AND THE GREAT STRENGTH IN YOUR HEART, YOU SLIP AWAY, LITTLE BY LIT-TLE, UNTIL ONLY THE STORY REMAINS.


THE STORY OF ONE MAN AND HIS CONSCIENCE, HIGH IN THE SKY OVER KAESONG, NORTH KOREA.

# AUTHOR'S NOTE

I started writing various versions of this story at least fifteen years ago, and it has evolved during that time to this final form. Please bear in mind that though some historical characters, situations and details are based on fact, this is a work of fiction and is therefore primarily a product of my imagination.

I'd like to thank Brian Cook, my agent, who helped to shape the book along the way. This was the story that gave Brian the impetus to offer me a contract, and I know he'll be pleased to see that it's finally seeing the light of day.

I am grateful to Lieutenant Colonel Matthew Campbell of NORFORCE who was so open and helpful, answering all my questions and providing such valuable background information on the operation of NORFORCE in the period I was writing about.

As always, my friends, family and readers mean more to me than I can express in words.

Greg Barron
April 2020

# CAMP LEICHHARDT
## BY GREG BARRON

Ben Mulligan is a cop from the Northern Territory town of Katherine, with more than his share of problems. When he heads down to Camp Leichhardt, a Grey Nomad camp on the Roper River, to fish and get away from the stresses of life, he finds that all is not what it seems.

Ben uncovers a criminal conspiracy that will destroy lives and wreak havoc on local communities. With the beautiful Malea as his ally, he has to face his past head on, and tackle a cartel intent on making money at any cost. Yet, in doing so, he risks everything, even his own future.

get it at ozbookstore.com

# OUTLAW: THE STORY OF JOE FLICK
## BY GREG BARRON

When anthropologist Robert Morris arrives at the old Doomadgee Mission, at Bayley Point near Burketown in 1934, he's intent on learning local languages and customs. One very old woman living there, he discovers, was originally from outback New South Wales, and is something of an outcast amongst the Waanyi and Gangalidda locals.

On delving deeper, Morris discovers that the old woman was the 'wife' of a white stockman for more than thirty years in the frontier days, and claims to be the mother of one of the north's most notorious outlaws. Determined to record the facts of her son's crimes from her perspective, he sits with her each afternoon.

This is the story she told ...

Get it at ozbookstore.com

# RED JACK AND THE RAGGED THIRTEEN
## BY GREG BARRON

They called her Red Jack, for her hair was as bright as an outback sunset, hanging to her waist from beneath a stained cattleman's hat. On her jet-black stallion, Mephistopheles, she roved the north in the 1880s and 90s. Where did she come from, and where did she go? No one knows for sure, but the mystery lives on.

The Ragged Thirteen were a band of thirteen larrikins who put their stamp on Australian folklore with their devil-may-care journey across the wild Northern Australian frontier. They were not bushrangers, but were certainly inclined to bend the law. This fictional account is based on the recollections of settlers and pioneers, but is, most of all, a yarn in the best traditions of the word.

Get it at ozbookstore.com

www.ingramcontent.com/pod-product-compliance
Lightning Source LLC
Chambersburg PA
CBHW030636110726
47901CB00002B/467